BLUE SKIES,
NO CANDY

BLUE SKIES, NO CANDY

GAEL GREENE

WILLIAM MORROW AND COMPANY, INC.
NEW YORK   1976

A part of this book was written at The MacDowell Colony in Peterborough, New Hampshire. A second part was written at the home of the Four Wynns.

An excerpt from this novel originally appeared in *Playboy* Magazine.

The title *Blue Skies, No Candy* was suggested by Walasse Ting's poem, "Blue," in *Hot & Sour Soup*, published by the Sam Francis Foundation, California.

Printed in the United States of America.

6   7   8   9   10

Library of Congress Cataloging in Publication Data

Greene, Gael.
    Blue skies, no candy.

    I. Title.
PZ4.G8Bl   [PS3557.R3797]   813'.5'4   76-17870
ISBN 0-688-03082-3

BOOK DESIGN   CARL WEISS

For DHF

And for Margie. She believed love was more than life.

I especially want to thank William Bayer, Don Congdon, Joni Evans, Murray Fisher, Deborah Harkins, Carol Hill, Mildred Newman and Eleanor Perry.

BLUE SKIES,
NO CANDY

I

SKIN FLICK. My skin. Open scene inside my head. Deep nothing. Camera moves into bosky afternoon of a bedroom. I would like this a little more early Jeanne Moreau. But he alas is somewhat hardcore porno, all ego, rough, armored Michael. And I alas am not Moreau. I am just your everyday late-blooming adulteress and when this scene gets really kinky, I have to grit my teeth to keep from laughing.

Am I rushing things . . . beginning the scene in bed? I cannot resist. Bed is where I'm making it these days, friends, and sometimes it seems I'm only limping along elsewhere. Of course, no one would ever suspect. On paper my life is beautiful, meaningful, creative, posh. Sensitive devoted husband. Perhaps slightly anxious about my success but it scarcely shows. Good marriage. One fine offspring, our remarkable unfuckedup wise little Maggy. *House and*

Garden real estate, overlooking Central Park and on the dunes in the fiercely stylish Hamptons. Booming career. I am a screenwriter. I am *the* screenwriter, Katherine Wallis Alexander. Not too many hassles these days. They are talking Redford, Fonda, Coppola and $150,000 with a very nice percentage for my next script. Everyone is thinking Woman this year and I am the woman to write it. I looked thin and not a day over thirty-two at the Zanuck-Brown party in *Women's Wear* two weeks ago. Donald Brooks wants to dress me wholesale. Elaine never denies me a table. "Great Kate," writes Vincent Canby. "Gentle Kate." Life is spectacularly beautiful. But bed is best. I can't seem to get enough. I'm hungry all the time. For so long I was sheltered in the nunnery of my ambition. My fantasy was Oscar the status doorstop and love letters from Pauline Kael. I was caught up in the joys of monogamy for a long time. And while I was on ice, a lot of guys seem to have learned some very fancy fucking. Even the bastards are more fun in bed than they used to be. And so am I.

Michael could be a bastard. And Michael is killing me softly in Room 828 at The Algonquin. His pose is butch but he can be sweet. He is dynamite bright, confused, a beautiful guy. Pink cheeks, ice-blue eyes, ash silk hair. Remember Wheaties. Michael is a dirty Jack Armstrong and his hands know my body as if he invented it. Never mind Kate Alexander. He knows who I am but he is utterly uninterested. He doesn't ask if I hated what those clowns did to my last movie. Or what happened between me and Max Palevsky. He wants to know: "What do you think when you're eating me?" "How does it taste?" "Would you whip me if I asked you to?" I am my gender. "Woman, eat me," he says. "Woman." Never Kate.

"Why me, Michael?" I ask. "Why not some of those cute little groupies that lurk in the corridors waiting for you?"

Brutal Michael: "You could catch the clap fooling

with that trash, love. Kids today all have the clap." Flexing
his wrist, admiring fist framed in leather and heavy chain
links. "They talk. They sue . . . crazy jailbait. I have to
be careful."

Michael could be a bastard. If he were ever in town
long enough. Michael wrote that book of love poems for
the illiterate and the retarded. Made a fortune. But he's
even richer from writing jingles for television commercials.
Does the music too. Whenever he comes to New York, he
checks into The Algonquin and between his appointments
and mine we fuck like there's no tomorrow. And there
rarely is. Tomorrow he is gone. How often do I get to Santa
Fe? Never since location for *My Friend Larry*. That's where
I met him, playing the loony crooner in the nightclub scene.
And he comes to town now maybe three times a year—
a beautiful crazy from Santa Fe "direct in concert" or im-
ported to orchestrate a chorus of dancing toothbrushes.
Ideal transient bedmate for the wife who strays and stays,
superKate, loving hausfrau. I wouldn't need these free-lance
Don Juans if my once-a-month lover weren't so goddamned
elusive, you prick you, Jerry Glass. In a halfway amusing
George Segal film, Jerry Glass would be a constant of my
afternoons, tempting me away from the typewriter to Con-
necticut hideaways, waylaying me in the laundryroom and
Gristede's. Instead, I pursue the bastard and his primitive
insults. So I need the Michaels just passing through. Michael
loves to do all these things as much as I do. "The stranger
who desires you and convinces you that it is truly you in all
your particularity whom he desires, brings a message from
all that you might be, to you as you actually are." I cut that
out of *The New York Times Book Review*. I feel more official now, acting out all my erotic fantasies with the *Times
Book Review*'s cognizance as it were. I come and I come
and I come again and then when I don't think I can stand
it anymore, Michael grabs the soft little hill of my pussy
bone and does diddle diddle diddle till I am nothing but a

pussy on fire. Out of my head and into the cunt. That glorious sense insanity just one screaming millimeter this side of unconscious. That must be what this is all about.

"Does your husband know about you?" Michael asks.

"Does he know about *you?* No, of course not."

"That's impossible. How can he not know? He must know."

"No. That's part of the love contract. I promised to love honor obey—surprised? Well, everybody promised to obey in those olden days. And lie. It's cruel to tell. I'll lie and lie and lie. If he walks in that door and finds us here together, I'll say it isn't happening."

"He's no good in the sack," says Michael.

"He's wonderful in the sack but it's none of your business."

Well, now Michael puts on his skin-grazing black leather jeans with the grin of zippers up the calves. He couldn't get into them otherwise. And the shiny black tunic with the hardware that makes me think of whips and chains. He tilts a shiny lizard-skin cap at a menacing angle on his straw-blond hair. His goggles are mirror so you can't peer in to see if maybe, please, Michael's just kidding. I'm too numb to laugh. Then he's gone. Michael is my Hell's Angel gangbang. He fucks hours before coming and he could go on forever if Bristol-Myers and Hunt's Tomato Sauce didn't demand his attention. He's gone now to do some bubblegum rock for iced tea in a can and I can lie here bruised and fragile till the flesh heat ebbs and the compulsive writer's ego reaccelerates the motor of my mind. I feel full of pleased giggles. I am trying to imagine hustling Harry Hinkenstadt's eyebrows if he suspected how Kate Wallis Alexander likes to spend her afternoons. Harry is my agent, loves to talk about my integrity (when he says it, the word has five syllables). His eyes get moist when he catches me holding hands with Jamie. "You two," says Harry, "give me false hope for marriage." Billy Hutch,

infamous producer of slick shlock, told Rona Barrett he
lets me have my way because I have balls. Two-faced bastard. Only Kate knows Kate. I get my way yes. At least
I think that's what happened in Paris yesterday. With movie
people, you never know. Except for that Cowboy, the beautiful smartass know-it-all. I'm not going to think about that
now. I'm going to concentrate on my knees now, make them
stop shaking so I can get out of here.

"The script is beautiful, Kate. Ryder loves it. You're
going to love Ryder, Kate," Billy Hutch promises. "Women
lose their marbles over Ryder."

"You've been reading *Photoplay*, Billy." If I were
meeting Ryder Meade in bed, I wouldn't be so nervous. I'm
not reduced to reading *Photoplay* but I hear he's something
of a cocksman. Of course that could mean anything—stud,
scorekeeper, narcissist, only rarely, a lover of women. Anyway, on the vertical I bet we're going to make static. Fox
has stashed Ryder down this sedate corridor of the Plaza-
Athénée. My favorite hotel in Paris. I am in a broom closet
but Ryder is behind gold-piped doors at $175 a day. Billy
Hutch just happens to be producing a movie here in Paris.
Ryder is on tour promoting his newest film, with time to
talk about the next. So at the drop of about 1,000 tax-
deductible dollars, I have been flown in for a little talk. My
agent, Harry Hinkenstadt, reluctantly in attendance at my
insistence, Harry the Great Compromiser, is digging his
fingers into my arm. He has read the color of my outrage.

"I wasn't sure how Ryder'd go for that big fight scene,"
says Billy. "But he likes it. Now that is what I call a sense
of self. Ryder is amused he should get kicked in the groin
by a skyscraper chick. In fact, he thinks it might be better
a whole regiment of Amazons."

I have no choice. Ryder is it. Guaranteed box office
My wonderfully sophisticated and wryly witty futuristic vision of a colony of wonder women is rapidly being de-

stroyed by a triumvirate of cretins. "I can't wait to meet
the legendary cocksman."

Harry coughs. "No need to be bitchy, Kate. So, Ryder
likes women. Women like Ryder. You two could get along
like—"

"Not if Ryder is talking about bringing in somebody
like Ernie Tidyman to do a major rewrite."

Snorts now. That's Billy. "Bullshit. You know we
can't afford a big gun like Tidyman." Do these dumb doors
open? Someone on the other side can't decide whether to
push or pull. "Besides," Billy is saying, "if we didn't want
that special Alexander quality, we wouldn't have killed ourselves bidding on that script, Kate."

Ah, the salon of The Star. Gucci shoulder bag. Hermes
attaché case. Professional hairdrier. Champagne on ice and
white, starkly funereal gladiolas. Somebody dead. Probably
me. What looks like a very elegant streetwalker is on the
phone to Room Service. "Five slices of lean bacon, lean,
l-e-a-n, *bien cuit, pas de* fat." Red sateen sleaze and purple
snake platform anklestraps, Dracular crimson fingernails.
It's not Ryder's mother so it could be his Gal Friday or a
loan-out from Fox. Two blondes in licorice hip boots flutter
over the custom-crafted Vuitton wardrobe trunk. Could be
fan club. Traveling *avec* The Star, perhaps. One of them
smooths the nap of a royal-blue suede blazer, caresses The
Star's tweed pants, inhales deeply as if feeding on his scent.
The room is heavy with Brut.

"And Raquel Welch as Wonder Woman is just about
the cliché casting of our time," I am saying. "Ryder is
always saying he hates Raquel Welch. Now all of a sudden
he wants her. I say he just wants her because he's afraid
of looking vulgar next to an actress of Lydia Rowan's
class."

"Or being upstaged by Rowan's boobs," Harry chimes
in.

"Boobs, shit," says Billy. "It's Lydia's balls that worry him." He pours two inches of gin into a tumbler of ice cubes. "Shall I start with Alka-Seltzer or finish with Alka-Seltzer? Oh God, decisions, decisions."

Harry is whispering. "Don't go into this with a chip-on, Kate."

"A chip-on. What, dear Harry, is a chip-on? A hard-on for women?"

"Are these men assaulting you, lady?"

Behind me, just emerged from Ryder's inner sanctum, lazy Texas vowels, some kind of cowboy, lean, tall, sulky mouth, piercing blue eyes. Matching blue turtleneck. Doesn't look like a man who would put that much thought into a turtleneck. Boots, dungarees, Mississippi gambler cigar in the teeth. Curiously young face for that wild salt-and-pepper hair. Kate is cool. Nothing shows, I swear it, but the man's presence is like a blow. Cool Kate laughs.

"No, I mean it," the Cowboy says. "These men are being damned rude." His glare is ice. Hutch and Harry freeze, Hutch in the middle of a belch.

I feel a sudden flush. There, you see. I wade knee-deep in psychological abuse and I don't even notice it anymore. I've become oblivious to the hostility in Harry's patronizing humor. "Oh, it's just a manner of speaking." I shrug. I don't like the look in the Cowboy's eyes. "But . . . well, you are sweet to . . ." His eyes dismiss me. Abruptly he wheels and settles at the desk phone, back to us all. A very peppy cheerleader in a pink knit tube, midriff-bared, forehead edged with a jagged silver crewcut, sticks her head into the salon. "Mr. Ryder says where the hell is the champagne and what you-all want for breakfast? He won't be but a minute on long distance."

I can't let that arrogant blue-eyed Cowboy just get away. He thinks I'm a fool. Or worse. Doesn't see me at all. "I think I'll need espresso and two orders of raspberries," says Kate. The wild mane of silvered, sun-bleached hair curls against his neck, sun-brown, sharp etched wrinkles and a scar. He does not turn.

Now the peppy you-all summons is for us.

Ryder smiles at me as if no one else were in the room. "Our lady of the raspberries." Oh those teeth. He is handsome, that self-mocking grin even more attractive close up. He is shirtless and booted, collapsed in a buttress of pillows against the backboard of a giant bed, with kicky slanted heels digging into the ivory satin bedspread. He is handsomer than I'd imagined. The scar across his chin, the furrows of his forehead and the squint lines around his eyes save him from unbearable prettiness. He is smaller than I'd guessed. Most movie stars are. "Well, the legendary Mrs. Alexander," he says. He takes my hand. Not quite a handshake, more intimate, a lingering melding of our flesh. Greetings from Hollywood's celebrated exhibitionist ladykiller. "I'm just a simple country boy myself," he says. "I like a simple breakfast, fried eggs and ham and home fries."

"And simple Dom Pérignon."

It is the Cowboy, come in behind us loosening the wire around the champagne cork. Definitely an expert. Where do these country boys pick up this fancy stuff?

"Have you met Jason O'Neill?" Ryder asks, receiving the bottle from the Cowboy. "My land broker and cattle consultant." Ryder grins. "Tax shelters. Jason is a genius with tax shelters." Ryder pours just two glasses, full to the top, mostly bubbles. The silver-thatched cheerleader lurches forward on her Carmen Miranda clogs to pour some for Harry and Billy. The Cowboy declines. He's into the bedroom fridge for some grapefruit juice. He looks like a movie star. Lean and languorous like Clint Eastwood, but steelier. I have a feeling some tiny part of the Alexander fortune will be moving into cows. Beef. Whatever Jason Whatchamacallit is up to.

"There are almost no problems at all, nothing major," Billy begins, shifting porkily inside his black velvet jumpsuit, studying the reflection of the Eiffel Tower or God knows what in his mirror-shiny black patent loafers. "If Kate is anything, Kate is flexible, a sweetheart, Ryder. You are *her* choice for the part of the last surviving twentieth-century man."

"That's true, Ryder," Kate concedes.

Ryder winks at me and presses his thigh against my thigh. I am not moving my thigh. "Do you like your champagne that way?" he asks. I stare at the fading froth of bubbles. "Look at this," says Ryder proudly, dropping a tiny swizzle stick from a purple felt bag. "See, these are diamonds."

"I thought you said you were a simple country boy."

"Diamonds are clean."

"What's that dirty one in the middle?"

"That's a sapphire." He frowns and swizzles away at my bubbles. Across the room the Cowboy has settled onto the chaise with the Paris *Trib*. I can imagine the smirk behind the newsprint.

"Will you pour some coffee for us civilians, Kate," Harry says.

"No."

Silence. "Jesus, Kate, I didn't know you were one of those Women's Libbers," says the startled Compromiser, grabbing the pot and spilling the coffee into three or four saucers.

"I wasn't till sixteen seconds ago."

"You've only got to read Kate's script and you know she's not one of those foulmouthed dyke feminists," Ryder observes. I am very impressed. I knew he could read figures but prose I wasn't too sure. "What bothers me, Kate"—he's got my hand again, pressed in his—"the script is just too funny. Ha ha."

"You've been saying for years that you want to do comedy."

"I was thinking of the old Cary Grant. This guy is a

schlep. More like Woody Allen. There's got to be a middle ground."

Kate agrees: "Definitely middle ground."

The *Trib* rustles.

"Definitely," echoes Harry.

"The audience is not going to accept Ryder Meade as a schlep." Ryder hunches forward, gazing into my eyes. "Do I strike you as a schlep?"

I put my hand on his thigh. "You are not a schlep." He takes my hand and moves it onto a remarkable bulge in his skintight pants. Why does gangrene not set in? Surely no blood can circulate in the constriction of that gabardine. "You are *not* a schlep," I repeat. "You are the hero. You are the only male known left in the world who will not die like a used-up praying mantis in the act of making love to an Amazon. You're the sex bomb of our time, Ryder. And if you could concentrate on delivering a line with a measure of whimsy and gentle self-mockery instead of reverting to the clown, you could be devastating."

Ryder releases my captive hand. And pulls back. "She isn't flexible for a minute. She isn't interested in anything but what *she* has to say. I say the hero needs two or three good scenes by himself. What's his motivation? Why the hell does he fall so fast for this bimbo, Lydia? Athena is much more his type if you ask me. And I don't get the ending. She doesn't kill him. No way. It couldn't happen. Not even an Amazon would just choose to live the rest of her fucking life without a man. That's garbage. No way. No one will get it. Let her give in to this guy. All she needs is a couple of good fucks to soften her up. I like women, Billy. You know me. In my personal life I always have gone for real women. I'm not interested in twenty-year-olds who don't know who they are yet. But this Lydia character is tougher than what's her face, not Gloria . . . the other one. Germaine Greer."

Billy butters a croissant with dramatic intensity, contemplating the fall of a pastry flake. "Ryder has a point, Kate. The guy needs a couple of solid scenes."

"Give me depth or count me out," says Ryder.

"Now wait a minute, Ryder." Billy is talking around half a croissant. He chews. "We need Ryder, Kate. He's hot and he can do comedy. Give him some motivation. Ryder, you need this movie. That last thing you did was a bomb. I'm a blood and guts man myself, you know that. Who invented the slow motion blood and guts explosion—"

"Arthur Penn," I say.

Billy flushes. "I'm not so sure about that, Kate. You don't remember a film called *The Assassinator?*"

"Nobody remembers *The Assassinator*, Billy," I snap. "And you're lucky they don't."

"Kate." Harry leaps into the fray with the coffeepot. "Anytime you can't get work writing films, Kate, you can always get a job at Sea World . . . as a barracuda." Then to Ryder: "You need a change of pace, friend. And you have a brilliant comic touch. You got something there nobody's had since Cary Grant."

Ryder falls back into his pillow, stroking himself. I've seen women do that—play with their naked breasts inside a deep V neckline, absently stroking . . . but I must say this is the first time I've been sentenced to sit watching a grown man play with himself inside a gabardine Ace bandage.

"Ryder, if this is going on . . . I haven't got that much time." The Cowboy folds his *Trib* and stands. "I'm meeting the Swiss bank people after lunch."

"Jesus, Jason. Sorry. I'll get this shit wrapped up."

"Shit. Listen here, Ryder," Kate protests. "You may be the Jayne Mansfield of the decade but this is my script. I'm co-producer here too."

"I like the ending," Billy announces. "I feel it. Trust

my feelings, Ryder. You get two scenes, good solid scenes, good solid motivation. The ending stays. Lydia stays. I'll handle her."

"Wait, Jason. One minute. Okay. I trust you, Billy. And I sure hope those boobs of hers are real because if they're silicone I won't be able to get close to her in the clinches."

Billy sighs and stands up, brushing off Harry's effusive congratulations. "See you at the urinal, Kate," he says, exiting, licorice-booted blondes in tow.

"You were kind of tough," says Harry, stopping to slip in a long-distance call at Fox's expense.

"Oh Harry, I'm not tough at all. I wouldn't have to fight like that if you'd be tougher. You sit there nodding your head like you've got palsy."

Well, I won. No battle scars. Now why am I so depressed. My hands are shaking . . . I hide them in my St. Laurent pockets. What a rage I feel. I can see my face in the mirror. In the crackled smoke-grey glass, I see the red splotches of anger and that funny little white spot on my cheek that comes out when I'm upset. Maybe I need a drink. If I get a drink maybe I won't cry. Everything is going blurry. Why am I waiting for Harry? I'm not waiting for Harry. I'm waiting for the Cowboy.

There he is now, coming out of Ryder's bedroom, taking it all in, Harry on the phone, me in my blur and blotches.

"A drink, I think," says Kate.

He disappears, returning with a tall glass of . . . I sip . . . grapefruit juice.

"Feel that jolt." He drops his arm around my shoulder. "Sour, right. Acid. Vitamin C. Better than Scotch." He dips his hankie into the champagne bucket, is mopping my cheeks with it (there goes my artfully-painted "natural" look), smooths my hair. "Take a deep breath."

"You should have been a Jewish mother," says Kate.

"I was just going to suggest a big bowl of onion soup. But if chicken soup would be better?"

A brunette giantess about six foot three walks into Ryder's bedroom. "You want a Swedish massage?" Ryder sticks his head around the door. "Jason, before you go. You too, Alexander, no hard feelings." The Cowboy waves good-bye, and pushes me through the door.

"Harry." I throw him one of those phony little kisses it took me no time to get good at.

"This is the famous Chez Lipp and they have no onion soup." The Cowboy is disappointed. "What is a croak monsieur?"

"Croque Monsieur. Grilled cheese sandwich."

"I didn't come to Paris for a grilled cheese sandwich." He drops the menu and pins me with . . . I know they are only blue eyes. They feel like laser beams. "You should have a lawyer or an agent to handle these conferences for you," he begins.

"I have an agent. That was my agent, the man with no guts."

"Well, a lawyer then. Someone. It's not dignified for a woman to get involved in that snarling."

"You don't bring along a lawyer. It just isn't done. Lawyers frighten people. Lawyers mean it's past the talking stage. And besides, being a woman has nothing to do with anything. I'm a writer. This is my work."

"I'd never let anyone talk to my woman like that."

"Well, that's . . . sweet. But I'm not abused. I'm not a child. I'd be furious if my husband butted in to protect me."

"You're wrong." Flat. No argument possible. "This soup is awful. You can get better cream of chicken soup in Houston. What's wrong with your marriage?"

"Wow." I feel winded. "I didn't say anything is wrong with my marriage." I am falling in love with the Cowboy's mouth. Selfish mouth, rather arrogant, full and soft, a tiny cupid's bow on the top and the bottom comes up and out like a spoiled kid when he's delivered an ultimatum he knows you're going to attack.

"But something *is* wrong. You're like an animal in heat. I feel you sniffing."

"That's not a very attractive image. There's a difference, you know, between 'might' and 'must.' "

He touches my hand, playing with the stem of my wineglass, tracing the valleys of my knuckles lightly. Inside I feel that reflexive electric shock. "Here is little Effie's head whose brains are made of gingerbread."

I am truly dazzled. A Cowboy that quotes e.e. cummings.

"Are you really catching a plane?" I ask. I'm not especially good at enticing men. My strength is more just being . . . um, available.

"Is your husband bright, bright as you are? Is he successful? Does he give you the kind of attention you need?"

"You don't waste time on superficialities, do you?"

"I hate small talk. My plane leaves in seventy minutes. I'm forty-one years old. This is awful soup."

"Stay for dinner and we'll find the best onion soup in Paris."

"I wish I could stay but I must be in Zurich. And it's not just idle curiosity. I'm not interviewing you. I'm interested. I expect to see you again. I read your novel . . . you expose yourself perhaps more than you guess in *Sequential Suicides.*"

"That's a funny book."

"It's not funny at all."

"People laughed like hell. Gore Vidal said—"

"Vidal, shit. People are fools. Nervous fools. You have the most beautiful hands. I'm imagining what you do with those hands." He shakes his head in exaggerated pain.

"Oh yes, thank God for Zurich. I have a feeling something is wrong. Does your husband wince when people call him Mr. Kate Alexander?"

"People call him Mr. Alexander because that's his name."

"Point for you, Kate. An old-fashioned woman . . . uses her married name. I'm surprised. Wouldn't have guessed it."

"I don't have to prove anything."

"Well something *is* wrong. You go to bed with other men? Lots of other men? Do you hate yourself in the morning?"

"Wait a minute. That is a cliché supposition. I love myself in the mornings. Morning . . . why are we talking about morning? Unfaithful wives don't have mornings. We have afternoons."

"I don't mean guilt. Are you looking for a way out of your marriage?"

"No. Absolutely not. I'm . . . why am I telling you this? I'm restless, I guess. I go to bed with other men because sex is one of the great joys of life and it's all out there . . . I want some. I want everything. I think you can be unfaithful to the man you love with tact and delicacy. It's good manners. You're discreet. You don't go to bed with his friends or his enemies. Nobody knows. Nobody gets hurt."

"Sounds deceptively neat. He's not good in bed. He's not enough for you."

"What he's like in bed has nothing to do with it—or with you. I'm not about to discuss my husband's sexual performance with a stranger. Or anyone."

"Emily Post would approve."

"You're infuriating." I wish I hadn't let this go so far. The Cowboy is probably a voyeur.

He nods solemnly like some goddamned Freudian psychiatrist. "Were you ever monogamous?"

"Of course, what kind of a question . . . I loved being monogamous. I was monogamous for years and years. Now I realize monogamy is a tragic waste of our natural resources. And you? Are you monogamous?"

"I find I've become monogamous. How long can you go on, balling a different girl every night?" He closes his eyes. "I'm imagining you in bed. You touch." He touches my arm. The Cowboy is a cunt-tease. And I am wondering now if he is about to postpone that flight to Zurich. "There is a woman I live with. Very beautiful, not very bright but funny, and healthy, not the least bit neurotic. That's what attracted me in the beginning. That's so rare."

How does my face look? Does it show? I feel whipped, used, so hurt. My mouth feels frozen. I want to throw up, I think. Why doesn't he stop? Why don't I get the hell out of here before I make a fool of myself? Where does he get such arrogance . . . playing with my skin, touching my arm, my cheek. "You are going to resist my charms, aren't you?" I worry about Kate. Trying to sound casual, in control. The hurt is showing. Oh for a measure of cool.

"You and I would make quite a contest," the Cowboy announces. "I'm at least your match. You need that. When was the last time you were involved with a man you actually respected? I bet you go for the pushovers. I saw you with Ryder and Hutch and your agent. You mow them down. You numb them with overkill. I see you chewing up little boys for breakfast." He laughs. "But I see something else too." He grabs my wrist, opens my hand, examines the palm, tracing the mounds as if they were Braille. "I could talk about your sensuality."

"That's enough." Pulling my hand back. He won't let go. "This conversation seems to be getting sadistic."

"Everything turns you on. This brie. The wine. My fingers."

"Stop that."

"I've been watching you. Your hands. Look how you

touch yourself. How you eat. I'm watching your tongue
on the edge of the glass. How you inhale . . . the sauce,
these pathetic little flowers. You don't miss anything. Nothing gets by you. All your senses are clicking. Your teeth.
One tooth is slightly crooked. Did you know your mouth
tastes like brie and oranges?"

"This is crazy. Shut up. You're going."

"The timing is off for us, that's all. We met at the
wrong time. If we'd met a year and a half ago , . ."

"I don't believe you. You're some kind of a nut . . .
talking like this."

"I have to leave now or I'll miss that plane. Let me
put you in a taxi."

"Don't go."

"We're going to see each other again. I promise." He
leaves a pile of franc notes on the table and slides off the
banquette. I think I'm going to cry. He stands there—
very corny slow fade. Then he bends down surrounding
my mouth with the warm softness of his mouth. He is
gone. I am sitting here like a used napkin. Cognac and
another pot of espresso. That's what I need. What a long
morning it's been. Win one, lose one . . . which one?

Emerging from The Algonquin to reality after Michael
is like coming out of a movie into bright sunlight. Hmmmm.
What a high. I feel like I own this town. Some women
sign themselves up for A Day of Beauty at Elizabeth Arden.
I sign myself in for a day of body. I feel glorious, alive,
sore. Only instead of feeling sated, used, through with all
that for a week, I am curiously hot . . . hungry for more.
Walking along 44th Street toward Fifth Avenue, all I see
are crotches and hands. Am I mad? Is it a disease? An
affliction carried in a recessive gene by the late-blooming
adventuress? No man is safe while this sex-crazed monster
walks the streets. Who would I cast as the sex-crazed
monster? Dyan Cannon, maybe. Anne Bancroft in the old

days. Not much call in Hollywood for female sex-fiends. That's how far movies are from reality. I had hoped all this athletic ecstasy would make me feel like work. I owe rewrites I can't bear even to think about. Instead I am so turned on to my body I am thinking I'd like to see Glass. Only Glass is off on some mysterious mission to Miami, probably got some hooker sweetheart stashed away. I could trap some gullible young man. I consider the possibilities for the evening. There is a screening at Rizzoli's. Slim pickings there. I don't go to pub day parties but it's Michael Crichton's new book so I could make an exception. There is that benefit Susan Shiva talked me into buying tickets to. I could sort of amble through Elaine's and maybe find someone to buy dinner for.

In the polished steel face of the bank on the corner of 44th Street, I see this flushed, to be cruelly frank, blotched and frazzled harpy. If you were its mother, you might say, "But what a blissful glow." So I skulk into the first amenable taxi, persuade him to pull up near a Baskin-Robbins while I buy a quart of pralines 'n' cream, then we double back to Central Park West. I'm going to work after all. In the struggle between Kate and cunt, Kate is still a contender.

The key doesn't turn. My heart pounds. Blood chills. Of course the key doesn't turn. All the locks are open. What outrage is Manhattan fate testing me with now? Junky-rapistsecondstoryman. Should I call the elevator man?

"Kate . . . that you?"

"Jamie, you're home. You forgot to lock the front door."

"Did I? Sorry." Jamie comes out of the kitchen. I'm never sure he'll look the same to me. When we're apart for more than a day I have to get used to his face again Was it that way before or only since I started kissing all those other faces? You see, his face *is* oddly different, tense, masked. Now it adjusts. He kisses me. Maybe we're too much apart. I think he is afraid someone will steal part of me away, leave him behind abandoned. "I didn't expect you back from Paris this fast," says Jamie.

"I wasn't expecting you at all, Jamie. You said two days in Albany, at least. I got back last night. I need a hug, Jamie. Harder. Harder." This is the bad part. Walking into Jamie's arms covered with all the smells of Michael and me. I never get caught like this. I'm too thoughtful, too careful. Just because I'm committed to adultery doesn't mean I'm a heartless insensitive bitch. I love Jamie. I protect him. I guess nothing shows. Now his face is more familiar, warm strong square face with grey-green eyes and a soft mouth, maybe vulnerable, or perhaps, simply sensual, and those baby fine ash-blond ringlets, greying now, thinning a bit, he is convinced, and longer now, curling over his collar, over his ears. I need to get into the tub and scrub away the ravages of the afternoon.

Jamie follows me. I'm talking too much but he doesn't seem to notice. "They love the Amazon script so naturally they want a thousand changes. Predictable. The new director wants more action, more guts. Ryder Meade wants motivation, a new ending." The bathroom is filling with steam—obscuring smells, blushes, bruises, torn underwear, whatever . . . I hope, everything.

"Kate, what are you doing?" Jamie switches on the cold water. "You'll steam the paper off the walls."

"Sorry." He's sitting there, watching me as he always does. I have to take off my clothes now. Damn. You see, Kate, adultery isn't so simple after all. "Let's see, where was I?"

"They want a new ending."

"Incredibly enough, Billy Hutch likes my ending but he wants a less sentimental beginning. They've signed Dory Previn to do some lyrics." I should have taken a shower. Showers require shower curtains. Maybe some bubbles will make me feel less exposed. Bubbles. Making bubbles. Slapping the water like a madwoman making bubbles.

"You're supposed to put the Vitabath first, then the water, Kate."

"I know. I know. I just forgot. Oh Jamie, I hate these constant movie negotiations. It's like submitting to behavioral conditioning. First they have to humble you . . . then they love you up . . . then they stomp on your fingers. I feel violated, you know, robbed, even when I get my way. I scream and snap at them. I don't like to scream. I hate to hear myself talk so damn tough. It usually ends up with everyone saying, 'Brilliant Kate. You always win.' Saluting me and hating me. Pinching my cheeks with a smile and calling me a cunt behind my back."

He kisses me. "If there's one thing you're not, Kate, it's that."

Pure and sweet again, only slightly damp in a terrycloth caftan, I stretch out beside Jamie on the sofa.

"I'm not really tough, am I, Jamie?"

"If they only knew. Tough as Jell-O." He buries his face in my hair, purring and rubbing my neck the way he likes his neck rubbed.

"Here, I'll rub yours." Shifting bodies . . . the sofa is precisely wide enough for two. I designed it that way, had this platform built so we could lie here together, see the tops of the trees and the lights of the buildings across the park. "I brought the script back to do the revisions. I rushed back because Cinema Adventures is talking about doing some kind of contemporary version of *A Star Is Born* and besides I didn't want to miss my silicone."

Jamie frowns.

I am in love with silicone. Dr. Orentreich is plumping up my nasty little wrinkles with liquid silicone. Perfectly proper. Totally ethical. A holding action pending the full-scale overhaul I will soon be needing from some discreet and skillful plastic surgeon in Switzerland. Katherine Alexander is thirty-eight. Let that read, thirty-eight going on thirty-eight. Mean how they keep track of numbers. Can't they just say Kate Alexander doesn't look a day over thirty-two. Feel that thigh, gentlemen. Feel that firm silky rump. Feels no more than a voluptuous twenty-five. Jamie doesn't like this subject. Doesn't want to hear age panic, wrinkle-talk. Now and then I suppose he notices some infinitesimal flaw, but I'd be a fool to provide a running non-stop catalogue of real and imagined withering. In the beginning he was totally opposed to silicone, but now he understands. He tolerates . . . with suspicion. Jamie rolls on top of me and hugs me as if we've been months, not mere days, apart. I love to feel his tummy and his resting prick and to rub into him. I love to tease. "We never neck anymore," I complain. "Remember how I used to call you at the office and make you come over the telephone?"

"Uhmph." Into my shoulder.

"And you always had to carry your old rotten raincoat just in case. Walking around with a constant erection." Maybe I'm an incurable adolescent. I love it when the man I'm with rubs up against me in an elevator or pushes me into a doorway—exquisite desperation, we've no place to go, can't wait. Playing in the taxicab. He folds his arms in the movie, one hand cunningly pressed against my breast. Jamie and I used to be crazy like that. What happened? I guess this is it. You can torment a stranger and tease, hurt a love who's hurt you. Then you fall in love, good love, and you're not angry or frightened or threatened or insecure anymore. So you take off your clothes every night and slide into bed.

"I couldn't find anything to eat," says Jamie. "Don't you eat when I'm out of town?"

"I was going to have an ice cream binge. Pralines 'n' cream. Want to share? And there's caviar left from last weekend, hidden way in the back, and I know there's sour cream. How about a caviar omelet? And homemade bread in the freezer."

"You know I shouldn't eat bread. Besides, I just finished the sour cream."

"Remember those wonderful days when we ate the most beautiful bread?" Nobody ever worried about thin Potbellies. Dowager's hump. Crepey throat. No, we only worried about frivolous things. Mortgages. Miscarriages. Would Maggy have chicken pox scars? "Remember we used to eat pizza every Friday night on the way out to Fire Island? When was the last time we had pizza? Oh God, pizza." I look at him. He never used to diet. "You're not having an affair, are you, Jamie?" I ask, but I know the answer. He isn't. Jamie is a terrible liar. If he were having an affair, I'd know. Still I have to ask. When you lie so much yourself, you never really trust anyone.

He laughs. "You know I'm not having an affair."

"There are suspicious signs. You're always on a diet these days. And you're doing something different with your hair. Last time I knew you were having an affair because you quit smoking cigars."

"Do my cigars bother you?"

His cigars bothered *her*. Audrey. That terrible time we never talk about. Sad what you will give up to please a lover, never for the beloved mate . . . cigars, torn underwear, dowdy nightgowns. Audrey was very moral. Wouldn't go to bed with a married man unless he was separated from his wife. "What's wrong with you two?" I'd cried. "Everyone else has their little affairs like grown-ups. Nobody else goes around breaking up families." That was the only time for Jamie. I guess. You never know. Still I think Jamie has to tell. "You look good smoking a cigar," I say.

"Listen." He stands up. "We've got a whole long weekend. Let's drive out to the beach. We'll stop for pizza on the way. I'll pack now for Aspen and you can drop me off at the airport Monday morning." Jamie is leaving for a seminar in nuclear architecture at the Aspen Institute. Something to do with the center city in the nuclear age. Then he has a workshop at Berkeley. I'm glad for him, really. Even teaching would be better than working for this hopeless city. He went into city planning with such contagious enthusiasm. Now he realizes no one has any intention of implementing any of the ideas they've worked on for years. Even zoning is hopelessly frozen. But he will be away most of the month. I probably could visit him at Berkeley if my work goes well. Crazy how this is depressing me. I'm scared. I go away all the time but I don't like Jamie to go away. He's never been away so long before. Unless you count the six months four years ago when Jamie moved out because Audrey was so moral. And I'm not blaming Audrey exactly. Except for her fucking morality. She just happened to come along in the year of our disenchantment.

11

THE BEDROOM LOOKS like Big Bargain Bee at Bloomingdale's—shirts and underwear and shoes scattered everywhere. The suitcase is already full, the jackets folded meticulously inside each other. He's waiting for me to organize his duffel roll . . . shoes and underwear. "Jamie, you promised to throw out those shorts. They're a hundred years old. They're all stretched out. They're torn."

"They suit me," he says. Jamie doesn't like to throw things away. We were married six years before he would let me give his high school graduation suit to the Thrift Shop. "It isn't even worn," he protested. "They made clothes to last forever in the old days."

I grab the torn shorts and rip them apart.

"Bitch," he cries, twisting my arm till I fall into a pile of socks and polo shirts on the bed. "You're the one that has time for an affair."

Out of nowhere. I bite the inside of my cheek, not

quite able to look at him. "Oh sure, that's what you think. But it isn't that easy, you know. No wholesome single man wants a woman who has to go home at midnight and isn't free on weekends. And how many married men are free in the afternoons? And where shall we go? To cheater's motels. I'm too elegant, darling. I just can't crawl into bed with the florist's delivery boy. I'm much too particular."

"For one, there was Fred Geller. You were with him two weeks on location in Utah. I remember you talking about him a lot. What else is there to do in the wilds of Utah between setups? And I want to believe you have better taste but I am sure there was what's his name, the singer."

"Not Kris Kristofferson." If questioned, lie. If caught, lie. If interrupted in the act itself, lie. I put it in a movie once: the etiquette of adultery. "Kris Kristofferson was knee-deep in teenage bodies. I was never even alone with him. And Geller was sleeping with the script girl. You know that. She's always with him. On all his movies."

"Somebody calls and hangs up when I answer."

"Jamie. I wouldn't go to bed with anyone that stupid."

"If I die promise me you won't do anything crazy." He curls away from me into a cocoon of sudden misery. Jamie has a flair for the dramatic.

"If you died, I'd die."

"No. Promise. Promise you'll be strong and take care of Maggy and not let some smartass bastard marry you for all your money." Jamie is actually crying. I love that vulnerability. We are one family that doesn't need much gender liberation. I am hugging and kissing his eyes and licking the salt from his cheekbones. "I know you might go to bed with someone," Jamie is saying. "I just want you to respect yourself. Don't get crazy, Kate." He is so spooky and giving and sentimental.

"We aren't dying, Jamie. You're just going away for a few weeks."

"I love you."

"I love you."

"Is Kris Kristofferson good in bed?"

"Oh shit, Jamie. Nothing ever happened with Kris. You want me to tell you something sexy. You want me to do you a dirty movie?" He shakes his head no and smiles. "Well, hmmm . . . let me think. Jamie. Did I ever tell you about the time I went to bed with the Steinbergers while you were in Ithaca."

"I don't believe it. Not the Steinbergers. Come on, Rabbit, you can do better than that. The Steinbergers. With their rare old porcelains and that eight-thousand-dollar couch you can't sit on. I bet she has an import China teapot between her legs."

"Shut up. It's my story. Actually her body is quite beautiful. Her breasts are high little moundy round things and she has the sweetest tasting pussy I ever tasted."

Jamie smiles and sighs and shoves all the shirts and shoes off the bed. He knows I am making it up but the idea excites him. I can see the hardness growing against the pale grey twill. "You all just fell into bed together," he prompts.

"Oh no. We're all much too shy for that. Sally Ann and I were in their bedroom looking at all the beautiful lacy underwear she had made in Spain and the real silk nightgowns and the see-through chemise and I said, 'Oh Sally Ann, put it on and let me see. I'll send away to have some made too.' And she said, 'Try the café au lait panties on, Kate, you have such super thighs.' And I said, 'Oh, Sally Ann, I wish I had little titties like yours.' And she said, 'Mine are so tiny and boring. I wish I had nice round ones like yours,' and she reached inside my bra to feel them and I got terribly hot all over. And she said, 'Touch mine, see how boring they are.' So I pushed down the straps of her chemise and held both boring little titties in my hand and they weren't boring at all but very silky and firm with hard pink nipples and a kind of raised aureole."

"Can you tell it a little faster?"

"So she wiggled out of her chemise and pulled down her bikini panties and took my hand and put it on her furry pussy. So I started to play with her and I had my tongue in her pussy when Gregory walked in . . ."

"What did he do?"

"Oh, you know Gregory. He cleared his throat twice."

"You're spoiling it."

"He tore off his clothes and put his prick in her mouth and his fingers in my pussy and he did the most unbelievable things with his fingers. Wait. I want to tell you. No, wait. I've got to tell you what he did. With his . . . fingers. Not that. Hmmm. Well, yes, that. Yes. That."

"Am I good, Jamie?"

"You're fantastic," he says. "You fuck so goddamn good."

Jamie has been to bed with hundreds of women. He was the Don Juan of Cambridge the first time we met and I sort of dismissed him as "that charming young boy." He was the insatiable cocksman of East 65th Street years later when I realized the little-boy ways were calculated seduction weaponry. So Jamie knows good fucks. I know I'm a spectacular good fuck. But I do love to hear it.

"Am I really good?"

"You know you are."

"Am I your best fuck?"

"Yes."

"Do you think I'm one of the best in America?"

"Probably."

"Probably?"

"I'm not sure I've had enough experience to say."

"In your experience."

"One of the top ten."

"Top ten in America or in your experience?"

"In America, Mexico, Guatemala and the South of France. In the entire Western Hemisphere and Samoa."

"I want to be the best."

"There are no Olympics in fucking, Kate. No Oscar. You'll never know."

"You're angry."

"No."

"Yes. I can tell by your icy voice."

"No, Kate. I'm just sorry. Because you mean it. You'd like billboards, gold medals: First Fuck. Best Blow Job. Rabbit, I love you. The Steinbergers love you. Kris Kristofferson loves you. George Cukor and Adolph Zukor and Vincente Minnelli and Vincent Canby and Pauline Kael love you. You really should see somebody—a therapist, analyst, somebody—find out why you keep beating yourself up."

"I don't beat myself up. I just . . . I'm ambitious. I like to be best. I'm hungry. I'm not going to be satisfied with small triumphs. If you stop, you're dead. I can't sit still for therapists. You want me to be like Eric Banfer with his East Coast shrink and his West Coast shrink and he still can't get a hard-on unless he watches his wife making it with another man."

"Well, yes," says Jamie, "that thing with Eric is sad."

"I do give sublime blow jobs. I think I will have my mouth insured by Lloyd's of London."

"Tell me you're kidding, Kate."

"I'm kidding."

"I wish you *were*, Rabbit."

So it's not impossible to sleep with two men in an afternoon. It isn't easy either.

How long did we sleep? The clock says ten. I am tucking a little wooden mouse into the pocket of Jamie's terry-cloth beach shirt. Our love is special, very strong, protective, very needful, I told the Cowboy, wanting him to know that, yes I stray but I am a paragon of the thoughtful adulteress. Jamie brought me the little pink mouse once when I had the flu. The year we were married. She is hinged and when you push her down, a sign pops up: "We need each other."

"We won't ever be grown-ups," Jamie used to say.

I hide the mouse in Jamie's shirt. He will be lounging at the pool in Aspen, painting some Lolita's toenails and he'll feel a lump in his pocket and find Madelyn Mouse. So much for Lolita. I know Jamie.

Jamie wakes up ravenous. "It's too late to drive to Bridgehampton now. I'm too tired."

"Let's send out for pizza. Oh God, pizza. I can't bear it. Pizza, I'm so excited. How do you send out for a pizza? It's been so long I've forgotten."

"Yellow Pages."

I warn Goldberg's Pizzeria it's an emergency. They don't deliver to the West Side but I tell them it's me and I'm feeding Robert Redford so won't they please put it in a taxi—I'm not sure Kate Alexander means anything to the East Side snob on the other end but Robert Redford—the pizza is coming "rush."

"Let's have a special wine, Jamie. Something really stirring. Something too grand for pizza. Something that will move me to tears. After all, this is a landmark pizza."

Jamie comes back in a paint-stained sweatshirt with a bottle from the wine closet. " '62 La Gaffelière Naudes," he says. "An insouciant Saint-Émilion to complement Madame's mozzarella."

"Can a Saint-Émilion be insouciant, Jamie?"

"I don't know, Rabbit. I'm just faking it like everyone

else." He uncorks the bottle and pours a bit into two glasses, sniffing. "Ahhh." Stretching out on the floor. "Come into the cave, Rabbit."

I am stretching out beside him on the floor. "It's so long since we played in the cave, Bear." This is too corny even for Erich Segal, but, sorry, it's how we are.

"You're so busy now. Deadlines. Screenings. The flying expeditions to Hollywood. The damn conferences. The telephone calls."

"I don't really need to be so busy maybe."

"Probably you do."

"Do you hate my being mildly successful?"

He laughs. "Mild is not the word, Kate. I'm proud of you but—I'm proud of you."

"But what?"

"It *is* consuming."

We are hugging in the softness of the kit fox rug where we used to play every night before Maggy came and later the three of us, and then very self-consciously desperate in that terrible winter just before Jamie moved out to live with Audrey. I am never going to be too stiff or arthritic to make it into that cave. If Pancho Gonzales and Margot Fonteyn can leap about madly at their advanced age so will I. Jamie is asleep now, his full weight on top of me. The twilight stubble of his beard on the unlined cheeks is scary. White here and there. Poor baby. My arm is paralyzed. The doorman's desk is ringing. That will be the pizza.

We tear into it right out of the cardboard box.

"The wine is slightly over the hill," says Jamie.

"If you say 'Who isn't?' I'll kill you."

"Hey, is it too late to call Maggy? Yes, midnight. It's too late."

"We'll call her tomorrow from Bridgehampton. You want to open your birthday present? . . . It's not till Sunday. The package came while you were away."

Maggy made the card herself. She always does. "Remember how brilliant she was at drawing as a child." Jamie sighs.

"Well, she'll be brilliant at something else soon," I promise. I suppose it's too late to do anything constructive about Maggy. Sometimes I feel we've done everything wrong—defied Spock at every turn—and yet she has somehow emerged a prematurely wise woman, an earnest little guru at seventeen. She came to us at nine, exhaustingly verbal, a musical wunderkind, astonishingly gifted with paint and crayon, a Christmas gift package for Jamie from his first wife, Edna, the hit-and-run ball-buster, who'd rematerialized as abruptly as she'd vanished years earlier. Maggy the nocturnal waif. Edna had toted her everywhere, camping out, freaking out till three or four in the morning. Maggy had learned to sleep anywhere. On the floor. In a bathtub. She brought her little satin eyeshade. She would sleep through the afternoon. We tried to break her nocturnal rhythm but she would sit awake drawing or leafing through Jamie's art books till dawn while we yawned. She'd never gone to school. Edna didn't believe in the educational system. "Motherhood is a farce," Edna wrote. "It was my mistake, James, but I couldn't have done it without you. Now it's your turn. She's allergic to a few things, strawberries, feathers, but she knows. She'll tell you." No forwarding address. Dispatched Maggy by messenger and gone off to Morocco, friends said. A few years ago we heard she'd remarried and divorced a sexually confused flooring heir and was conducting a spectacular literary salon in San Francisco on her flooring alimony. Sometimes she wrote to Maggy. Four or five times a year, once not for fifteen months, once twice in a week, postcards and once a poem in a letter illustrated by an Indian she'd met. We always gave Maggy her letters but it killed me to hand them to her, to see the nose quiver and the lip tremble. They're all there in her room, in a ruby velvet doll clothes trunk. Once she said to me, "Kate, if she ever calls, I don't want to talk but I do wish to receive her written communications." Agreed.

I don't mean to say we haven't loved Maggy enough. You'd have to be catatonic not to love Maggy. But she came to us so *old*. I guess we treated her like a small-size adult from the very beginning. What a burden that must have been. Jamie and I were just so determined never to grow up. We were grateful that she bent when we pushed and was strong when we were weak and brave when we were terrified—over broken bones and old men exposing themselves behind a stoop on 74th Street. We let her be the grown-up and we the children. I don't feel guilty. Well, maybe I do. Why didn't she ever scream or tell us off? Why no tantrums ever? Once we sent her to a very relaxed gentle child therapist. They played together. Played house. Maggy drew pictures. Dr. Hull was knocked out by her pictures. The detail. Her Rorschach. Her imagination. Her cheerfulness. "There's nothing wrong," he said. "I would say inside is . . . basically a reflection of the exterior . . . how shall I put this . . . healthy. Yes. A supremely stable little girl."

"Maggy is not working at the ashram any longer, you know, Jamie." He is ripping away string and tissue paper. "Apparently a lot of the commune dwellers were quite disillusioned when the guru died and left everything to his mother in Brooklyn. The dissidents moved into a big old farmhouse somewhere near Woodstock, not far from Bard. Oh look, Jamie, brownies."

Jamie has a hand full of crumpled foil. "Two brownies."

"Hash brownies, I bet. Give me one. We'll get high."

"I can't eat brownies, Kate, damn it. Brownies and pizza in the same day. What are you trying to do to me? And you shouldn't either."

"Hash brownies." Oh Jamie, you're so uptight. When was the last time you let yourself get high? Sucking a joint self-consciously, never really inhaling, never the least bit stoned. I put the brownies in the freezer.

Jamie is asleep again. I lie there in the dark drafting brilliant dialogue in my head. "Have you ever taken mescaline?" the Cowboy had asked. "You have to lock yourself away somewhere secure with someone you love. And make love. Incredible." Jamie says we're too old for drugs. I want to try everything. How did he get so stodgy? I'm not concentrating on dialogue. If I think about deadlines, I'll lie awake all night. I have to say Yes or No to CBS about adapting that maudlin Emily Berman book. I try to imagine being seized by the Cowboy. That kiss. His lips are so full. He makes them soft. There are pursed lip kisses and impersonal pecks. Mouths that are tight, dry, perfunctory. His mouth is sex, totally carnal. I try to imagine the rest. And next thing I know I am dreaming, only the man is John Lindsay. He has noticed me at last. He has cornered me in the butler's pantry. I am protesting but not strenuously. After all, John, be cool. Mary Lindsay is standing just a few feet away grilling cheese sandwiches in the toaster oven. Big John presses against me, his hands under my sweater. Gradually and with a tiny flare of annoyance, I realize it is Jamie and not Lindsay. He has awakened from his own erotic dream and reached for me, provoking mine. I am creamy and ready. I force myself to come awake and give myself to it. When was the last time we made love twice in a night? Only slightly sore from the exercise at The Algonquin. The afternoon whore. I am Catherine Deneuve in *Belle de Jour*. Can't stop. Can't get enough. I love it. I wonder who Jamie was dreaming of. Three years ago I might have asked. Now I am much too clever.

III

Not quite 8 a.m. yet. And I'm not quite awake. But Jamie says, "I'm up, let's go." And here we are on the Long Island Expressway heading toward Bridgehampton. And today I feel absolutely beautiful, sexy, insatiable. I feel used, abused, exhausted, tingling. My bottom is on fire, raw. I smell my forearm, the skin smells so sweet. My arm is smooth and firm and the gentle curve of my own arm turns me on. Surely it must show. I am the tattooed lady. Hester. Emma. Jamie is turned on too, though of course, he doesn't know why. Last night was extraordinary. We haven't been like that for . . . how long? Long, long. I am trying to concentrate on plot lines and characters but my mind keeps slipping back to mouths, the Cowboy's mouth. How dare he resist temptation. And Michael's mouth, all teeth . . . Michael resists nothing. Not nice, Kate, Unfaithful brain isn't nice at all. But sex is so much on my mind, crowding my head. Suddenly I see Michael's face—

the way his eyes ice, his hand crushing my breast, painful, really painful.

"Do you have any idea how it hurts when you do that?"

"No. No, I didn't realize."

"Well, it hurts."

"You should say something."

"I guess I don't want you to stop. I want you to stop but I don't want you to stop. I'm on the edge, close to unbearable pain, close to the edge. And I'm scared. I'm never sure you won't become really violent. I love that."

"Would you like me to tie you up?"

"If you like—"

"It's no fun if you let me. You have to struggle."

"Oh please, please. Don't tie me up."

"Stop moaning, bitch. You have no choice."

Remembering, I get that lovely hot flash cutting through me.

"What are you thinking?" It is Jamie. I can feel my face flush.

"Nothing."

"You can't think nothing."

"No. Really. Nothing."

"Nobody thinks nothing. You're always thinking something."

Now I am furious. Can't I even have a private thought? Isn't it enough Jamie has to come into the bathroom and sit on the edge of the tub to talk while I'm on the toilet? Does he own my thoughts too? End of rage. Of course he is entitled. It's in the contract of our old-fashioned marriage: love, honor, italicize *obey* when it pleases me and share everything. Red eyes, runny nose, mysterious rashes, bathroom sounds, togetherness.

"I was just thinking how much I have to do on Monday when I get back to the city. I have a feeling they're not through yet with the Amazon script. Ryder Meade isn't sure how far he can push me." If I wanted to reach the Cowboy, I'd have to do it through Ryder. Yes, and why are we pursuing the Cowboy, Kate?

"You had such a funny expression on your face," says Jamie.

"I was just thinking how brave the trees look this time of year. The green is so tender." He is silent. Does he believe me? All that instant tender green crap. "What are you thinking, sweetheart?"

"Nothing," he says.

"Hey. I'm not allowed to think nothing. Nobody can think nothing." I know very well nobody thinks nothing. My horny little head is going full speed all the time.

Michael has me face down my feet tied to the bed frame with a belt and a sash from his karate coat. I am struggling against the bonds, crying and pleading to go free. "What do you want from me?" I cry, "What are you going to do to me? No. No. Not that."

"Shut up," he snarls.

"No. No." I am struggling so much he has a difficult time getting into my pussy. I aim it right at him crying, "No. No. You're hurting me." Sobbing. Fucking. Fucking and crying. "No." I don't know if this is his fantasy now or mine. I'm so hot. I love it. He comes and collapses on top of me. For just an instant as all sense perception moves from my pussy back to the brain I am sure he is the Cowboy. Then I smell cigarettes and Dentyne and open my eyes. That is Michael's nicotine-stained hand, wrist wrapped in leather. "Did you love it, Michael?"

He groans and rolls away. "It was all right."

"Just all right." I feel foolish and maybe insulted.

"You're supposed to stop struggling in the middle and give in. You're supposed to beg for more."

"Well, hell, Michael, you didn't tell me. I need to know the rules."

"Did you hear that?" says Jamie. "That song. I'm not imagining it, am I? That song was about people going down on each other, wasn't it?"

"I wasn't listening."

Silence. Jamie is smiling. Maybe he is thinking how nice it would be in bed with her. If there is a her. I rather think there is not. Jamie is a terrible liar. And Jamie is monogamous. But one doesn't ever really *know*. He says he's due in Aspen Monday. For all I know, she'll pick him up at the airport after I drop him off and tomorrow night they could be at some windswept love cottage at Montauk. She might be nineteen years old with terrific tits. She is so innocent, so unworldly, he will eventually tell me, and yet what innate sagacity. Shit. I know all about innate sagacity. I know all about big tits. They're great fun for about six years, dear. Just wait till she confronts gravity.

"What are you thinking now?" Jamie asks. "The expression on your face . . ."

"Nothing." I laugh. "I was just thinking how much I love your neck."

He smiles. Oh God. You see. I suspected it from my demurely cautious beginning four years ago. Adultery is infinitely complex. How clever of Nabokov to concentrate on butterflies.

Camera closes in on Oskar Werner at the piano. But it is Jamie at the keys, intense, absorbed, like a scene from Interlude. *Suddenly his attention is caught by the entrance of his leggy girl friend. She is nineteen years old.*

"I've been turned down for the Playboy *centerfold," she says.*

"If your tits are drooping, don't come mooning around me," says Jamie, slamming the piano shut.

In the next room Jeanne Moreau smiles existential triumph. But why is she playing with those cowboy boots?

I V

ADULTERY IS MY FAVORITE way to spend the afternoon.
And to think once I found a stolen afternoon at the movies
the ultimate in wickedness. Kate, Kate, Kate, for shame.
What's a nice bright supposedly busy girl like you doing
in Room 828 of The Algonquin Hotel? In the beginning I
suspected restlessness born of underutilization. And I told
myself, Kate love, prim tentative wanton. Kate, you're reborn. You are celebrating the sheer joy of animal passion.
I'm going to admit right here (in the pursuit of honesty and
insight) that I like to see Kate cast that way: a great lusty
uninhibited sex machine, all flesh and nerve endings. Here
is the control center, in my clever lovable little pussy instead of the wrinkled old cerebrum where all the uptights
and innocents of the world imagine it must be. But obviously adultery is more than just sheer orgasmic euphoria.
Now and then I put myself wantonly in the hands of a
few poor clods who can't even find the magic button.

The danger is irresistible, the elaborate camouflage, and the brilliant falsehood, the stammering, the scarlet flushes, the harrowing escapes, the complexity of logistics and arrangements. How intoxicating. What an aphrodisiac.

The Adulteress. She is not Jezebel. Not a backstreet Susan Hayward. Not a Hemingway Catherine. There will be no more dying in the rain, sisters. No more falling off toboggans to be crippled for life. I want to write a screenplay about the New Adulteress. Nobody has done her with precisely the tone I want to convey. I want to see joy and a little clumsiness; the sheer ridiculousness of naked strangers. My heroine is not a Tuesday Weld catatonic nut. She isn't all hung up with hives and regrets and whining recriminations, no Sandy Dennis. She is an unleashed Barbara Harris. Somewhere between Eugene O'Neill and *I Love Lucy,* reality lurks.

I was going to be faithful always. I was thrilled and tamed by till-death-do-us-part. I was in love with the idea of fidelity, one body, Jamie, the man I love, loves me. Musical beds can be arid, wearying. I'd done all that. Men were universally pigs in those days. The late fifties. Before Cockmania, our current golden age. Just when Kate got to feeling wondrously, voluptuously free, some guy would bring her down quick. The essentially demoralizing fuck. Not that Kate was discouraged. I still have a list of the first thirty-three boys I went to bed with, names, dates and how many times, tucked into a ratty old suitcase with pressed brown gardenias, stuffed animals and straight-A report cards. Finally kicked the habit of keeping score. That seemed too weird even for me. What prudes we were then, back in the constipated fifties.

Happily there were scattered free spirits like the Don Juan of Byron, the sexual adventurer, not a victimizer but a willing victim with a spirit to heal all wounds. Like Kevin Deems-Millar the shy and seductive teaching fellow from Oxford. Shocking even the unshockable Kate by coming through the Pi Phi window at Northwestern after curfew, minus underwear, erect already and naked inside his corduroy, to romp and giggle as if fucking were sheer fun rather than a tiresome challenge and a moral tug of war. Like football-player-poet Max Chernecki who went to Vienna for a Communist Youth rally and learned to eat pussy between the thighs of a Marxist siren from Verona. And brought that souvenir home to me. No resisting the early lure of Max. By comparison all local youths were hopelessly callow. So I dropped out of Northwestern and suffered in the lukewarm welcome of Max's fourth-floor walkup when he moved to Manhattan's Avenue C. Forbidden to move or speak as he worked on his poems, I wrote longhand, producing *Standing on My Head,* the novel nobody wanted to publish. Then Max simply disappeared one day, run off, a friend informed me, with a pudgy but rich little dance major from Bennington. Fickle Max. A pudgy dancer, for God's sake. The tragedy of my loss (oh, it was real) and a borrowed typewriter did something for *Standing on My Head.* I rewrote and it became *Sequential Suicides,* perhaps the best thing I've ever written.

About then I met Jamie. He was a sweet hurt little puppy. We flirted and went to bed. I remembered that in a vague blur. But it was his wife Edna I could never forget. Edna haunted me. She was some kind of early Amazon, part Welsh, part French, part Indian, part scorpion, very tall with a strong beautiful body and the most astonishing eyes, deep gold, sometimes yellow. I remembered those eyes long after that tense weekend in Cambridge. I didn't want to go, afraid to come out of the cocoon so near to finishing the revised version of *Suicides,* preferring to live with the fantasy of Chernecki remembered than to see Max in the outrageous flesh. But Max insisted. Max never let go of his victims. He still kept me on a long, idly permissive leash. Edna was his newest find. Or he, hers. The undisguised fact of their affair made the air electric. Edna played the flute, also the French horn, the recorder, the banjo and a slithery zither and she looked like a killer. Max was a challenge. Jamie made choucroute garnie.

Jamie and Edna were a bizarre mating. Jamie never quite understood either. Jamie had played baseball, serious baseball, steel steady, he told me when we met again four years later in New York. "A young Bob Feller," local sportswriters used to call him. But he'd given up baseball his sophomore year because architecture labs cut into batting practice. What a relief for his family. To the Alexanders, Jamie's fleeting fever for baseball was somehow embarrassing—baseball, how amusing, how common, how lower class. No one till Edna had ever paid the mildest attention to Jamie's head. Edna thought he ought to write poetry. He wrote sonnets. At her urging, he began to paint, heavily with the palette knife, crude expressionism vaguely architectural. Architecture was his own idea. Edna chewed away at him and when she stopped chewing he felt like a hero. Edna's consort. Edna's prince. Worthy of the extraordinary Edna. "I can't imagine why she wanted me," he told me later. Did she fall in love with her creation? No. She lost interest in it. She grew to loathe it. The Alexander money seems too obvious a motivation. Edna hated Jews, even elegant Episcopalian Jews like the Alexanders. "You think you're better than everybody, insufferable snobs," she said. She asked for $100,000. "I don't need a divorce," she told Jamie. "If you want a divorce, you should pay." She got $25,000 and his little red MG and all the lithographs collected by Jamie even as a child. But why did she take Maggy? That was so uncharacteristic of Edna. "I won't have Maggy in the clutches of those reformed kike snobs," she said. And $1,000 a month in child support made a pleasant cushion too. How stubborn she was, dragging Maggy around for years, sometimes parking her with cousins or a friend till finally she delivered Maggy to us. "You'll love her," she wrote. "Maggy is the motherly type."

Out of all that, Jamie emerged brimful of compassion and understanding and wary of women. He did not make it commercially in New York and he did not make it as a rogue womanizer. Too soft. Too needful. He fell in and out of love every few months, burning and getting burned a lot. He had just surfaced from a seventeen-month love siege when I ran into him again. Jamie wanted to please. He needed to please. Perhaps he was afraid not to please. In bed with him, I learned to be free. No more doubt nagging, "Oh shit, Kate, you've done it again. Too soon. You're giving too much. You didn't resist enough. You didn't hold anything back." Jamie despised those games. Jamie would take everything I wanted to give. Jamie wants it all. He needs love. He loves. No desperate needful excessive love is too much love for Jamie.

His face was softer then, even with his fine ash hair trimmed in severe brush cut, and his body was hard, the muscles smooth, not mean stringy sinew, a body utterly unselfconscious. And he embraced the bruised embryo of the marvelous-to-be Kate, the wondrous Kate we all know and love, only then she was plainer, mousy with that scrubby gamin haircut and the dopey little bounce-walk. Jamie made me walk around with my clothes off and nagged me to let my hair grow. I gave up Kents so I could live long enough to be his widow. He insisted. "Promise me you won't die first." He let me suck my thumb and taught me to touch my breasts till I fell in love with them. He made me stop saying "it" and "doing it" and "do that." Made me say fuck and cunt and prick. When he lost his temper he would cry: "You're just a cunt like all the rest." And I would laugh because now I knew. I wasn't. I was different. Special. Remarkable. Wonderful lovable loved Kate.

And I planned never to look at another free-lance cock again. For a long time I didn't even see other men, never stopped in my tracks on Lexington Avenue numbed by some craggy blond beauty. Then one day I began seeing necks, cheekbones, crotches pressing against tweed, muscled backs above bikini swim trunks. Seven-year itch. It's such a cliché. For me, it was six and a half. I began dreaming at night of necking with Paul Newman on a bicycle and fleeing from the papparazzi for a stolen afternoon with Richard Burton. I dreamed I went down on JFK. I flirted at parties and fantasized. Jamie and I talked about the scent of restlessness between us the night of our seventh anniversary. He'd worked late and come home exhausted. I cancelled our dinner reservations at Chauveron. Jamie was too tired even for the Roederer Cristal and caviar I carried to bed for us on the wicker bed tray.

"Caviar is so grown-up," he said.

"I bet you'd rather have cookies. I just happen to have some beauties. Chocolate leaves, macaroons, crunchy things." I ate all the caviar, bursting the eggs one by one with my tongue, and Jamie ate most of the cookies.

"If you brush your teeth, I'll kiss you," Jamie said.

We made love because, after all, anniversaries, you kind of feel obligated to ecstasy and in the middle I felt the intensity of Jamie's love and a familiar pattern of his movement. I was overcome with a sudden vision of a thousand years of boring dutiful fucks. "That wasn't too terrific, was it?"

"It was fine," Jamie said.

"It couldn't have been too fine . . . you didn't moan or groan or carry on too much."

"It can't always be dynamite, Kate."

"Is there somebody else?"

"You mean besides Elsa Martinelli and Rita Gam?" Silence and then: "Well, I seem to be obsessed lately with young bodies. In the office, on the street, that screening last night—I find myself wanting to fuck them all."

"Why don't you?"

"I love you. I'm afraid I'll get caught. I'm afraid to risk what we have."

"If you do it, even if I didn't know, somehow you'd be different. We'd be different together."

"You think about it too." Jamie wrapped himself around me. "I can't imagine growing old without you. I always see us gumming our gruel together."

"We could try harder. You could have a fantasy about Rita Gam and make love to me with your eyes closed. We could fall in love with another couple maybe."

"Oh Kate."

"Orgies."

"Kate."

"Not a desperate orgy but a nice relaxed spontaneous orgy."

"I'm not interested." He knew I wasn't idly teasing and was annoyed.

So Jamie resisted. For a while. But Kate kept playing cunt tease games. A few weeks later in Hollywood (on some frantic casting conference and deadline-rewrite schedule) after hours in some dark and dowdy steak joint with a slightly boring near-alcoholic black Irishman, I was burning. Pussy on fire. Like naked in the back seat of an old Dodge parked in the high school parking lot when I was a virgin, determined to stay a virgin, unchaste in every way. But I sat there in that splintery booth, my thigh pressed between his and that night I went home to my Beverly Hills Hotel bungalow . . . alone. Still reworking the scenario. Knowing next time, I wouldn't resist.

Home again on Central Park West the virtuous Kate. Kate playing intensely now with the naughty notion that one could stray, might stray, would stray. Worried too. I'll be different. Keeping secrets will drain away the joy of Jamie and me. To risk it all, the beautiful life, our exceptional marriage, our nurtured oneness. For what? For the terrifying unknown. New body, strange cock, unfamiliar fingers. To put your arm around a body, not his body. After all these years, your arms expect to curve a certain way. You fit. Where will noses go, and what about strange stomachs? What if there is coarse hair on the back of that strange neck? Jamie's neck, I love it so. How can I imagine involvement with a new neck, new smells? Will he snore? Do I? How will he taste? That first night with a stranger, will he undress me? How do you get your clothes off? How do you get to the bathtub? Oh Lord, you have to buy all new underwear. I am committing myself to put two hundred dollars in lacy bras and filmy negligees and flattering diaphany for a vaguely tipsy Irishman or some twenty-five-year-old filmmaker groupie who thinks a roll in your fate-kissed sack will somehow make the blessing contagious, as if he could draw your unique talent out through your creamy little cunt.

Four months sorting through that nonsense till finally, back on the Coast again, I tasted the beautiful black Irishman. Risked it all for one night in bed with a semi-alcoholic who couldn't engage Kate's mind for more than twenty minutes but had engaged her fantasies for eight months. Risked all, everything. And risked, nothing. No risk at all. It didn't show. Well, I suppose there was a nice residual rosy glow. Eye sparkle. I started remembering to use perfume again, smelled a lot like country mornings and sometimes like lemon and once in a while like sandalwood and spice. I walked taller. I did Audrey Hepburn things with my neck and Loretta Young back bits and signed up at the gym again after a delinquency of four years. I threw away faded underwear and torn nighties. Kate was sexier. Jamie sensed it too.

On camera now, Kate the eros scholar. A walking laboratory of sexuality, observer of anatomies, cataloguer of erotic responses. I am curious about cocks. They are often smaller than imagined. Eager runty stubs. Sharp thin hooded tumescences. Thin and curved, listing to the right or left. Rarely as awesome or formidable as *Screw* and dirty movies promise. But many are handsome, straight and sincere, rosy and smooth, with that neat little ring naked and brave without its foreskin. And a few are enormous, terrifying rape-fantasy rods demanding admiration, exciting vestigial anxieties of submission. Cocks that want to be licked, tongued, bitten, surrounded, swallowed. And listen to me, poor radical lib ladies, running around insisting there is no difference between he and she. No biological difference, only what culture introduces. It just isn't so. Men are not made like women. I would say the primary physiological difference is that men like to make love to music. Every man I've been to bed with in my late-blooming years remembers to turn on the music just before the denouement and exactly when I'm itching to turn it off, they turn up the sound so it will carry into the bedroom. Even Jamie did it to music years ago, except I guess I teased him out of it. But I remember when we were courting—courting? Correction. In the beginning it was a dueling to the death. Does that make marriage death? Nasty question. Not fair. I have been to bed with men who loved Baroque ("Play anything as long as it's Bach"), Beatle freaks (under the age of forty Beatles are their Bach). Some men like to fuck to the football game. I have made love to the last half of *Raintree County* dubbed in French on the telly in a suite at the George V. Jerry Glass likes WQXR. For God's sake, doesn't he hear those commercials for Vita herring? I believe that is the crucial anatomical biological difference between male and female. Gray's *Anatomy,* take a footnote: Men and women are biologically alike except that women tend to be distracted by the commercials. It's in the chromosomes. Once the prick goes up, men don't hear anything anyway, I suppose.

* * *

"And whatever happened to Spiro Agnew?" Bob Hope breaks up at his not-very-funny. The audience guffaws. "And now, here to announce the Academy's Scarlett O'Hara award, our town's delicious adulteress, Kate Alexander." Kate hugs Hope affectionately. Hope giggles. The spotlights weave and lash the audience, illuminating the trembling nominees. Raquel bites her lip. Shirley lowers her head as if in Zen prayer. Vanessa throws back her head in an ecstasy of hope. Liza wiggles. Kate puts the silver Scarlett on the rostrum and reaches for the envelope.

"The winner, for her rapturous performance at The Beverly Hills Hotel and at The Algonquin is . . . me. Kate Alexander. I can't believe it." Kate wipes away a tear. "I can't accept this award without saying how much I owe to so many people. I want to thank Sigmund and Betty Friedan and Helen Gurley Brown and my gynecologist and Norforms and Emma Bovary and Jeanne Moreau and silicone and Dr. Orentreich and Yves St. Laurent and Monsieur Marc and most of all, my husband. Thank you, Jamie."

V

LAZY WARM LOVING weekend in front of the fire. None of
the usual weekend people around. The enchanted cottage
in the middle of our Bridgehampton potato field is half
hidden by fog. "Sleep a little. Sleep till noon," Jamie urges,
knowing how Kate likes to creep slowly into Sunday. Jamie
never sleeps mornings. The birds wake him and he invents
important projects—storm doors to hang or remove, immaculate sashes to be repainted, the woodpile to be rearranged. He is a born cook and now he is waking me with
French toast. From the bedroom I can barely make out the
woodpile through the fog and the ocean blurring greyly
into grey sky. Jamie's French toast is always perfect,
sodden with egg and golden brown, sometimes dusted with
sugar, sometimes pressed together with nutty yellow fon-
tina or even brie. Once he made French toast of a tunafish
sandwich. That is his bizarre bent. Apricots in shrimp
curry. Foie gras tucked inside chicken Kiev. Sometimes his

madness is brilliant. Green crêpes filled with sour cream and a puree of avocado. And his chocolate rum milk shakes are demonic.

"I wanted to bring you breakfast in bed because you're going away, Jamie."

"But I'm really neutral about breakfast in bed," he says. "You're the one who loves it."

"Crawl in and eat this with me." He has squeezed fresh grapefruit juice and arranged toast and sour cream in odds and ends of precious unmatched dishes on a Lucite bedtray elegantly spread with a lemon-yellow napkin. There is a yellow tulip next to the fork and the entertainment section of the Sunday *Times* folded into a see-through side pocket. Jamie props himself on the pillows next to me, tearing off bits of toast and dipping them in sour cream. He never makes any for himself. Prefers to nibble mine. He is always on a diet. He is studying Craig Claiborne's recipe for the week, contemplating a great hunk of beef brisket, a carrot, some shallots and a bottle of wine—still life for a Sunday morning.

"I'm going to miss you," he says.

I set the tray on the floor and crawl into the side of him. "I'll miss you, Jamie."

By three o'clock sun has cut through the fog and warmed the sand. Still it is cool and we lie on the beach wrapped in old Army blankets. Reading. And touching. "Are we being too cavalier with Maggy?" Jamie asks. "She may be wise but she's only seventeen. I worry about her doing nothing all summer in some kind of commune."

"Would you call it a commune? They're really just sharing the rent on a house. And they are making a movie. And anyway, Jamie, I don't think we have any choice." I must drive up there and see what Maggy is up to.

"Are you considering the CBS thing? Adapting the Berman book?"

"It's a real tearjerker, you know. Another brave teenager dying young. Half a box of Kleenex at least. Why do you ask?"

"When I get home I'd like to have you around for a while."

"There is the Cannes Film Festival, you know."

"You have to go?"

"Well, I usually do. You come too."

"Cannes is a bore for me." He sighs. "I liked us less successful."

"Oh Jamie." I put down the novel my friend Vivian has sent me. How depressing . . . a woman in her forties having an affair with a Harvard sophomore. In Italy. Poetic. Is someone trying to tell me something? "What are you drawing, Jamie?"

"My foot."

I'm not going to do the Berman book. I'm tired of doing easy crap. Well, I'll think about all that tomorrow at Tara.

Let's get one thing clear about my being forty. I'm not. I'm a voluptuous ingenuous thirty-eight. Now, according to certain cruel and malicious documents, an alleged birth certificate, an irrepressible passport, Katherine Wallis Alexander was scheduled to be forty February 9. I was not ready to be forty. I could not even say the word. Forty is Greer Garson. Irene Dunne. Dame May Whitty. Wrinkles, liver spots, cellulite, frizz and flab, tired blood.

I am remembering my mother at forty, how dry and fussy and finished she seemed to me, her pale blond hair pulled into a beyond-style French twist, the perfect transparent skin stretched over high cheekbones. She was . . . she is . . . painfully thin, with the pelvis-thrust-forward, hand-on-hip stance left over from the late twenties. I have a snapshot from Grandma's album, Mama in a Ziegfeld

Follies pose with her four brothers lined up behind her in their tank-top bathing suits. I see her smoking, one cigarette after another with that exquisite tortoise shell and mother-of-pearl holder, ruffling fabric swatches, swearing over meticulous floor plans for her interior decoration projects, always with that alert expectant look, always waiting for a word from Daddy.

"Don't ask me. Ask your father."

Daddy so handsome and clearly bored peering into the backs of people's eyes, into their brains, cutting out of his office, fleeing the dilated pupils and clouded retinas at four o'clock, to sit motionless in a marsh or lightly wooded field watching an anthill, taming a chipmunk, writing angry poems full of blood images and violence.

> "I lose touch with the late lamented me.
> Stubborn carrion, forgot to die.
> Well, the flesh is full of mangy tricks, Death.
> Don't despair. My blood will feed your roses."

Mother would read the poems, silent, smiling a nervous half-smile, fastening on a single safe image. "Roses," she would murmur. "Lovely, Peter, lovely."

Daddy would press the back of his hand against her artfully flushed cheek. "Your mother is an extraordinary woman."

He would take me along on his walks, hand me a notebook and a fat red fountain pen. "Choose an object, or even a word. Write what it feels like to you, in you. Not what it means but how it feels. Make it rhyme if you like, don't if you don't." He would read what I wrote.

> "I am
> Shazam
> If you don't believe it.
> Punch me."

And laugh. And hug me.

"I want to believe in God,
God.
How odd.
I want God to believe in me."

"Keep a diary, Kat." He called me Kat. "A writer must keep a daily journal." In our cellar back in Evanston there are boxes full of aborted journals, term papers, clippings from The John Burroughs High *Spectator,* a Kate Wallis short story that won a National Scholastic award, scraps of poetry, a four-page nine-act play by Kate at seven, even notes to M&D left by six-year-old Kate on their bed. "Wake me when you come home whatever time. I have a scary poem in my head." "Don't kiss me two loud when you come into my room tonight. Amy is sleeping over." At dinner we rhymed words. And traded impromptu haiku.

"Asparagus is
A miracle I cannot
Speak. It might answer."

"Of course, she's brilliant," Mama would always say, pulling out a ragged clipping of Kate's latest triumph. "She's her father's daughter."

"But you can't possibly be forty," Jamie lies to me one morning last January. "I can subtract and add and you are about to be thirty-nine. Let's go away for your birthday. You'll wake up the morning of February ninth and you'll be thirty-nine if you like and we'll have breakfast in bed, something decadent . . . champagne and lobster. Nobody will know the difference. I promise."

"*Time* magazine will know."

"Now, aren't you glad you're not the Queen of England, with everyone keeping yearly score. *Time* magazine won't even notice."

"If I ever get on the cover—"

"Let's worry about it then. This year you're thirty-nine. Be thirty-eight if you like. Kate, you look great. Look at those legs." He strokes the long tight lines of my thighs. "Your best anatomical feature," he has often assured me. "Pussy excluded. That pussy is beyond all competition."

"How old do I look?"

"Not a day over thirty-two."

"Thirty-two!"

"Kate. Do you want me to say twenty-three . . . nineteen?"

"If it were true, I wouldn't complain."

"Kate, you look great. Great. But you're not twenty-three."

"All right." Flexing and stroking an admirable thigh. "But let's make me thirty-eight because thirty-nine sounds suspicious."

Waking up in Martinique. Sunshine. Radio Antilles. And Jamie kissing my ear. He's been up for hours lying beside me quietly reading Updike's *Museums and Women.* Brilliant short stories about infidelity and domestic war. I read some on the plane flying down, the unfaithful Marples, very familiar. He looks at me anxiously. Will I be thirty-eight cheerfully or am I going to be forty fighting and angry? He strokes the inside of my elbow. Sweetly, not very sexy. Vacations are usually sexier for us. But our time here in Martinique has been strangely tame, close, loving, tame.

"Happy Birthday, Rabbit."

Jamie pushes the drab beige curtains all the way back, letting sun, blue sky, palms and enough Caribbean into the tacky beige room to save the day. The terrace is hot and buggy, the air conditioning defiant. True to promised fantasy, Jamie has managed to provoke the kitchen to exquisite heights: cold boiled lobster, wedges of fresh pineapple, freshly made mayonnaise and icy champagne. The thin black waitress teetering on green platform shoes is laughing at such unabashed excess as she sets the tray at the edge of the bed.

"My head is strong enough for this madness," says Jamie. "I hope my liver can take it." He puts a small red leather jewel box on the tray. "Happy Birthday, Rabbit. It's not a floor-length sable."

"And it's not an umbrella." I feel weak, anxious. Whatever it is I must love it. You must always love Jamie's gifts because he suffers so choosing them and a flicker of disappointment may cause serious wounds. I close my eyes and open the box. Now, eyes open. "Oh God, Jamie, an emerald."

"David said you would be happy with a cabochon but I wanted a real cut gem. I said, 'Set it with sapphires.' David said, 'Yes, sapphires and that carved jade behind.' The minute I saw it, I knew it was Kate."

"Oh yes, it's me." Kissing his ear, his eyes and crying. Fast flashes of regret. Why isn't this man enough for me? "I can't bear it, Jamie. It's too beautiful."

He's crying too. "You deserve beautiful things. You're so good. Nobody but me knows how wonderful you are. They think you're tough, super chic, witty, steel. They don't know. Nobody knows." He lifts my hand to admire the ring. "It was actually a very good buy."

He wants to tell me how much. "Don't tell me. I'll be too nervous."

"I was surprised it was only—"

"Stop. Later. Tell me later. I might get sick."

He puts down his champagne glass. And reaches for me, fingers on my nipple, hand lightly circling the breast. His I-want-to-make-love-to-you signal. He kisses my shoulder and buries his head. "I can't. I don't know why. I want to make love to you," he whispers. "But I can't."

"Oh Jamie. We'll make love later." Does champagne and a birthday make fucking obligatory? Did I read it somewhere in *Larousse Gastronomique?* I'm not going to think about it now. Maybe Jamie has come to resent the command performance. Kate is up, wiggling into a clingy low-cut jersey maillot, slamming drawers, hunting for the white beach clogs, throwing them back into the closet, trying on a snappy panama and a floppy cartwheel, discarding them both for a neat white turban. Pretending that forty is not the end of the world.

"Don't you want to hear your horoscope?" asks Jamie. He is fascinated by the Voice of Radio Antilles with its daily morning horoscope. "Here's a warning for all you Gemini," sings a lilting West Indian voice. "What a best friend says may hurt you. Do not take it to heart."

"Jamie. I don't want to hear my horoscope."

"And this is for you Cancers. A loved one may disappoint you if you don't let him know what you have in mind."

"Jamie. It's silly but if it's something bad it will ruin my day." He ignores me. "I'm locking myself in the bathroom."

Kate is making her "natural look" face for the sun. Screeners, moisturizers, blushers. Jamie knocks. "It's all over. You can come out now. 'Good news for all you Aquarians,'" he mimics. "A legacy that will grow in value." He hands me a crystal of brown sugar from the breakfast tray. "Put this in your pussy and see if you can produce a pearl."

"Jamie. If I put that in my pussy all I could produce would be a mackerel."

"Kate. Bite your tongue." He hugs me studying our embrace in the bathroom mirror. "I could never leave you. You're so funny."

"I didn't know you were thinking of leaving me."

"I'm reaching that certain age, Kate."

"My birthday seems to be depressing you more than me, Jamie."

* * *

The French tourists here on Martinique are so relaxed. This is a bourgeois European family crowd at La Marveille. The children run naked. A lean sun-dried woman with the body of a prepubescent girl is sunning topless at the pool. She stands, places a hand over each near-nonexistent breast and steps into the pool for a swim. No one stirs.

On the beach ten feet in front of our low reclining chaises are two girls, not that young but young, topless, bikini-bottomed, backs to the sun. The blonde is golden with a lot of hair and a puffy blurred face. The other must be a brunette gone henna and deeply tanned, nails painted kelly green. She keeps examining herself in a round hand mirror rimmed in chartreuse plastic. Tossing her hair into a studied disarray. Jamie is fascinated. He lies there slicked in Coppertone with Updike open on his chest, deceptively uninterested, watching. Watching the two women turn and adjust themselves for a frontal toasting. The blonde is silkily languorous, knees up, knees open as if the sun were a friendly gynecologist. But the redhead keeps fidgeting self-consciously, turning on one side, cradling a breast in her arm, examining that position in the mirror, arranging her hair, touching herself in a glorious self-love affair.

Jamie sighs.

"Are you going to get a hard-on watching all that?" I ask.

"I don't think so."

"You can always hide it in Updike."

I am reading Joyce Carol Oates in paperback, *Marriages and Infidelities*. I am suddenly struck by the lush femaleness of so many words: silk, ripe, peach, open, full, creamy, bloom, wanton.

There is a marked increase in traffic at this end of the beach. Men strolling out along the jetty glance casually to the left as if the two girls were not the whole point of the exercise. The redhead is flashing her mirror. Is she looking to see who's looking? The two girls are singing in chorus. How wonderful to be so silly.

What is Jamie thinking? A few weeks ago coming out of a movie across from Bloomingdale's he groaned and blurted out: "All those naked bodies. So eminently fuckable." Why does he tell me? Why doesn't he just quietly go out and fuck a few eighteen-year-old bodies and come home turned on and love me.

"You can sun topless if you feel like it," Jamie says. "I won't be embarrassed."

"I'll think about it."

Midmorning rain. Very light drizzle. Everyone ducks under the palm-thatched clubhouse roof. Jamie leans against the wall, reading Updike. Close up the blonde is coarse and the redhead in a prim little shirtdress and big round spectacles is a bit blotchy and plain. At the edge of the concrete stand a beautiful young couple, teenagers, perfect bodies both. She is long-legged, near-naked, with high small breasts.

"Is that what you want?" I ask Jamie.

"I don't know," he says. "I had that and I still don't know."

"You could leave me, Jamie."

"I'll never leave you. I couldn't live without you."

"Then stop torturing me. Buy me something rummy."

"Let's get dressed and explore the town."

The sidewalk is narrow, lined with tin shacks painted pale pastels. Inside a small green-painted hovel there is a counter and a display of pitiful fruit. The oranges are green. Perhaps that is some wonderful organic secret. We buy three oranges for a franc. The shopkeeper stares.

Exploring a tiny inn on the water, I follow Jamie up a steep drive edged with magnificent tropical flowers. The terrace is deserted except for a sullen black girl at the bar. Jamie orders rum and pineapple juice for me, the house ice cream sundae for himself. She does not smile. Or nod. We sit opposite each other at the edge of a white stucco wall overlooking the sea. Incredibly sad. I am crying.

"I'm afraid to ask why you're crying," says Jamie, pouring melted guava jelly on his ice cream.

I will never say. I am thinking how it would have been how many years . . . eleven years ago when we were brand-new, when we couldn't get enough of each other, when the sweet softness inside my thighs made him crazy, when we would wake at night in the dark and come together, half-awake at first, then suddenly all the way conscious, Jamie banging so much love into me.

Walking home through a light drizzle. The hotel seems deserted. The room is cool and starkly ugly. I shower, watching the pale pink burn, ever-so-light not really a burn at all, a blush.

"See Jamie, how pink I am. Less than an hour did that. The rain saved us from epidermal disaster."

He touches. Puts down Updike. And makes love to me. Doing all the things he knows I like him to do. Fingers. Mouth. Coming into me from behind like a dog. Fierce. I feel myself flying out of myself brought back too quickly by a sudden awareness of his deliberate design.

I feel unfinished. He is collapsed on top of me, eyes closed, far away. "So good, Jamie. You do me so good." Oh Kate you sweetass liar.

The orange is not an organic triumph. It is sour. Jamie tosses his into the wastebasket. "This orange hasn't made up its mind yet if it's an orange."

Perhaps I just need someone to look at me . . . new.

V I

BAD DAY AT GREY ROCK overlooking Central Park West. Jamie gone a week. Kate six days overdue on the final revisions. Got a really keen and adoring lover but she's lucky to connect with him once every three weeks. "Maybe Thursday," he says over the phone. "We can meet with the bankers to finalize that deal." Get that. Code. Glass is very discreet. Always in code. Thursday the answering service has a message for me from Mr. Soot Factor. He's funny too. Mr. Soot Factor was suddenly called out of town and will not be able to make our conference this afternoon. The bastard. That could mean anything: The IRS has descended or his wife wants to go to Parke-Bernet or it's daddy's day at Dalton or some teenage hustler on Sixth Avenue gave him the eye and he's getting laid or rolled.

Telephone rings at 4:15. That will be Jerry Glass to proclaim the obvious. Not coming by this afternoon. "This day has been unreal," he begins, already on the defensive.

"Big shipment of wine just delivered and we've got to get it stashed away in the cellar. Fabulous wines. Nobody can afford to buy wines like these anymore but I have my sources. So here I am getting my rocks off lugging these cases—"

"Oh my God, Jerry." Now there's a fine delicate phrase. Getting your rocks off. "This has been going on all week. I'm sitting here, waiting for you, turning down invitations, waiting."

"I don't ask you to wait. You're making me feel guilty. Look, I don't need you to make me feel guilty."

"Right. Good night." I slam down the phone. Oh Kate, remarkable Kate. The best blow job this side of Central Park sits here waiting for some clod who is just as happy getting his rocks off moving crates of adolescent Bordeaux around the basement of his overpriced restaurant. Getting his rocks off. Okay. So Glass is honest. Damn. I used to think honesty was some kind of virtue. I try to be realistic. I have examined the intricacies of adultery and I have to admit that most probably I could not handle a more demanding lover when Jamie is in town and I am working. Glass loves his wife. Glass loves his children. Glass loves his restaurant. American-owned, German chef, but as good as the best French food in town. Glass loves his wines. And his cellar *is* a tiny marvel. Never have I seen him quite so aroused as the day he gave me the cellar tour, cradling the rare old magnums, stroking his treasury of '61's. "I'm a genius," he assures me. "Everyone said fifty-nine was the year of the century, but I went easy. Then came sixty-one and I knew. They said I was crazy and I was. Like a fox. I cashed in stocks and borrowed from my mother-in-law to buy sixty-one." Crazy is a word I do not use loosely. Jerry is mad. He hears voices. He sees auras. Mine is early Picasso blue. I could have told him that. He picks up vibrations walking down Lexington Avenue. "I don't like the vibrations near Lamston's today," he once said. "I'm selling all my stock and going into silver." Never mind that he was right, damn it.

He's priced his best wines so high no one but a drunken conventioneer would actually order a bottle. He is splintered by mixed emotion even if he himself is about to consume a great old bottle. Torn by unabashed joy for the taste and cruel regret for the loss from his cellar. He keeps plying me with "great little country wines." This goddamned cellar could turn into a sea of vinegar from age and the vibration of East 63rd Street before he will grudgingly share the intoxicating finesse of some truly great bottle with me. He pulls out a magnum of Petrus '61. And trembles. This is my first sight of a vulnerable Glass, a Glass who actually . . . cares. I am annoyed I guess, or maybe even jealous. He treasures Petrus more than Kate.

"Fuck me standing up like Marlon Brando," I command.

"Here?" he says, aghast. "Not here, darling. We could break something. You bitch. You make me so fucking hot." He leads me past a walk-in cold box, pointing to what looks like a small pizza in a dark corner. "Even the rats eat good at La Canaille. The chef makes them a poison quiche, see that . . . cheese and tomatoes and rat poison sprinkled on top. They love it. Don't be shocked. There's not a restaurant in town that doesn't have rats, you know." He laughs. La Canaille means the rabble. Glass's little joke.

I let him talk. Whenever he isn't actually fucking, he talks. He fucks well. Once-a-month for three years. Who would believe it? Me and Jerry Glass. I don't believe anyone has guessed, not even my secretary Holly who misses very little. For years I never really looked at Glass. He was always there at La Canaille, ignoring Babe Paley, pretending not to recognize Truman Capote, putting John Fairchild at a tiny table near the kitchen. Sweet revenge. "How vulgar," they say. "He can't even speak French."

Glass snarls. "I'll show them *de gustibus*."

I'm scarcely a regular on the big-time lunch circuit. But now and then I let myself be pampered or wooed. And one afternoon near the end of a forty-five-dollar lunch, I suddenly became aware of Glass as a man. Till then he was a background blur, Jerry Glass, primitive host with his mocking smile, the martinet restaurateur. Now he comes into focus, standing at our table, Glass the sexual man. His thigh presses against my arm and stays, not an accident. I look at him over the large expensive mock sheepskin menu contemplating dessert. He is very handsome, a little too Hart Schaffner, Jerry the barber does his hair, teased, sprayed, suspiciously blue-black. I'm not mad about that manicured look but he has a very natural rhythm in bed that suits mine. And he's safe. No professional or social overlap. Would anyone even believe it if they caught us coming rumpled out of a hot-sheet motel on 11th Avenue? Never. Looks like her, they might say, but couldn't be. Glass doesn't yet believe it himself. He doesn't trust me. He feels more comfortable in bed when he's paying. Or if some semi-pro offers him a quick lay. I'm not making this up. Glass will fuck anything. The poor dear primitive can't quite figure out what I see in him. "You're an intellectual," he says. "I'm just a slob. You're famous. And you don't like the way I treat you. When you want, you can go to bed with movie stars. Why do you put up with me?"

Glass and Kate in bed. He is running his hand over the curve of my hip. "Did anyone ever tell you you're stacked?"

Stacked. All right, stacked. Nobody booked this guy in as a poet. "Oh yes, every once in a while someone mentions it."

"Let's stay like this," he says. "Let's always look good. I'm going to start really working out at the club. Take a steam every afternoon. Swim." He slaps a slightly thickened midriff and sucks in trim muscled gut. He plays squash. The muscles of his right arm are like steel. Amazing shape for a roué of forty-seven. Forty-two, he tells me.

"Yes, we'll stay beautiful always," I agree. Brilliant idea. Charles Revson sailed a yacht financed by that idea. I've already invested several thousand dollars in the concept myself. Neat little $3,000 tit-lift, artful stitches fainter now, scarcely telltale. Stretch and bend. Stretch and bend, forty-five minutes every day till the end of time. "I feel beautiful with you, Jerry." That voice, Kate, how breathy sweet . . . vintage Marilyn Monroe. Well hell, I am feeding the ego that feeds me. In some perverse atavistic way I sort of actually almost love this dear old lug.

Mustn't be too harsh with Glass. Rough as he is, Glass is also sweetly romantic. Perhaps the last of a vanishing species. From the moment he clicked into my consciousness I knew we were fated for bed. But that was too straight for Jerry. Too simple. Not sufficiently devious. He needed to play out all the moves of the ritual seduction. Candlelight. Innuendo. Dialogue that begins with "what would happen if" or "where would we go if we were both totally free?" Kneesies and thighs pressing. Rubbings and humpings in darkened doorways. Greatcoated wrestlings and hungry kisses in the taxi home. Bare tit under the sweater, stolen. I loved it. I love to neck. Who has time for teasing foreplay these days? Jerry Glass, free once-a-month from 3 to 6 P.M. (I am later to learn) is time's prodigal. Kate is putty. Now Jerry has choreographed the consummation. In his head, he sees a bed. Where is it? Oh shit. There's no place to go. I had assumed so seasoned a Lothario must have an understanding crony to lend him a key to his *pied-à-terre*. The Glass ménage's rented ski lodge is three hours away. Anyway that's where Glass's wife is, else what would he be doing here?

Kate is no help. "I think it's bad manners for a wife to sleep with lovers in her husband's bed," I say, exasperated, my voice sharp. The taxi has made half a sweep now of the circle drive in Central Park.

Glass doesn't think it's bad manners. But at his apartment there's a Haitian maid, so that's out.

Kate groans. For a year I have kept my no-affairs-in-Manhattan vow. Now I am about to break my rule and this clown hasn't even plotted the logistics. "We could hire a limousine with curtains and do it in the backseat. I'd love that."

"You're joking, aren't you."

"There's a book, you know, French. About a brother and a sister. They hire a taxi because they have nowhere else to make love."

"To each other?"

"Hmmm. I believe that's the point of it. They're both virgins. So each finds someone else to show him . . . ah, her . . . how. Then they get into an old-fashioned taxi with the shades drawn."

"It wouldn't work," says Glass. "I'm too tall. And so's my sister."

With the instinct of a homing pigeon, our taxicab pulls up at some cheater's castle on the nowhere edge of the West Side. Glass takes the corner suite, forty-five dollars. He signs the register: Mr. and Mrs. Craig Claiborne. The clerk doesn't crack a smile.

Next time we'll go to my place. Fucking strangers at home is bad manners but forty-five dollars for a hotel room is criminal.

"I'm not good enough for you," Glass likes to say. That's the ritual signoff when he calls to explain why he can't find time for us this week.

"All right, I'm crazy," says Kate. "I want you anyway. You must come." I am crazy. I am begging. Weeping. Prowling around the typewriter waiting for Glass, vowing never to call him again . . . calling . . . "Please . . ." This can't be me, not me, *the* Katherine Wallis Alexander, Susskind's favorite wit and panelist, scripts adored by

Zanuck, raves from Canby . . . assorted horny young men tumbling at my feet. I've been to bed with America's hottest young filmmaker and with the brilliant, spoiled, charmingly neurotic son of my very close friend (what would she say if she knew?) and a certain supposedly bisexual textile designer . . . He has a hard, inexhaustible cock, can fuck for hours without coming. In the middle of all this uninvolved sport fucking, I find myself missing Glass. With Glass, you see, I'm me, not merely a convenient orifice. More than sex but less than love . . . nothing to threaten Jamie and me. I wouldn't be restless at all if I could have my measure of Glass once a week. And Jamie when he's in the mood. And eventually an Oscar. Ah, that would be a Captain's Wife's Paradise.

I fell in love last May. Just lightly, friends. Just epidermally, with a certain Italian director. Now, I thought, Glass is out of my life, banished. He is zero. I'll tell him "Goodbye forever." Paolo writes love notes, sends a chocolate bonbon inside an eighteenth-century Battersea box from Manheim Porcelain on 57th Street. "Love the Giver" it says on the lid. Paolo can't get enough of me. I don't have to put up with Glass's crap. Inevitably Paolo returns to Rome and Signora Paolo (as I knew he would). But for a time I am feeling too precious, too dignified, to fall back into the Glass routine. Then Glass calls. I thrill at Kate's hauteur, her chill ennui. Glass is casual, mocking, sounds as if he could not care less. Two days later Kate falters and is off again like a plastic pulltoy. "Why don't you stop by for a drink, Jerry, this afternoon when the lunch crowd leaves."

On again, off again, once-a-month Glass if I'm lucky. I am caught up in work again, on location in Utah, then a whole sweetly loving month with Jamie at the beach. Glowing with color, tanned prudently twenty minutes a day per Dr. Orentreich's warning, calm. And a grass-scented ten days with Maggy, very intimate and funny, just back from music camp. An assignment from Paramount. And plans to produce myself, maybe even direct, my Eudora Welty script nobody else has wanted to do all these years.

One afternoon in September I walk into La Canaille with Gideon Kennecky, the publisher. Gideon is rich and social, handsome in a strong tweedy battered way and flirtatiously attentive not because he is trying to bed me, as Glass instantly supposes, but because he wants me to try writing another novel. Glass is discreet, very proud, eyebrows just perceptibly out of control. He suggests a "nice little Bordeaux" and sticks Gideon with a twenty-eight-dollar Château Palmer puckery with tannin.

"I've just gotten back from a week in the vineyards," Glass ventures. I ignore him.

As we leave, Glass makes a great fuss, helping us into raincoats and presenting umbrellas with mock military snap. He pulls me back. "I jerked off twice last week thinking about you."

"Oh Christ."

"I thought you would be pleased," he says, brown eyes wide, face tanned and handsome. "I think about you more than you think I do."

Mantovani could do a lot with that lyric. Oh hell. You want to know something disgusting? I *am* pleased. This morning I learned I am the protagonist of a very flattering anecdote in a Robert Towne interview in the Sunday *Times* but knowing that I am the fantasy object of Jerry's jerkoff is at least 50 percent more pleasing.

What a spectacular day. One of those rare clear intoxicating New York spring blue-sky afternoons less than a month ago. Swallow your pride, Kate. It has no calories. The equinox is on my side. I have actually persuaded busy Innkeeper Glass to play hooky. Spring has got to Glass too. He is very big on nature. He says, "You're right. It's too beautiful a day to work, let's go for a ride." It would be fun to explore Dutchess County, if only there were time. Once

around the Palisades, since we're a bit pressed? Alas, today
there's no time even for the discount tour. Today we are
driving twice around Central Park.

"Oh God, I love the country," Glass says.

Twice around the park and home to get laid. "You
should have known me when I was a playboy," says Glass.
"I didn't get into business, not seriously, till ten years ago.
Boy was I a bum then. I did nothing. Squash, tennis, fuck.
I got laid every afternoon and then I went to the club for
a workout and a steam." Get laid. I hate that expression.
I love to fuck but I never . . . get laid. Yet here I am
smiling sweetly, tolerantly, lovingly at an arrogant clod who
doesn't know the difference. Glass is a man of habit. Gets
laid in the afternoon. And you, my dear paranoid-schizo-
phrenic late-blooming adventuress, are today's lucky layee.
Lay-away.

"That was some workout," says Glass kneading his
belly muscles and flexing his thighs. "We're terrific together.
You're a great piece of ass." As if he'd forgotten. I really
am special today. The tender earth mother and the crazed
wanton. I have surpassed myself on the Richter scale. "You
could make a fortune doing this professionally," he observes.

"Jerry, for God's sake."

"I thought you'd react like that. But I mean it. Six
thousand a week . . . I'm leaving a little free time for me,
that makes, ah . . . six thousand times fifty-two. Maybe
six thousand is slightly optimistic, make it four thousand.
That's two hundred grand a year, tax-free, minus my cut,
of course."

"Minus time off to get my hair done."

"No problem."

He's serious. "You really think I could . . . do this
professionally?"

"Absolutely."

"I'd make you pay too."

"Wait a minute. I'm the one bringing in the action."

"And cash only. I don't take checks. Or credit cards."

He leaps out of bed, stretching to touch his toes. "That was some workout," he says. "I don't know about you, but for me, that was some workout. Better than an hour of squash."

At least there are no witnesses. Just when time and success and the pressure of late blooming have brought me to the ideal balance of ego and wholesome narcissism, I discover fucking me is only slightly more invigorating than a game of squash. Doubles, that is. What am I doing here with this clown? Why aren't I beating him with a shower clog? Why am I stroking his arm, giving his shoulder fluttery little kisses, for God's sake? If it's true about the meek inheriting, I'm overdue.

Now I'm so restless it takes every ounce of discipline to keep myself at the typing table more than ten minutes at a stretch. I have rearranged one shelf of books—all the autographed first editions and books by friends, all my leatherbound scripts and the books I've adapted and my own novel and published screenplays in custom binding and gold leaf. I'm staring at Jamie's face in the tortoiseshell frame. I love him. And I'm depressed to see someone has left a wet glass that made a ring in the finish of the Renaissance chest Jamie loves and worked hours to restore. I need something to pick me up. Vitamin C. Grapefruit juice, I think. The Cowboy. Now that would be a worthwhile challenge.

What did he say at Chez Lipp? If only we'd met a year and a half ago. What shit. I'm too finished for him, I bet. Too much uniquely myself. I bet he likes to start with fresh clay, something younger, innocent . . . someone he can mold. If I were Hepburn in *The Rainmaker* he'd love to be my flimflam man, the mesmerizing Starbuck.

"You're a woman. Believe in that," Starbuck tells the eager spinster Kate.

If nothing else, I believe in that. And I do believe in Vitamin C. A practical Kate should be grateful Jason O'Neill is nowhere in sight. A practical Kate takes 1,000 units of organic rose hips in tablet—fewer calories than grapefruit juice.

Each time the phone rings, I wait till the service answers, then I pick up the receiver to sneak a listen, too depressed to talk to just anyone. What am I waiting for? Adventure. Carlos Underwood is having a few friends in after a screening tonight, I hear him tell the service. Mostly fags, I suppose, some of my good friends, and a sprinkling of neuters. But I'm going stir crazy. I *did* work all morning, a very funny little column for *Playbill,* so why not . . .

"Hi Carlos, it's me, Kate."

"Oh, you're home," the answering service operator says brightly as if she didn't know.

"I've ordered dumplings from Pearl," Carlos volunteers, "and tons of lemon chicken and Nino has promised to bring Bertolucci."

"Hmmm. I'd love to see you, Carlos. I'll be there."

VII

WAKING UP MORNINGS next to strangers used to worry me. Long ago in another century waking up next to a stranger created anxiety, an unreal appetite for breakfast, rashes that lasted till afternoon, once even a false pregnancy. Time and the times cured that. Now I don't mind morning strangers at all, though I feel residual guilt seeing them here in Jamie's house, less guilty because at least it's the guest room and not Jamie's pillow and our own shared bed. This stranger is baby-faced, cocker spaniel eyes and all over freckles. With a deviated septum. Or so it sounds. The snore is what woke me. He looks scruffy and tough, sort of like a hustler I might have picked up outside a deli in the jungle at Times Square and 42nd Street. Perhaps that's where Carlos actually found him though he insists not: "Don't you love it," Carlos is saying. "He came with the groceries from Waldbaum's."

I stalk him stalking the dim sum as fast as Carlos'
houseboy gets them heaped artfully between poufs of fresh
green coriander on Imari platters atop the long T-square
table.

"I'm only just into Art Deco and it's already démodé,"
Carlos confides.

Only rarely, in moments trading domestic confidences,
does Carlos become mildly faggy. Even at gatherings of
the gay faithful, even tonight, surrounded by delicate,
mannered friends, rough trade and the usual amusing and
decorative women of a certain age with their rotating
escorts, Carlos reigns witty, rich and above it all. Success
as a playwright seems to have liberated Carlos from most
homosexual clichés. Yet I can sense how intent he is on
seducing the kid from Waldbaum's. Am I a bitch? Am I just
perversely competitive? Am I newly militant—unwilling
to surrender one male body to the enemy? Mostly I just
don't feel like going to bed alone. Well, it looks like I've
captured the prize. I am already sloshed on stingers and
now as we leave together, Waldbaum's Mercury and me,
Carlos, good old Carlos, laughs and shakes his head and
drops two joints into the kid's pocket.

"Don't forget to return him to Waldbaum's," says
Carlos.

The kid says he is Phi Beta Kappa in anthropology
at Yale but he hasn't got it all together yet, so for the
moment, he delivers groceries for Waldbaum's. "You meet
some very predatory people." He turns out to be a sur-
prisingly skillful lover. He moves so lazily and talks so
softly, his philosophy of life is so indolent, you figure he
could crawl into bed and forget what brought him there.
Sloshed now, stoned later, I might forget too. I remember
weird athletic diversions. I remember . . . oh shit, I can't
remember.

The morning light is strangely grey. I'm embarrassed

to ask his name. He is propped against the headboard reading Kate Millett. He looks even younger than he did last night. I run fingers through my hair letting it veil the eyes. I must put this bed against the other wall so I get morning key light. If the lights hits you fierce head-on, it's as kind as a filter—erasing shadows, lines and hollows.

Camera dollies in on Princess Kosmonopolis in sunglasses, dazzling key light and dramatic deshabille on a satin chaise longue. "Who are you?" She lifts her sunglasses to study Waldbaum's Paul Newman. "God knows I've done better. And God knows I've done worse."

Fade to Kate in the bathroom, neutralizing the ravages with Erace and Ultima's pale green toner. "Do you want to take a shower or . . . something?" He seems so settled in. And Holly will be here at eleven to do the mail. "I'm going to work now," I announce, walking through the guest room in stern black pants and prim black turtleneck.

"Good." He wanders into my office, naked in his snakeskin boots. I ignore this but I can't help noticing how curious he is, picking up the silver snuffboxes and bronze cats, studying the malachite cigarette case that once belonged to Cole Porter—Jamie got it at auction from Parke-Bernet—blowing into a pre-Columbian whistle shaped like a fox and running a careful finger over the big black Nevelson boxes, lightly, not to catch a splinter. "I guess I'll have a glass of milk," he says. "And then I better go." He reappears dressed and I walk him to the door. He pats my fanny. "It's the Waldbaum's on Lexington at Sixty-fifth Street."

I feel weak and wet, gripped by raging paranoia. Kate you fool, he could have been the sexfiendjunkierapist- secondstoryman you're always waiting for. Quick inventory of treasures. Purse tossed carelessly on the entrance table.

Untouched. Kate is getting out of hand, friends. My face in the crackle of the antique mirror is flushed and damp.

"Kate. Who was that?" Holly emerges from the kitchen with our breakfast on a tray.

"Jesus Christ, Holly. I can't decide if you're terribly discreet or downright sneaky." I'm not going to ask how long she's been lurking.

"I try to be graceful, Kate."

I can't face the day without thick black espresso. Holly is allergic to coffee. She makes herself rosehip tea and always indulges us with some goody. Drake's crumb cake or maple pecan doughnuts, sometimes carob cake and organic brownies. This morning we have raspberries. Holly is dieting again. I share Holly with Buddy Canfield, the moldering but still brilliant "new" journalist (Buddy is too old to be new but I'm not going to debate the point with Tom Wolfe). Buddy had Holly first, three days a week but she was getting restless, he said, and needed more income so he graciously agreed to share her. Quite frankly, Buddy is four years overdue on his long talked about nonfiction "novel" and he's smashed most of the time and doesn't need Holly that much anymore. So gradually I am inheriting this dear chubby asthmatic little dilettante. She hates typing letters. Dictation gives her colitis. And she has only recently mastered the filing system, after a fashion. Letters signed from Miss Braelis for Richard Zanuck got filed under *F* for Fox which wasn't all that impossible till Zanuck moved to Warner Bros. For a time I was collecting clips on freezing the dead—that all got tucked into the ice cream file (Jamie is mad about homemade ice cream).

"I want you to know I would have quit months ago if you weren't a woman," Holly confided to me one day. "You're a sister and you need me," she explained.

"That doesn't explain your loyalty to Buddy," I reminded her.

"To me Buddy is beyond gender. Besides Buddy is pathetic. He *really* needs me."

Holly has absolutely no ambition. She is convinced my life would become hopelessly boggled if she left so she cheerfully totes my scuffed sandals to the shoemaker for new soles and picks up Jamie's cigars at Dunhill. She is wonderful with caterers, loves helping out at parties and adores running amok for me at Bloomingdale's. She can scream at clumsy window washers—"How dare you soil our woodwork." And cow the most arrogant dry cleaner. And she's a demon when it comes to filing complaints. We are the Consumer Affairs Office's most constant correspondent. When $400 dresses come back from the cleaner minus buttons or manmade fabrics disintegrate overnight or the bathroom carpet rots from humidity, I sic Holly on the goddamned bastards. She reads law books all the time and has won two cases in a row in small claims court. She saved us $358 in taxes last year on some obscure IRS ruling. The accountants were awed. Holly knows everything about me . . . everything except perhaps a few minor specifics. And some of it depresses her.

"You and Jamie are the two most loving and devoted unfaithful people I know," she moans. "Why do you do it, Kate? Jamie adores you. You adore him."

"Fidelity is a waste of natural resources," I say.

"I'd die before I'd be unfaithful to Mitchell MacGhee."

"No one is unfaithful to lovers, Holly. Just husbands. Longtime husbands."

"I think it's Mount Everest for you," Holly once analyzed. "There it is and there you are . . . can't pass up a mountain."

I like the metaphor. But as challenges go Jerry Glass is more of an anthill than an Everest. And Waldbaum's kid is not exactly an Alp. Perhaps my body has been somewhat underutilized. Still, loving and tamely predictable sex once or twice a week is probably a statistical average. It can't be that I don't have better things to do—stealing an hour for The Algonquin requires unbelievable juggling and lies. I don't know . . . it just feels so good. I missed the drama, the danger, the game . . . not till I finally found myself in bed with that demon black Irishman being fucked out of my head did I realize how good it would feel. To exist mindless, guileless, out of control . . . all pussy, all female. If I had an analyst I suppose we could make hash out of all that. Mostly I can think about it tomorrow. But I do worry about Holly's telegraph system. She swears to me on the honor of Mitchell MacGhee and the Scum Manifesto and the Radical Coalition that she reveals none of my confidences to Buddy Canfield but I am not altogether convinced because she tells me absolutely everything about him. Most of it too disgusting to repeat. He buys the cheapest vodka and pours it into an empty Smirnoff bottle. He wears a retainer brace on his teeth at night . . . unless he has company. He writes letters to his folks on the back of studio press releases. He pees sitting down. He shaves his armpits. He watches *General Hospital*. He has a crush on Burt Reynolds. He keeps a lacy orchid bed jacket in the farthest reaches of his closet. "For god's sake, Holly, you don't actually go through his closet."

Holly is outraged innocence. "He wears it when he's sick in bed. It was his mother's." I want to trust Holly. "I would never betray a sister," she says. Still, Buddy Canfield is sort of a sister too. I shudder to think what wide-eyed observations about me fall from the petulant Vaseline-slicked lips of Holly Bernstein. No wonder I am so good to Holly. Theater passes, screenings, peanut-butter fudge sent by a longtime fan in Buffalo, a slightly scuffed Gucci bag, the kid gloves with harness chains at the wrist from Jamie's mother. Holly gets more than half the books that come touted as "so right for Kate Alexander." This week it was a wonderful poetic memoir too sweet and too plotless for today's film industry and some incredible garbage about a Baldwin, Long Island, housewife who invents a bust-developing cream synthesized from Gerber's strained peaches, wheat germ and hair-spray, and leaves her husband and three children to become a topless go-go dancer in Las Vegas.

Jamie wonders why I keep Holly. Well, there aren't too many uncompetitive humans with an I.Q. over 102 who would remember where they misfiled a really important clipping, four months later . . . or cheerfully hit five hardware stores in search of an elusive tensor light bulb. And besides, she lies. Holly is the most convincing and imaginative liar I know. She is truly gifted. She ad-libs fabrications with an icy chill, not a hint of a stammer, never a feint of regret. "Mrs. Alexander walked out the door just five minutes before you called" is child's play for Holly even with my typewriter keys clacking behind her. "I put it in the mail last night" is nothing. On a letter two weeks overdue, she types the proper long-passed date and then walks all over it. "It probably got lost in the Post Office," she will suggest. "Oh yes, she was reading your book yesterday afternoon. I've never heard her laugh like that before . . . but she'll want to tell you herself." Lies. Lies. Lies. "She had appointments all afternoon," she will tell Jamie. Or, "They drove to Westchester to look at locations." And "There's a meeting with some money people in Chicago . . . she'll try to fly back tonight." Holly doesn't like lying to Jamie but she likes lying so she psychs herself up for the kill.

The phone rings now. I sense her winding up for a smashing line drive to my agent. But I can't duck Hinkenstadt any longer.

"This isn't like you, Kate," Harry says. "You have a terrific reputation for meeting deadlines. Nobody's asking you for a treatment, just a conversation. I know you're working on something you're not ready to talk about. But these people are waiting. Is it something about this particular story that has you blocked?"

"Harry, I'm not blocked. I'm distracted. I have a few other things on my mind. There was some family business . . . with my mother, trust things, Jamie's mother's." Next to Holly I'm a pitiful liar. "Give them some really impressive legitimate reason and I'll get to it this afternoon. Tomorrow, definitely."

Holly is shaking her head. "If you'd warned me . . . I'd have had a story ready. Whatever happened to the jiffy bag?" she cries. "Why do they mail books now with these two-inch staples? I bet it's a plot against the Women's Movement. They know we break our nails trying to open these damn things."

"Holly, for God's sake. Not Jamie's boning knife. Use a screwdriver. He'll kill us." Holly does not wear makeup. She is allergic to almost everything. Now she has stopped wearing bras. I can see the brown of her nipples through the wide crochet of her sweater.

"Aren't you nervous walking down the street with your nipples exposed?" I ask.

"I look everyone straight in the eye."

"If I did that, I'd trip."

"It does sort of scratch. Do you find it lewd?"

"I don't know what keeps the rapists back."

"An old woman on Broadway hit me with her umbrella. She called me a witch. Perhaps she meant bitch. I want to be a natural woman. It makes Mitchell nervous too. And it hurts like hell when the taxi goes over a pothole and your breasts start flying." She picks up the unbound galleys of Lorna Neilsen's new novel. "I'm going to bind these for you somehow," Holly offers, knowing how I hate to read rough galleys.

I don't really feel ready to tackle the morning mail.

Careful not to bruise Jamie's pampered bamboo palms at the window, I watch the traffic on Central Park West. I do talk to the palms but mostly I just breathe on them. It's the carbon dioxide not the dialogue that counts. There was a spider fern but it was dying so I gave it to State Senator Sidney Blumberg. Once a fern needs intensive care, I just give up. Sidney is a fern specialist, he said. Now, there was an unrewarding adulterous diversion. I knew Sidney from benefits and fund raising and I knew exactly what he had in mind the day he invited me to lunch. "I'm just a peasant from the Bronx," he said. "I wouldn't know what to order at La Grenouille." He pronounced it gren-oo-ly. So we drove down to the Lower East Side for knishes at Yonah Schimmel. Even Sidney wasn't peasant enough to finish his. So we picked up blintzes-to-go from Ratner's and a carton of thick sour cream. He was very direct. He wanted to go to bed. I wondered why he'd even bothered with the lunch.

"Well, why not," I said. "Let's go."

He was too excited and really not very good. He came in a stroke and a half and seemed quite pleased with himself.

"Was that good for you?" he asked.

I smiled mysteriously, too polite to answer.

It was obvious he had another appointment. Annoyed, I stood at the window breathing on Jamie's palms while he redid his tie.

"This little fern has white bug," Sidney observed.

"Oh no. Does it really? Damn." I snatched it away lest it infect the palms. "I'll throw it down the incinerator."

"You don't have to do that," he said. "It can be saved. I happen to be an expert on ferns."

"It's brown and spindly anyway."

"Then give it to me." He walked out very dignified, cradling the fern and handed it to his chauffeur. He calls once in a while but I say I'm busy. I haven't got time for men who aren't marvelous in bed. I don't mind guiding and expanding the sensory awareness of some twenty-three-year-old but a man of forty has either got it or . . . he's beyond remedial therapy. What exquisite power I feel. Back at Northwestern, my best friend Louella used to say, "reject before rejection." Well, I finally have.

My office looks like New Year's Eve. Holly is attacking the Neilsen galleys with a hole punch and the holes are flying like confetti. "We don't have a looseleaf binder anywhere," she says, "And no binder rings, so I'm going to use a couple of bangle bracelets till I get to the stationery shop." I can only marvel.

Speedread *Variety* and the *Hollywood Reporter.* If only Holly could read them for me. "It's your mother's birthday today," she announces studying the calendar. "You sent her a moderately sexy nightgown by John Kloss . . . hyacinth-blue, and a basket from Bloomingdale's made of real bread."

"Oh shit, she'll hate them both."

"I loved them both."

"I'm not up to actually calling her just now. Get me Maggy in Saugerties or Woodstock or wherever she is."

Maggy sounds light-years away and awfully Goody-Two-Shoes. She must be up to some really monumental evil. "Oh Kate, why are you calling in the middle of the afternoon? You should wait for the 'rate change at five."

"I can't count on being alive at five, Maggy." Then sorry to sound so irritated. "You're very thoughtful, dear, but I like to follow my impulses. What are you up to, darling?"

"I've been planting lettuce all morning and I'm doing research on the compost question. And I'm keeping a journal and of course I'm in love. You'll meet him when you come up for a visit. Just as soon as we get a little more settled."

"You haven't changed your mind about summer school or visiting the Bayers in Porto Ercole."

She sighs. "Oh Mom . . . I'm not interested in frivolous things anymore. I'm not running away from reality. I'm facing myself."

"Summer school is not quite running away."

"You know, Kate. I love the way we are on the telephone. Remember the Loud family. They had nothing to say to each other. We really try."

"Well, communication between the generations can be dangerous, Maggy."

"We live dangerously." She giggles. "Oh, almost forgot. Thank you for the goodies from Bloomingdale's. Do you have any idea what Holly sent . . . it must have cost a fortune."

"Holly is on a diet and Bloomie's fancy food shop is her big noncaloric outlet."

"Well, Mom, I personally adore brandied peaches and marrons in vanilla syrup and lobster bisque. But everyone here is pretty rigid about eating organic. I don't want to sound ungrateful, but next time maybe she could do her transference number at Brownie's or The Good Earth up on Lex."

"Okay, sweetie."

"I love you, Kate."

"I love you, Maggy. You're sure everything is all right? Honest?"

"A Gemini never lies."

"Geminis always lie."

"Oh Mom."

Leafing through the mail. There is a slim envelope from my clipping service: late rage from a small-town housewife who's only just gotten around to seeing *He Loves Me, Loves Me Not* at the Peachtree Corners Drive-In. Finds it shocking. Is disgusted to discover it was written by a woman. Writes angry letter to the editor, Peachtree *Gazette*. Five clips of the Earl Wilson item about a supposed exchange of rat poison and roach spray between me and Ryder Meade. What flack made that up? Rat poison and roach spray. How banal. I should have asked Bobby Zarem to think up an elegant denial for me. And this from *Women's Wear*: Elena the manicure wizard confides she does my pedicure. Elena says I use Earth Plum on my toes. Guess I've got to be grateful she doesn't ooze into the iggly piggly details of pumicing my calluses. What would *Women's Wear* say if they heard that now and then I use Peach Whip blusher by Yardley on my nipples?

Jason O'Neill isn't listed with Houston information. Ryder Meade is out . . . or possibly not taking my call. Ryder's secretary has three numbers for Jason. I am muttering something about cattle as a clever tax shelter. Now what will I do if I find him? A long-distance tease?

Enter Holly, face streaked with tears. "Oh Kate, this book . . . *Diary of My Obsolescence*. It's poetry. Like *Ariel*."

"Harry said it's about a great beauty in love with an irresistible bastard."

"Oh Kate, it's all about growing old."

The page is streaked with Holly's tears. "I am not a shallow woman," the paragraph begins. "I have given enormous chunks of myself to the men I have loved. And they have always disappointed me. I was just a decoration to the painter. He saw me thrashing in the act of love with the Minotaur. And now the social-climbing journalist taunts me in the morning: 'What is it, Serena, afraid of the sunlight? Don't dare open the blinds.' He pinches me with play-masked hate. 'I love your plump thighs.' When did my thighs become plump? Where did these plump thighs come from?" Oh hell, not another hysterical aging female. Enough. "Holly, this is garbage."

"Kate, you know nothing about thighs. *I* have thighs. My hair is getting grey. What will I do if Mitchell Mac-Ghee notices my thighs?"

"Holly, you nut. For every kind of thigh there is a man who will love it. You must get undressed at some point in your relationship with this man. Don't tell me. Get yourself a fresh cup of tea, Holly, and we'll do this mail."

Memo to Harry Hinkenstadt: Not interested *Obsolescence*. Too sentimental, too exaggerated, too close to home (that's off-the-record, HH). Adore the new Barbara Greenspan book. Her agent sent it to me directly in bound galleys. It has a wonderful manic madness. It's angry and funny, very real. It could be Streisand, could be Burstyn. Find myself underlining passages we could use. Can I take an option myself? Then you could make it into a package. I hear Friedkin has read it. Get a copy and let me know.

Memo to me re Greenspan treatment: I want to convey a sense of her anger and her appealing capacity for self-mockery. What's wrong with Marina? Incredible to think that a woman as bright, witty, attractive (she *is* handsome in a crisp, fashionable, sexy way . . . crisp *and* sexy, yes) would simply drift through life letting coincidence and the whims of men decide her fate. In her work, she is a force. Emotionally she has a kind of fatalistic passivity. A straight summary of the plot reads like *Mildred Pierce*. The book's pace and wit make it funny and contemporary. Marina is today's woman, confused. There is no mention of the Movement, thank God. Too easy to fall back into cliché. I'm beginning to feel uncomfortable with certain lib auto-think. I hate flashbacks that start at funerals. At least she has on shoes and it won't be raining. This is a New York City funeral, sandwiched in between deadlines, contract signings, Halston fittings and lunch at "21." Both widows in black. Sons kissing first one and then the other. The older woman, Richard's wife, comforting Marina, Richard's mistress of sixteen years. Then the cut: "Before he died, Richard asked me to give you the De Kooning and the red Rothko and both Lindners, Marina, but I'm not going to give them. I'm telling you so you'll know he cared. We need the money and I'm too old to start all over again." Marina, of course, has the real De Kooning, Rothko, the Lindners—his wife, the fakes. Gothic funeral, very black, garbage strike, lovers in the distance so romantic in the cemetery close up turn out to be . . . fags, of course. Maybe that's a bit much.

I am dialing Houston. His voice. My hand on the phone is wet.

"Kate Alexander. The sensuous movie writer. The expert on the etiquette of adultery. How are you?"

"Was I that outrageous?"

"Outrageous? Not at all. You were a charming evangelist. Very tempting. I think about you often."

"I'm pleased," says Kate in a breathy little Jackie voice. Where does that come from? And how do I segue into cows? "Would you believe that I've been thinking of cows?"

"If you say so, I'll have to believe it," he says, laughing.

The bastard knows.

"Next time you're in New York I was hoping you'd take time to speak to our accountant. Explain, you know."

"Of course. But why don't I send you some brochures and a prospectus we have."

"Oh." Silence pregnant with dashed fantasies. "Please. Yes. Do."

"And how are the Amazons doing? Especially you,

Kate? Your life still full of champagne and conquests?"

"Hmmm. I'm fine. Very busy. My life is glamorous. As always. And yours, Jason?"

"Fine. Really fine." He pauses. "Listen, Kate, I'll be in New York soon. I'll call you."

Good for you, Kate. The meek may inherit after all. But they'll have to hire a marshal to evict the aggressive.

VIII

NEW YORK is the heartland of ritual decadence. And lunch in New York is my favorite quagmire of decay. Any two people of minimal intellect could contrive schemes more efficiently by phone. But one must eat now and then and the cunning of the income tax system encourages big-bracketed folk to drop everything at noon for the tax-deductible salmon in brioche and a golden Corton-Charlemagne. Even when cottage cheese and a hard-boiled discipline would be infinitely wiser.

Noni Gelfan loves Maxwell's Plum. Since Noni is a critic-writer-journalist, I am a tax-deductible mouth to her and she is tax-deductible public relations for me even though we are dedicating 7 percent of lunch to pure pleasure in salmon, 12 percent to innocent gossip and 81 percent to outright assassination. Anyway, it's not an outrageous stretch to argue that journalism and movies are 7 percent pure salmon, 12 percent innocent gossip and 81 percent outright assassination.

Growing up in the dry, muted gentility of Evanston, Illinois, I came to associate food with prim flowered Spode plates on an old, slightly warped gateleg table in a white-washed sunny dining room. Lunch downtown was a tuna-fish sandwich on toasted white. Dinner was roast beef at the Club, gently boring and overdone. I cannot believe to this day that I am about to shell out (or is it Noni's turn?) thirty-five dollars for lunch in this hysterical cacophony of art nouveau and nouveau nouveau chatter.

"What is Gloria's problem?" Noni is musing. I cannot get used to what Noni's done to her face. She has bleached her eyebrows and plucked them to vampish parentheses. Her mouth is drawn in a perfect Cupid's bow stained the color of chicken liver. And her hair is hidden inside a twist of white jersey. And still the silly little bitch is beautiful.

"You mean Vanderbilt, Swanson or Steinem?"

"Kate. Stop toying with me. You know. I know you know. Never mind Gloria's cosmic problem. I'm talking specifically about this thing of hers with body hair. I shall never forget that thing she said in the *Times*. You must remember. What do you do about body hair?"

"Body hair?" My computer comes up blank. I must have missed the segue staring at that remarkably sexy man —bald, bristling eyebrows, dimpled vital face, gravel voice and Slavic accent, lecturing the woman beside him . . . she in an exaggerated pose of boredom. "Body hair?" I look at my arm. I'm very fair. The hair is blond. It doesn't show. Noni's arm is hairless as an egg. "This isn't something new due to the Pill?"

She shakes her head. "I mean shaving your legs, Kate, and under your arms."

"Oh Noni. Not you. *You* would stop shaving your legs?"

"Kate, I don't know how you manage to stay so isolated. You can't simply ignore the Movement. I'm not a militant but I'm committed financially, emotionally."

"Now wait . . . I signed the abortion statement. I give money to Bella. I make my airline reservations in the name of Ms. Alexander. I hate that sound. Miz. But I use the goddamned thing."

"You may think Gloria is pretentious—"

"I never said—"

"I mean that thing in the *Times*. Gloria said . . . it's engraved in needlepoint on my heart . . . 'women who shave are a symbol of a smooth, hairless ideal, the perpetual child . . .'"

I shudder, pursued by a sudden inescapable vision of stubbled legs in white bobby sox. "Manifestos like that alienate the hausfraus, Noni. Manifestos like that alienate *me*. That's where I feel Gloria makes a mistake. In fact, I've been toying with the idea of shaving my pubic hair."

"You're kidding, of course. Anyway, pubic hair is in. Even *Playboy*'s consciousness has been raised to recognize pubic hair. All right. I know you're kidding." She sips her wine. "Did we really finish a whole bottle?" She waves across the room at someone in a turban precisely like her own, the same stylish plucked chicken look. I must renew my subscription to *Vogue*.

"Money isn't enough, Kate. If you care about women, you've got to put your body on the line. I do what I do at the gravest risk. The word *Sisterhood* is like a red flag to Herb. I made a sort of a joke once about maybe God was a woman and he smashed the fish tank with his fist. What a mess."

"I don't get the connection."

"He said he'd sooner believe God was a gerbil."

"Why didn't he smash the gerbil?"

"The gerbils died months ago. You certainly don't want to seem to be rejecting the Movement, do you, Kate?"

"Nobody asks me much. Maybe they don't think I'm . . . sincere."

"You are known to be something of an Aunt Tom. Anyway, maybe the dykes have got something, screaming how all us straight women should get rid of the men in our lives. Maybe in some nutty way, sex is to woman what alcohol is to the alcoholic. In order to be free, perhaps you've got to eliminate sex from your life entirely."

"Sex is the last thing I'm eliminating. The only thing I'm eliminating is body hair. What is existence without sex, Noni? What is life without men?"

"That's approximately what Gloria said."

"Maybe too many women are afraid of disappearing into some great man's aura. Are you afraid of being swallowed by the force of Herb's personality? Frankly, when you're in the room, Herb's aura fades into the wallpaper, Noni. I'm not unhappy at being seen as a sex object. I love it. If I spend an afternoon with a man who doesn't see me as a sex object, I'm depressed for a week."

"You're very lucky, Kate. You have Jamie and he adores you. And you have always been a liberated woman . . . long before there was a name for it. You go where you please. You do your work. You're independent, but you're too relaxed about it, too cavalier. Something's wrong. If you ask me, you need your consciousness raised more than I do." Noni is staring at the American Express charge form, struggling to compute the tip *a capella*. I'm afraid the whole Women's Liberation Movement is doomed unless women can learn how to multiply in their heads by 15 percent without visible hysteria. "Come to my consciousness raising group," she urges. "You've had a free ride, Kate. You've never really had to struggle. Think of your Sisters. Sisterhood. I know it sounds corny. But it's healthy, really. You begin to realize everybody gets the same kind of shit from guys."

Two tables away against the wall, a bouncy little

brunette is salting a daisy and nibbling at the petals. "The Movement has practically ruined my life," Noni goes on. She seems cheered by the observation. Almost ecstatic. "In the last year I've had colitis and said good-bye forever to Herb twice. I've picketed and sat-in and signed the abortion statement too. I've been disinherited by my family. I've learned karate, spent four hours in jail and been the victim of retaliatory impotence for months." She stands up and I brace myself for the sight of her hairy legs. Thank God. She's wearing wheat-colored dungarees tucked into ivory suede boots. "You're so lucky. Jamie is a mature, un-threatened man. He doesn't seem threatened that no one has ever heard of him and everyone in town knows you. Oh shit, there's my cousin Muffy. She's seen us, so we better walk by and say hello. She has no consciousness at all to speak of and my mom promised her mom I'd help her find a job. At least she found the courage to leave her husband."

"I've been so depressed," Muffy confesses as they exchange cheek-graze kisses. "But this month something mystical happened. I'm a Leo. So I wasn't expecting anything. But that man I told you about, the fabulous businessman from Chicago, married of course, naturally. He's coming for dinner tomorrow night on his way to Rabat. I'm doing Michael Field's Normandy chicken and Julia's tarte tatin and the tiniest baby string beans."

Noni groans, sitting down and helping herself to the dregs of a Bloody Mary. "Muffy, you are something out of the Middle Ages. One step forward and three steps back. The guys treats his wife like shit and stops by to ball you at midnight and you're falling all over yourself to spend the day cooking a four-course dinner."

Muffy's gel blush glow deepens. "I wish I were sophisticated like you, Noni. But I'm just getting used to taking my clothes off in front of strangers. I'm trying to be free."

Noni resists the impulse for overkill.

I am looking at Muffy. Muffy is 5'9". She weighs 128 pounds. She is twenty-three years old. She hasn't the tiniest suspicion that the world is populated by bastards who just want a quick fuck and a breast of chicken. Some people find innocence refreshing. Not me. I don't actually loathe her. It just feels like I do.

"Call me," says Noni, "they need someone in Senator Javits' office. Might be something for you, Muffy."

We walk out behind a man with a bulging briefcase and a radiant ingenue in marabou chubby. Man kisses marabou good-bye and she runs north on First Avenue. He hails a taxi. Noni snorts. "What did Lessing say? She never met a man who would stop his work entirely to have an affair and she never met a woman who wouldn't?"

Well, they can fly my consciousness as high as a kite. They can expand it like a Macy's Thanksgiving balloon. It's too late for me. Here I am . . . on the edge of my prime. I don't hate my gynecologist. I don't hate my Congressperson. I don't even hate my mother-in-law. (She's too silly to hate.) I once had a psychiatrist briefly and he was somewhat negative, but nothing to write NOW about. I love my husband and even my once-a-month lover is . . . a lot of laughs. Noni is like a lot of women these days, going through a stage. Or maybe it's a plague. I suspect I'm immune.

Noni has an appointment at Time Inc. She cheek-grazes me good-bye. I hesitate. What a spectacular day. I feel afloat in energy. And I feel wonderfully chic in my sailor-blue St. Laurent middy and brand-new boots from Mme. Danou. I am wearing twin gold cuffs from David Webb around each wrist, a present from me to myself. My Amazon bracelets. With these golden cuffs I can stop bullets in midair. Who are you kidding, Kate? Look at those hands. Suddenly then, I don't know why, oh shit, the bags, the wrinkles . . . my beautiful rejuvenated eyes . . . I start to cry. For Christ's sake, Kate. What if Warren Beatty came dashing around the corner and saw you crinkled up like this? I must try to think of something pleasant. Tomorrow is silicone day. I get my wrinkles plumped. Jesus, Kate, you call that pleasant. I wonder about you.

I X

LAST WEEKEND WAS STRANGE. Jamie was still away. I was
alone but suddenly I didn't give a damn about my empty
bed. I didn't give a damn about Glass or Waldbaum's who
called twice. The malaise mystifies me. Perhaps I am simply exhausted with being SuperKate the erotic wonder, or
maybe I need a real challenge, someone like that Cowboy.
(He said he was coming. But he never phoned.) I even finished the goddamned revisions and the Greenspan script
outline. I'm a good way into the script. I've stopped whipping myself. I'm clear. And I'm taking all the books I've
been wanting to read for months and treating myself to
four days' retreat. Not even the answering service will know
. . . only Holly. It's my favorite sandspit, Fire Island, mid-
week and nobody I know will be there. And just to confirm
that the gods are benevolent to good little girls, the great
mountain is moving. I mean the impossible is about to oc-
cur. The rhythm of the moon and tides is breaking. Once-

a-month-between-3-and-6 Glass is flying by seaplane to spend a day and a night. The Night! I want to believe the lure is me but it could be . . . nature.

"The beach is my place," he tells me. "When I'm at the beach I'm up at dawn. I walk for hours feeling the vibrations of the waves."

I foresee a real power struggle for Glass's attention between the tides and me. But, hey, I'm not complaining. I'm delirious. I'm manic. I'm grateful to dear Lillian Wyatt for insisting I hide away here where I can read and write "minus the temptations and fuss of the Hamptons." The Wyatts and the Hilsons share a house in the Pines. Why the Pines? Long before the great unliberated hordes of homosexuals came out of the closet, the Pines was almost wall-to-wall closet. "We're so square and straight we just don't belong," says Lillian. "Like being in a foreign country where you don't speak the language. We don't get caught up in the usual frantic socializing." And the house is empty Monday through Friday at least till July.

The Hilsons, the Wyatts, their two beagles and one freckled mutt and two little red wagons and I are headed toward the dock late Sunday. The community has converged at the ferry like dozens of extras thronging to market in a De Mille epic, lovers linked in the same consciously choreographed embrace, Romans, Christians, slaves and a sprinkling of concubines and offspring costumed by Edith Head, Levi and Giorgio de Sant'Angelo. And there is Glass, already arrived, sitting on the steps leading to boutique row a few hundred feet away looking like a Martian in his Petrocelli gabardine. I feel spectacularly wicked watching him amble nonchalantly toward the scrubby bayside beach as the Hilsons and Wyatts, oblivious to my lascivious plans, gather their yapping pups, their Gucci attaché cases, their Vuitton duffels and my distracted good-bye kisses.

Exeunt omnes. The scattered few mommies and kiddies and animals and other weekday beachhounds drift away. And as the ferry melts into shadow here is Glass coming up behind me, grinning. "I wrote a poem while I was waiting for you. Sitting there in the soda cans and the used condoms. I wrote a poem." The dock and wooden walks are almost lost in shadow now. Only Glass and me behind the flashlight beam hunting for the grey cedar-shingled cottage wrapped in blueberry brambles at the end of Wilderness Walk.

Glass is hungry. There is roast beef left from dinner. And for once Glass has really extended himself. The bottle he's brought is old and precious, La Mission-Haut-Brion, '53. "There are roses planted at the end of the vines at La Mission. You can smell the roses in the wine," says Glass, swirling the garnet liquid and sticking his nose deep into the goblet. We are freezing on the deck in the dark— nature boy and a tribe of mosquitoes. "Well"—he frowns— "sometimes you can smell the roses."

"You wrote a poem."

"It's about how—"

"You're not going to read it?"

"It's not on paper. I wrote it in my head."

"Well." I arrange my face for God knows what.

"I wrote about how the people get washed up on the sand, how the waves pull you out to sea, back to the city, back to the madding crowd. Only a few people can escape. Only a very few. They get thrown on the sand with the garbage of the sea."

I make an effort to follow him. Either I'm dense or some of the words are missing. So I spend a lot of time nodding my head. "Hmmmm. Hmmmm. Yes. Yes, I see." He never stops talking. I sit mesmerized by his stream of consciousness—tales of a man besieged by the restaurant union and the sommelier's sciatica and the inflation and uncertainty in Bordeaux. I swirl and inhale and sip. "The wine. I love it."

"I'm disappointed. I taste an edge of brown." He pokes

among the ragged remnants of the roast looking for a very
rare piece.

"Here's one, love."

"Let's go to bed. I need a little nap."

Nap. That's his euphemism for . . . you know.

"I've got to call my wife, but let's just take a nap
first."

"Call your wife first."

"I'll call her later."

"I'm going to take a shower."

"I'll call my wife."

Kate may sound tough. But Kate is not so tough. I
think of her as cool, coolly practical. I have never met the
much-appreciated Mrs. Glass, though we've spoken on the
phone. She called to enlist my aid on behalf of the Bank
Street School and I spent half a day persuading Richard
Levine of Colony Pictures to give the premiere of *He Loves
Me, Loves Me Not* as a benefit for the Bank Street kiddies.
Believe me, Levine doesn't go for featherweight philanthropy. I was on the Coast and missed it. Wretched Glass
never even said thank you. Anyway, I don't care to meet
the long-suffering lady (though I'm amused to hear we
look very much alike). But I love her narrow little town-
house. Snob that I am, I was surprised to discover how
comfortable I was in her chintz-and-down living room and
the subtle sapphire chinoiserie of her bedroom with
WQXR intruding over the universal sound system. Oh yes,
it was Haitian maid's vacation last summer. Mama Glass
and moppets lazing away in Amalfi. Anyway I am never
going to be so tough that I actually get kicks hearing my
once-a-month lover lie to his wife. Stealing off with a
married man isn't as stylish as it used to be. A good Sister
doesn't covet thy Sister's man. That makes Kate a wicked
stepsister. Unreformable Aunt Tom. But when I come out
of the bathroom, wet hair wrapped in a Siamese pink

towel to match the sunburn, wet nipples glowing pink as if I'd rouged them—turned on by the needles of shower— and glistening with Johnson's Baby Oil, he is still embroidering excuses. And he looks embarrassed too. I don't remember Emma Bovary ever getting caught up in the seamy mechanics of cheating phone calls. Adultery must have been much more elegant before the telephone. A man had to dispatch an epistle. By messenger. On horseback.

Now Glass is tossing his clothes all over. He collapses beside me. I roll right into his big bear hug. Are we really so starved, so desperate? He is in a frenzy. "You're so beautiful," he cries as if in pain. "Oh God, I can't wait. I'm too hot. Don't go down on me. I'm too . . . Damn you. Damn you. God damn. I'm sorry."

"That's all right. Really. We'll do it again later."

"We will."

"Of course we will."

"I was impotent last week. The first time in my life ever. You know all about impotence. It was in that movie you wrote."

"Everyone is impotent once in a while. It's nothing. Maybe you were mad at your wife. Maybe you were punishing her. Look! Isn't that amazing. It's waking up again. Oh you are really something, Jerry. So fast. I'm going to whip it with my wet hair."

"Not bad for a man of forty-two."

I smile. He was forty-two (he said) when we met and I'm not sure what that makes him now. And who more than Kate could sympathize with this peculiar mathematical ineptitude.

"My hair is starting to fall out," he says.

"Your hair is marvelous. You're crazy. Hey, don't. Not yet. Don't just push it in there, Jerry. Play with me first. Play with my nice little pussy." The bed is crawling with sand.

"All of a sudden my hair is starting to fall out."

"Oh for God's sake, shut up."

"You're my girl. You're always going to be my girl."

"Jerry, please shut up." Now he does the most insistent wonderful unbearable things to me. In his rough, blustery, stubborn way, Glass is a perfectionist. He isn't going to stop now till the fragments of me are scattered all over this bedroom. Not till I beg. Ahhh. Wonderful.

I'm so wet. I'm choking, coughing, drowning. We are lying in the sand, the surf breaking over us, Glass and me, except where did Glass get all those perfect teeth. He looks like Burt Lancaster. The camera sweeps across the horizon. A ship is passing. It is the S. S. Reluctance. *Ensign Pulver drags a wilted palm across the deck. Only Ensign Pulver is not Jack Lemmon . . . it is Jamie. He is crying. "I can understand how she could run off for the night with some persuasive bastard. But how could she let this happen to my palm?" The tide must be coming in. That last wave breaks over me and Burt is pulling me under . . .*

I wake. The bed is damp from our sweat. Glass has surrounded me from behind. He is squeezing my breasts and rubbing his hand between my legs. Hard. Too much pressure. Rubbing and pressing everything, teasing the clitoris, gently then hard. Too hard. I can't move. His body and his hands are like a vise. I am crying and biting the pillow to keep from screaming. Now he's trying to curve his cock into me from behind. He batters into me. Everything's black. All of Kate is between my legs. I am that thing. Just cunt. Is me. Afterward I can't stop crying. For once Glass is silent.

He is awake at dawn next morning, restless, out of bed at seven, does not eat breakfast—just juice. In three years of on-and-off-once-a-monthing it is our first night together. I am about to discover all his morning rituals and needs.

Now I am indulging his obsession for early morning
exercise because, after all, I must outdo the beach-loathing
Mrs. Glass. So here I am faking it like a track star in my
most vulnerable hour of the morning. We are sloughing east
along the water's edge, Glass with his strange rolling stride.

"Have you ever got laid in the sand?" he wants to
know.

"Yes. I hated it. The sand gets into your pussy. It
scratches. Fucking on the beach is one of those romantic
notions that just isn't practical."

I follow him to the top of a sand dune. We stretch out
in a hollow, overlooking the ocean on one side and on the
other, the bay. I untie my bikini. Feels so good naked in
the sun.

"What do you see in me anyway?" Glass asks halfway
serious, halfway teasing.

"Oh Jerry, why do you keeep asking such dumb
things?"

"Because I'm a slob."

"You are not a slob."

"Hey, I dreamed about you last week. A very sexy
dream. A wet dream. Violent. I was beating you."

"Oh for God's sake, Jerry."

"I think we should wrestle."

"Oh no." I retie my bikini. "I'm not interested in violence. Somebody spanked me once and I didn't care for it
at all."

"Well, let me just beat you a little bit with my dick."

Help. I'm staggering in the sand wondering what is a
nice girl like Kate doing in the middle of this unbelievable
dialogue.

"All right," he says. "I guess that does it for exercise.
If you're good I'll let you cook lunch and then we'll take a
nice nap."

He has ordered the seaplane at six. We are sitting on
the beach listening for its buzz. Glass is already miles away,

exhilarated . . . an athlete after a great track meet. Five times in eighteen hours. The man is forty-seven years old, at least. The man is a rooster. Kate is numb and triumphant too. Such good skin. He wanted to fuck me in the beagle's basket. In the canvas swing. Finally he found a narrow cot on the balcony under the eaves, still and airless. He scraped his ass on the roof. He pushed me onto the floor and came once fast, then again, slowly, angrily, brutally, again. He awes himself.

The seaplane can't come any closer because the tide is out. He wades through the water, gabardine rolled to his knees, attaché case held high and slams his head hard against the wing. I can hear the terrible smack even here. The pilot is pulling him into the plane. Glass waves goodbye. If that were Jamie smashing his head I would have screamed, thrashed through the water, made sure he was all right. But it is Glass my once-a-month lover riding off in his forty-dollars-one-way seaplane. Instinctively I know not to tarnish the glamour of his dashing exit. Adultery can be educational.

X

JAMIE HOME FROM ASPEN is like a stranger. He looks different. Some dumb haircut. At the United Airlines baggage claim he kisses me, shy . . . both of us, holding hands, nervous and stealing hard anxious glances. "What did you let them do to you, sweetheart?" Fingers soothing strange nakedness of Jamie's neck.

"It will grow. I think I look younger."

Sigh. "I'm afraid you do."

I persuade him to let me drive us to Bridgehampton. He looks tired and tense. "Let's stop somewhere and get drunk a little, Jamie."

"I just want to get home, Rabbit."

"Maybe a drink would sort of help."

"You don't drink, Kate, and neither do I."

"I feel sexy and I want to get a little bit high."

"We'll be home in an hour and a half. I'll make you something rummy."

"You're not a little bit hungry?"

"They served dinner on the plane."

"It was probably crap. You didn't put that crap into your beautiful tummy, did you, Jamie?"

"Kate, you're very strange tonight."

"I'm strange."

"Yes."

"Oh."

Silence.

"Jamie, let's stop in a motel. I feel so sexy."

"We're so close to home, Kate."

"Jamie, I mean sir, when I picked you up at Kennedy, a perfect stranger coming on to me in the baggage area, and took you into my car, I knew exactly what you had in mind. You don't have to be subtle with me."

"Katie, you're crazy. I'm tired, Rabbit."

"Oh Jamie, please don't be tired."

"Not tired, really, just hot and scruffy." He stares at the road. "All right. Where's a motel?"

"Damn. I don't know. Stop at a gas station and I'll look it up."

"This is hardly what I'd call spontaneity."

"The idea is spontaneous, Jamie. That's what counts."

The Somerset Arms is a fortress of fake Tudor with scrubby little pines planted at measured intervals, each pine surrounded by giant whitewashed stones. We are in the Falstaff Room, all red fluff carpeting that runs from wall to wall and floor to ceiling, brocade and gilded fleurs-de-lis, two giant king-size beds also carpeted in red fluff. "Not quite what I had in mind," murmurs Kate.

"Well the bathroom is definitely worth fifty-two dollars."

"Fifty-two dollars. Oh Jamie . . . I'll pay you back out of the house-running budget." Well, the bathroom is a plumber's fantasy of sanitary heaven. Speckled gold tile, giant tub, a peculiar low crouching john, infrared lights, heated towel rack, an ironing board that drops out of the mirror and even a bidet. Ashtrays big enough to toss a Caesar salad in. "I'll have to hang a spread across the room so I can protect my sense of decency," says Kate. "I am sure that you as a gentleman, sir, though a perfect stranger, will not violate my honor."

"Aha. We are doing *It Happened One Night*." Jamie smooths an imaginary mustache. "All right, kid, let me shower and I'll try to catch up with you."

He emerges from the shower wrapped in a towel. "I don't wear an undershirt, surely you noticed," he says. "By the way did Clark actually make it with Claudette? I can't remember."

"I'm the screenwriter."

"The bed is vibrating."

"Yes. It's something called Magic Fingers. I put a quarter into this little box. I hate it."

"So do I."

"Shall we neck and pet on the floor till it stops?"

"We could move to the next bed. I wish we were doing *Tea and Sympathy*. I could use a back rub and a cup of tea. Wake me if I fall asleep."

"Jamie. Sir. Are you going to rape me?"

"Is that what you want?"

It isn't fair, is it? Jamie just wants to be passive. But I don't often ask for anything, really. "Yes, I think I would like to be raped. Seized. Forced to perform humiliating acts. I mean . . . we are paying fifty-two dollars for this unbelievable room."

He is turned away from me. "I didn't know rape was your fantasy."

"It's a common female fantasy."

"You are a notoriously uncommon female. You must have a specific uncommon fantasy as well."

"I can't tell you."

"What could be so horrible, so disgusting . . . surely you can tell me, a perfect stranger . . . someone you'll never see again once I've defiled you."

Silence.

"Tell me."

"Jamie, please. I just can't tell."

"I'm going to sleep then."

"It has to do with black leather boots to my thighs and leather bonds and medieval instruments of torture."

"They're doing it to you?"

"I'm doing it to them."

"Oh." Jamie groans. "I'm turning off."

"Well, let's go back to rape. I really do like rape."

"You can't exactly rape a woman with her clothes off, Kate. You need a garter belt for God's sake or stockings, at least."

"You pussyeating fuck. I want you to rape me."

"Damn it, you cunt. I will."

Jamie grabs both my hands, pins me down. My legs are locked together. He realizes at once he cannot hold my hands and unlock those legs. We are rolling and struggling. I am almost as strong as Jamie. He grabs my hair and pulls.

"Hey. No fair. That hurts, Jamie."

"Who is Jamie?" He pulls harder, his other hand in my pussy hair, pulling too. "Spread your legs, bitch."

"Don't pull my hair. Hey, you bastard, that hurts."

"Oh Rabbit." Jamie releases me. "This just isn't me. Rape is not my style."

I sigh. Sit up, pulling myself out of my nice erotic terror. "Oh Jamie. You were faking it beautifully. All right, darling. Only I hate to just waste all that money. Fifty-two dollars."

He laughs. "That's my Kate." He takes my hand. "I love you, Rabbit. I don't need games to turn me on."

"I don't *need* games, Jamie. I just want to do everything. I don't *need* to go to Bali. Bridgehampton is fine. But someday I want to see Bali. And Nepal. And Africa."

Jamie sighs. Gets out of bed and stands there. "Your Majesty," says Jamie. "I am the new slave from Nubia. What does the Empress desire?"

"Are you a virgin, slave?"

"Yes, your majesty."

"Oh, how charming," says Kate in her most imperious voice. "Kneel here, slave. Between my legs."

"Is this the royal treasury?"

"Don't be smart, slave. Or I'll have to beat you."

"What do you call this, your majesty?"

"Our imperial twat."

I bite my cheeks to keep from laughing. Can't silence a giggle. Jamie breaks up.

"Oh God, I love you." His mouth closes on mine, his body presses against me, curled behind now, halfway to sleep.

Jamie is home from Aspen. I'd almost forgotten how much he loves me.

Now you know Kate, the Scarlett O'Hara of our time, Catherine of Russia reborn, the whore empress of all the Byzantines, the late-blooming adventuress. Probably it sounds like I'm boasting. Sexy Kate. All those sense-reeling comes. The Oscar-winning blow jobs. Is she really so special? Or is this a delusion of sexual megalomania? I want to be good. I love being best.

Here is a certain world-renowned cocksman collapsed on the bed beside me. "Where did you learn to eat cock like that?" he asks.

"I eat exquisite fudgicle too," I reply modestly. Mustn't take one's obsessions too seriously, friends.

What is a great blow job? The ego says it is nothing

like writing a great screenplay, but close, a more primitive triumph. It has to do with tongue and lips and fingers and teeth, swallowing and sucking and pressure and tickle and tease and come all over your face. You've seen porno films. You know. I guess watching me, it looks like I love it. That's it. I love it and tease and torture it and whip it with my hair and surround it with my mouth, crazy, furious, the cruel queen, adoring—the slave sentenced to hang a thousand years on this ridiculous bone, goddamn it, come.

Anyway, I never dwell on the erotic disappointments. Why bore or depress us reliving the bad times? There lies Kate's most enviable weapon, her talent for survival. Kate has an extraordinary capacity to remember only the triumphs. I erase all the rest. Those arid fucks. Strangers, strange bodies hungry, nervous, shy, not quite meshing. Timing off, cues missed, messages ignored, coming not coming, still hungry, embarrassed, wishing that just closing her eyes would force him to disappear. "Will you be spending the night?" Both hoping not. And the rejections: Not to be remembered. The supposed triumphs: Not to be examined too closely. Let us forget, for example, that Glass is a clod. That Glass picks up whores on the streets, tells Kate about it. Glass is a pushover, no challenge at all. That Michael of The Algonquin calls Kate "Woman." It's safer. With eyes closed, Michael may not remember Kate's name. Kate is not promiscuous. Kate is free. But I suppose not everyone will understand all this bedroom traffic. One lover yes. Even two. But five. And all these wild one-night cocks passing through. Kate doesn't dwell too much on the traffic. Only says, it's good to do something well with your body, to tickle all those nerve endings, to batter your senses with joy till your head is numb. What a shame to miss anything. Anything, Kate? Well, almost anything.

I have cut out this ad from the classified columns of the Los Angeles *Free Press*. It reads:

<u>GIRLS</u>

(Already a political miscalculation. It should say WOMEN)

<u>GIRLS</u>

who have multiple orgasms, nymphomaniacs or those who can screw steady ½ hour or longer only need apply. Inventer of new sexual device which enables the man to create & hold full erection & prolong the sex act far past the usual time will be in San Francisco, N.Y., Chicago, Los Angeles, Las Vegas, Indianapolis, Detroit, Peoria, Kansas City and other large cities during the coming weeks to further test this device. Write P.O. Box 927.

I have not replied.
I wonder how it works.

How does it happen that Kate gets so caught up in all those psychopathic sexual fantasies? These garter belt games. I don't get it. Submission and bondage in Room 828 of The Algonquin. Provoking her very own husband to rape. And if the once-a-month Glass pleases her so with their more-or-less conventional adulterous intrigue, why does she cater to his kinkier hungers? Or are they her kinks?

Well, what if they are. The games excite dear old Glass. And turn me on too. If we didn't have each other, we'd have to advertise in *Screw*.

Glass, you see, has a sweet little masturbation-surprise fantasy. He wants us to act it out. We are sitting naked in the Glasses' down-and-chintz living room, staring out at the garden, sipping the last of the wine. Mistress Glass is in the country.

"If you didn't have me what would you do?" Glass asks, stretching his long bony legs across Mrs. Glass's pale yellow sofa.

"I'd make twice as much money and get twice as much work done."

"No. I mean, if you didn't have me to get laid by. You'd masturbate. You'd lie in bed by yourself playing with yourself."

"Yes."

"And maybe I would just accidentally come into the room."

"I'm not following you, Jerry."

"But you don't notice me standing there."

"Ummm."

"So you just keep on playing with yourself."

"Yes. And then . . ."

"Go into the bedroom. I'll just sit here and listen to music for a while."

Off I go. Feeling sort of silly. Feeling very excited. Hot in the pussy. Shall I masturbate the way I masturbate or is there maybe something weird about the way I really masturbate? Should I masturbate more elegantly, the way women do in *Penthouse?* Should I lie on my back with my legs spread prettily, showing the pink, rubbing my clitoris and playing with my nipples? Acting out fantasies is basically improvisional. It's like making bread the first time. You read all the instructions and you know the dough is going to double in bulk but till you get in there and punch it back into shape, you can't even guess. I got all my cues but who knows what's in his head.

I borrow one of Mrs. Glass's terry velvet washcloths from the linen closet. Persimmon. The room is icy. Glass always keeps the air conditioner on full blast but the bed is still crumpled and warm from us. I will give him the real masturbating Kate, on her tummy with the rough cloth between her thighs, both hands and the cloth rubbing, her bottom working up and down, absorbed in her play, getting hotter, breathing hard. I hear his step.

"What is this?" he says. "Don't stop. Make yourself come." I shut him out, rubbing and pressing and squeezing. "Very good," he whispers. "You don't need me at all.

Wonderful." Squeezing my fanny, pressing his hand on top
of mine, pulling the cloth out from between my legs, pushing fingers inside and pressing his palm hard against the
pussy bone. He pinches and rubs. "Come." And shakes me
when I do. In a rage. I'm crying and he hugs me, swaying
back and forth as you would comfort an injured child.

What are we doing poking around in each other's
heads like this? Is this some Kama Sutra rest and rehabilita-
tion center? I say we're lucky to find each other, two uninhibited scholars of eros. Why am I doing this? Deep down,
I'm afraid, I'm that Cosmo Girl.

In the mail today I receive a clipping of a tiny UPI
item out of Pascagoula, Mississippi, about a man who horse-
whipped his wife because he discovered three copies of *Ms.*
magazine in her dresser drawer. "Don't pay to get uppity,"
is scrawled on the margin and his name. My new clipping
service, Jason O'Neill. A Houston postmark. The Cowboy who said he would call. And hasn't.

"Who is Jason O'Neill?" Jamie wants to know, picking up the clipping from my desk.

I feel my face freezing in a sheepish half-smile. Guilt
by fantasy. I haven't thought about the Cowboy for weeks.
"A business associate of Ryder Meade. He sat in on that
demoralizing session at the Plaza-Athénée, remember, with
Billy Hutch and me and the rest of Ryder's menagerie."

"Why would he send you this?"

"I suppose he thinks it's funny." I feel transparent,
caught . . . over nothing. My not very subtle attempt to
seduce the unseduceable Cowboy. "Wonder Woman, you
know, and the Amazons. He probably lumps it all together
with the Movement. He wanted to know if Gloria Steinem
is a lesbian. I can't tell you how much time I spend defending Gloria, Jamie. Why do men find women like Gloria so
threatening? Does it make them feel safer to believe she's
a lesbian? I get it everywhere, you know. There I am in an

airplane or a taxi somewhere and I find myself trying to explain to some hostile man what the Equal Rights Amendment is all about and that Gloria is definitely not a lesbian and I can see them looking at my raincoat and I begin to feel self-conscious about my epaulets or my grey flannel blazer."

Jamie turns up the sound on the ballgame. "You sure are chattering away tonight."

X I

AT NONI'S INSISTENCE I am here at her weekly consciousness raising session about to exercise my mildly elevated
feminist awareness. I've promised to try, really try, and if it
turns out I haven't a sisterly bone in my body, I can always
use the experience in a script someday.

Now, *that* is a classic Kate copout: do it as research.
Truth is I'm embarrassed that I've avoided involvement
with the Movement. Do I think I'm above it? Or beyond it?
Or that I might discover something about myself I'd rather
not know? At least I'm consistent. I never joined the Girl
Scouts either. For me it's always been my work and my
man (and lately my pussy) with not much room left for
the possible richness of being close to women. For one
or all of the above reasons, I am here.

Emerging from the elevator we see Maxine Raskin
standing in front of her own door ringing the bell. "I
locked myself out," she says, clearly delighted. There are

shrieks and hugs for Maxine and her absentminded bliss as we enter a narrow corridor painted purple. If I come back in another incarnation I want to have skin like Maxine Raskin's and I wouldn't mind her coloring either— pale, pink around the edges, a veil of pink-gold hair. She looks like a pre-Raphaelite madonna. Frankly she's a compulsive slob. The apartment looks like they just moved in— crates and cardboard boxes along the wall, breakfast dishes scattered, toys and Mallomars and bicycles everywhere— though they've been installed at least three years. And there Maxine sits utterly serene, barefoot in a rose-pink silk caftan (stained and ripped, of course) sipping camomile tea. And puffing a joint. Maxine is a poet and writer of children's books—nasty little grotesqueries that everyone adores. The last one, *Daddy's Wife Is a Witch,* was dedicated to her husband Bernie's two sons from Bernie's first go-around. Their own two—smeared with chocolate and Crayolas—are streaking naked across the room, snatching pretzels and taco chips. "Somebody do something with those monsters," Maxine cries. "Bernie promised to tie them in bed before he left."

"Mara, do something," Noni cries. The three of them —Noni, Maxine and Mara—were co-conspirators at Sarah Lawrence fifteen years ago and set some kind of record for seduction of male virgins "and other innocents" as Noni likes to put it. Mara drives in for CR sessions from Woodmere. "She was the brilliant one," says Noni, "but she couldn't wait to sacrifice everything for some podiatrist."

"Dentist," Mara corrects. "You know he's a dentist."

"It's the same thing," says Noni.

"May I say something before we start?" Rita Teichman vibrates with outrage. I don't really know Rita. I see her at screenings or in the Hamptons at parties. She got a little huffy when we were introduced for the fifth time and I said, "How do you do." It's beastly of me, I know, but I don't have super recall for small-sized innocuous women unless they have some memorable identifying marks—like an outright mustache or 12-carat diamond earrings or Robert Redford as an escort. Okay . . . crass. I'm crass. Rita has a faintly jutting chin in an otherwise marshmallow face and a scruffy ape haircut aping yesterday's Jane Fonda but not even that mildly successful. "Why are we bringing someone new into the group?" huffs Rita. "I don't care who it is, Kate Alexander or Eleanor Roosevelt. We've got rapport. How can we start from scratch all over again? It's disruptive."

Noni sweeps in from the kitchen with two pitchers. "This isn't urine, is it, Maxine? The last time we were here you were collecting for some blood test. Hmm . . . I do believe it's apple juice."

"Isn't anyone listening?" Rita punches her pillow and pulls two sticky moppet hands out of the corn chips.

Mara sets a box of Entenmann's brownies on the coffee table. She is skeletal and she never stops eating. Fueled with corn chips, she drags the kids off to bed.

"Oh damn," wails Noni. "All this junk food. Maxine, what are you doing to us?"

"I have Tab for the fashionably slender," Maxine offers, "and *crudités* . . . but you gotta peel them yourself, Noni. I had a killer deadline this afternoon." She drops plastic sacks of carrots and radishes and celery next to Noni. "I hope no one is sitting on the goat cheese. Beautiful goat cheese, Ariane, find it." Ariane is the sculptress whose latex vulva and ceramic genitalia flowers were in last month's *Art News*. She is divorced and about to marry again, a Frenchman, younger than she, says Noni, "but a thousand years more decadent." How can I know what Noni means by decadent? Perhaps he lisps. Maybe he eats nothing but raw beef.

Rita Teichman is determined to make an issue. "Isn't anyone listening?"

"I think Kate is fast enough to just pick up where we're at," Julia Sullivan offers. "And personally, I'm glad to see someone over twenty-three here because I'm forty-three and I sometimes feel absolutely obsolete next to you children." Julia runs Superfluous, that funny little thrift-and-gift shop on 86th east of Broadway. She has a son Maggy's age and a little girl, and a husband that simply skipped town pleading "the Gauguin precedent" as grounds for a life of sloth in Baja California. Anyway, that's Noni's version of the story.

"God knows Kate needs us," says Noni, settling on a bean-bag pouf. "If we can turn her into a militant feminist, she could set out to proselytize the great unwashed world. Anyway, Rita, I checked with everyone last week. No one objected. Your answering service stinks. I left a message."

"Why is it I always have to be the hatchetman—"

"Hatchetperson," Noni corrects.

"I'm not going to be the bad one. Kate stays. I assume you realize, Kate, what we say here is private. I'd hate to see us all parodied in your next movie."

"I wish Ava Gardner were young enough to play me. I wish *I* were young enough to play me," says Julia.

I feel detached. The life I live is what they're fumbling for. Rita is afraid I'm here as voyeur. Probably I am.

The last straggler is Gina Warden, daughter of G. G. Warden, the hotel and cablevision tycoon. Slim, tall, almost six feet, outrageous in her cutout, see-through gowns and the famous pop furs, the jewelry put together by her artist chums. Tonight she's in jeans, of course, by Courrèges no doubt. *Women's Wear* adores her. So have a motley parade of men including the playwright Richard Rafton till a few weeks ago when she punched him at the Shakespeare Festival Benefit. I didn't see it but Suzy did.

"The subject tonight is rape, what is rape?" Noni begins. "Do we agree with the expanded definition of rape?"

"Are you sure it's rape?" says Mara, peeling away a run of goat cheese with her finger and eating it. "I thought it was 'Feelings About Your Gynecologist.' "

Rita snorts. "It's rape. Last week was GYN. You missed gynecology."

"Oh damn yes. I was having my D & C."

"A D & C . . . Mara, you didn't tell me," says Julia.

"Oh Julia, it's a joke," says Noni.

Noni pulls a tattered clipping out of her bag. "Germaine Greer writes: 'We must insist that only evidence of positive desire dignifies sexual intercourse and makes it joyful. From a proud and passionate woman's point of view, anything less is rape.' That includes seduction, sisters, manipulation and doing a favor for a friend. Who wants to speak first?"

Rita, of course. "I've never been criminally raped," says Rita. "But I'm raped constantly, every day of the week. I am raped by the goddamned construction worker who hisses at me or eyes me like a hunk of meat suggesting to everyone on his side of the street that I'm a great piece of ass or says, 'Hi-ya, baby, why don't you eat me.' Sometimes I try screaming back, 'Hey, Mac, you sure are stacked' or 'Boy, is that bum hung.' My friend Carla and I practically started a riot on Fifty-eighth Street once."

"Why don't construction workers ever say that to me?" says Julia.

"You gotta flash 'em, luv," says Gina. "Try going braless under a raincoat."

How is Kate at construction sites? Not doing badly at all, friends. The fiercely competitive Kate is pleased to report: In the last four months alone on the construction sites in and around Bendel's and Orsini's, I have been verbally raped by at least a dozen hardhats. Sometimes they are actually sweet. "I like that hat," one freckle-faced brute assured me last week. Kate is big with our block's dashing garbageurs too. "Give me some of that, I know where to dump it," my favorite garbageman greets me. Dashing lad, with a silk foulard ascot in his coveralls, dead ringer for Mastroianni. "Here comes lunch," cries a steelworker sitting on the sidewalk in front of the little sportswear boutique on the corner of 56th and Sixth eating his hero sandwich. What do they see? The face in shadow beneath floppy straw hat, tiny eye-tuck lines hidden behind pale bronze shades, suntanned arms and tits bouncing inside a soft green cotton dress, tied at the side, not really me this dress, but I'm meeting Max Palevsky for a conciliation lunch at Orsini's and I want to paralyze him with my most vulnerable self as a pre-schizo Blanche Dubois.

"I agree with Greer," Rita is saying. "It's rape anytime you're not really in the mood, when some guy nudges you into it, or makes you feel you owe him because he bought you some lousy Szechuan dinner that's gonna burn right through you tomorrow morning. It's rape even if some guy you really dig makes you do something that you just don't feel like doing at that particular moment. Sometimes I get so bored sucking away at some dick, excuse me Julia, penis, while some guy moans and groans and thinks I'm in ecstasy because I'm choking on this thing. A lot of guys hated Lois Gould's book because she had the audacity to suggest what a bore it is going down on all those cocks, but . . . I don't know, maybe it's Jewish guys, they act like that's it, you know, that's the ultimate thrill. I lost where I was at . . . hmm. Oh yes, a long time ago I was curious about what it would be like, how shall I put this not to offend Julia . . . to get fucked in the ass."

"Anal intercourse," Julia offers.

"That way, yes. And the guy I was living with was

curious too but very cautious and careful, lubricating creams and all that, Vaseline, you know. But I was with a man last summer who kept trying to put his cock, his penis, in my ass and I didn't want to. And this one night he just wouldn't listen. 'When you're hot enough, you'll really love it,' he kept saying. He pretends he's fumbling around looking for the right hole, you know, and he did it. It hurt like hell, blood all over the bed too, and I really felt like I'd been raped. Violated."

"You didn't kind of love it too, Rita? It wasn't terribly sexy on some level?" Gina asks.

"I knew you were going to say that, Gina. No. No. Absolutely not. I felt totally violated."

"I've had that feeling too," Julia begins. "And nothing really happened. Still I felt violated. I was a senior in high school and these two boys I know very well decided I must be fast because I had ice cream cone bazooms in tight sweaters. I never purposely bought tight sweaters, just I was sort of chubby and sweaters were smaller then, you people are too young to remember. They drove me out to some country road and started grabbing at me. Probably they were virgins too. They didn't quite know what they were doing. And I was furious, kicking and biting and crying . . . finally they got sort of sheepish and drove me home, pretended it never happened. And I pretended it had never happened."

"God damn," says Rita. "The born victim. We're born victims."

Everyone has a rape story to tell, petty rape, sexual rip-offs, the unwanted lover or ex-lover who won't take no for an answer, the fucks passively endured because "it seemed easier than making a scene." Rita wants all women to learn karate. Julia wants to know if you can rape a man.

Gina grins. "It might take two of us to hold him down, but I'll tell you how."

"Oh wow, let's," cries Maxine.

"It's Mara's turn."

"You people seem to be getting raped right and left," says Mara. "I could expose myself naked at the next party in Woodmere, be accosted by a sexfiend and nothing would happen."

"Mara, you've been neglected so long you probably send out anti-sex rays," Noni observes. "I don't mean that hostilely," she adds hastily. "Mara keeps herself busy with the garbage of suburban existence so she won't notice how little Ted wants sex."

"It's true," says Mara. "I always know when Ted is sufficiently horny. He always does the same thing. Like a station break. He makes an X on my hand. You know, the way guys in grade school used to do to be dirty. Ted's still doing it."

"Mara needs a lover," says Noni.

"Here we go again. That's where we end up every time I open my mouth. This is an old story, Kate. I made a pass at my laundry man. He laughed. I came on with this beautiful kid who works at the gas station in Mineola. He didn't know I was making a pass. Let's see. Then I was really outrageous with my daughter's social studies teacher. He turned out to be a fag. Last week I almost made it. A drunken gin rummy friend of Ted's pushed me into the closet. Nice kiss, too much tongue and a little drooly, hands all over, but I really felt genuinely horny for the first time in years. We had nowhere to go," Mara goes on. "His wife is right outside the closet. Ted is finishing up the last hand of gin. Anyway, he says he's been hot for me for years, not too romantic but anyway, to the point, right. I never thought about him like that. He's kind of short and a little, hmmm, pear-shaped, anyway it's dark in the closet and he had his hand under my skirt inside my panties. I felt fantastic."

" 'Where do we go?' he says. Like I know. Like I do

this every day. 'Your house tomorrow afternoon?' he says. 'Oh God no,' I said. 'How about a motel?' 'I'll call you,' he said. Only he never did."

"I can't stand it," Noni screams.

"Too bad you don't masturbate," Rita offers.

"Rita, Mara doesn't need you to put her down. Masturbation is Rita's prescription for whatever ails you. Ulcers, loneliness, hot flashes, the shingles—"

"I believe that masturbation can be a terrific release, a fabulous sexual outlet, Noni, and it teaches you how to get pleasure out of your own body. Independently. You don't need a hostile two-timing fucking man."

"If you want to talk about masturbation, we'll talk about masturbation but the subject tonight is rape and besides I don't want us to get sidetracked if anyone has an idea to help Mara . . ."

"Masturbate," says Rita. "Ginseng root."

"The classified ads in *Screw*," cries Gina.

"You pigs," Ariane scolds. "You two are really bitchy tonight. I'm getting depressed about this group. Mara, I have a friend, he's married and he's looking for an escape, adventure . . . just like you."

"In Manhattan?" Mara asks.

"Well, he lives in Rye."

"So he sure as hell doesn't need a repressed housewife in Woodmere."

"You two work out the logistics later," Noni directs. "Maxine, back to rape."

I can see consciousness raising is not for Kate. Everyone thinks Jamie and I are spectacularly devoted. So loving. So romantic. I've been admirably discreet, painstakingly prudent. I am not suddenly going to spill it all out here to make some point, raise their consciousness, lift my own. What do they think of me, boring loyal old Kate, supposedly faithful to the same man for ten years. If only they knew SuperKate . . .

"What about literature?" Maxine is asking. "What about fantasy? Remember what Nora Ephron wrote in *Esquire* . . . what is going to happen to the female rape fantasy?"

"Yes," says Gina, "what about the rape fantasy? I love to be raped. That is, not literally, but I love it when I'm seized from behind. The man is rough, forceful. Rape by agreement. I find it exciting . . . to be taken."

"That's what feminism is all about," cries Rita. "To free us from our pathetic passion to be possessed."

"But I want to be possessed," says Kate. "I like being a sex object. I get nervous when I'm with a man who doesn't see me as a sex object. In the movie world, in the business world, a successful woman sometimes stops being seen as a woman. Or else she's seen as a mutant creature, a woman with balls. I'm a man's equal but I'm not a man. So I flirt and I might be a little seductive and if it makes both of us—me and the man I'm dealing with—more comfortable, I don't see the harm—"

"Oh Kate, I could cry," says Noni. "You've got such a long way to go."

"You can't change my fantasies now." I'm annoyed by their myopia. "It's too late. I do think about rape. In elevators, for instance . . . whenever I get into an elevator with a man, a young man, an attractive man, a black man, a tough-looking delivery boy. I imagine him grabbing me. I imagine the elevator locked between floors. I am terrified and yet somehow I wonder if I'm not looking for that man."

"What are you saying, Kate?" Mara reaches nervously for the last of the corn chips.

"Once I needed to be raped." There, I'm telling them. Kate goes on: "The first time I went to bed . . . what do I mean *went to bed* . . . when I lost my virginity on the floor of a darkroom, that was a rape. I didn't want to. He forced me. I was grateful that he did. I was furious, thought I was furious at the moment, but I was freed to be myself. Rape, a kind of a rape, was the only way it was going to happen. I was a senior in high school, ravenous for sex, still, determined to be a virgin on my wedding night. All the forces of evil were after me, bulging trousers, my own heat, D. H. Lawrence."

I was impressed. He was a first-string football player at Northwestern. In fall, he would leave for England to be a Rhodes scholar. He was impressed. To find me reading Yeats. 'Only God, my dear, could love you for yourself alone and not your yellow hair.' I had one fatal obsession. I loved to take my clothes off. He was patient . . . playing my game of carnal brinkmanship.

"What a waste. What a shame," says Sonny. "Feel this skin," he commands, stroking the inside of my thigh. I am naked in his photographic darkroom. To this day I can smell the chemicals, see the teenage Kate in the red darkroom light, nipples distended and scarlet. "You're a woman, Kate. You should behave as a woman."
     I won't let him undress.
     "All right," he says, sitting Indian-style on the floor. "Have it your way. Spread your legs," he says.
     "No."
     "Just a little bit." He slips his hand between her thighs and pushes them apart. She hugs and hides her breasts, hot and wet with fear and hunger, watching his fingers in the curly pussy hair. He bends his head forward and she stops it.
     "No."
     "Just one little taste. One kiss. Here." He touches. "This furry little landing field."
     Giggle. "No."
     "Yes." He rubs his finger against it. "See how sticky

you are. Isn't that lovely?" He puts his sticky fingers in his mouth.

"No. Don't lick it."

"Yes."

"You have such a sweet little cunt."

New word. Disgusting word. "Don't use that word."

"Cunt. What a lovely sound. Cunt. Say cunt."

"No."

He touches it. "Say cunt."

"Cunt."

He pulls me onto his lap and kisses lips, breasts, knee. What excruciating torture. The heat, the ache . . . Kate loves it. She moans. And squeals. She giggles. Hears the zip. Pulls away. He grabs her foot. "Sonny. We aren't going to do anything, Sonny, are we? Sonny. I'm not just saying that, Sonny. I mean it."

He surrounds her, against the wall, holding himself the length of that thing away, dragging it across her pussy bone and tummy, big and red in the light. He's trying to stuff it in between her legs. She wiggles free.

Now he has her, pinned against the wall, pushing his thing into her, pushing against bone, hurting, against flesh, tearing. "Sonny, stop. I mean it. Stop, Sonny." He picks her up, locks her to him. "Baby, it's for you."

Kate is furious, sobbing, gasping, lying there paralyzed, unbelieving, outraged. Filled with sticky come and . . . relief. For a long times she lies there silent in Sonny's hug suffering his comforting kisses.

Well, Kate thinks, that takes care of that.

"What you're trying to say, Kate, is that you provoked him," says Ariane.

"Yes. I asked for it. I was begging for it. All that year petting behind the tennis courts, I was begging someone to make the decision for me."

"Still, he promised," Julia says. "You said, 'We'll only go so far' and he promised."

"What right did he have to decide for you?" asks Rita. "Women are walking around getting raped, seduced, talked into it . . . what have you, and afterward they say, I guess I asked for it. Even the police like to make a rape victim feel dirty so she thinks somehow she provoked the attack. I mean, what kind of shit is it if some drunken slob can bully you into letting him spend the night. And make you feel guilty too because you had to be persuaded. That's bullshit. And we swallow it. I'm tired of being treated like a piece of meat. I want to be in charge of my body. I want to be in control."

They are looking at me. Waiting. I don't want to say another word. I'm so tired. I'm tired of being in control. Control of what? Do they have any idea what they're asking for? It's work . . . being your own self. Responsibility. I'm so tired.

"It's late," says Noni. "There was something I wanted to say about my mother." There is Bernie at the door. Ariane is looking at her watch. "May I propose 'mothers' as the topic for next week? No objections. Okay. My house then."

Noni walks me down Central Park West, chattering. "Is something wrong, Kate?"

"Just tired, I guess." I turn for Noni's cheek-grazing good night and I am surprised. Instead of aiming off behind my ear, Noni's lips touch my cheek.

I guess women in groups don't work for me. I'm too impatient. Or competitive perhaps. Noni's right. The evening *was* worthwhile as research. I may even sign up with Betty Dodson for a class in how to masturbate. But for me the group lament is terrifying. They are like mutating insects, women today, feeding on the poison they condemn, absorbing sexism and hate into the bloodstream. I worry they will immobilize the drones that adore them and become a tribe of queen bees with no males left strong enough to survive contact with their cunts.

Such anger. All the marginal men of our decade will be unmanned and then what will I do for playmates? Who needs the marginal man, you say? Let him go. Are you kidding? Can we afford to be so wanton? How many whole men exist out there?

XII

KATE WILL NEVER learn. Alone, she is desperate for company. In a crowd she panics, aching to escape. Jamie has been working late hours and is quiet, withdrawn, tired too. Won't talk about it. I need a glorious adventure.

Frymer at Fox spoke to my agent. Frymer is the third movie executive this month wanting ideas for a film about the Women's Movement. But the Movement isn't ready. Or I'm not. To treat it seriously is to risk a ponderous polemic. But if I dared to make fun, they'd all hate me. Why doesn't someone ask me to write about two good buddies pulling off some daredevil caper—Butch Cassandra and the Sunstroke Kid.

Holly has tacked an ominous quote on the corkboard. Her sense of irony stuns me. It is a poisonous thought from Ambrose Bierce. "You are not permitted to kill a woman

who has injured you, but nothing forbids you to reflect
that she is growing older every minute. You are avenged
1440 times a day."

Holly is writing a story for *Cosmopolitan* on "Women
Who Are Ageless." Needless to say, she plans to interview
and deify me. Ageless means old, of course. I am less than
pleased to be included. Holly is haunted by the specter of
aging. I find that premature if not rude in a woman of
twenty-eight.

I definitely need an adventure. I've finished the Greenspan script *Marina Next Morning*. Coppola is reading it
now. And with no immediate deadline, I am feeling aimless. Perhaps this is the moment I've been saving for the
Cowboy.

The phone is wet from my palm. My hand is shaking.
I have the high school prom jitters. He's not there. His
office says he's in New York at The Regency. In New York
and he hasn't called. Rejected. The confident Kate of high
self-esteem writes the bastard off her list. The real Kate
dials The Regency. Sorry, Mr. O'Neill has checked out. But
for the weekend he may be reached at Whitney Appleton's
on Fire Island. Would I like the telephone number?

No thank you. I have it. You see, Sigmund, the Kate
of high self-esteem would have blown the deal. The fates
smile on the real Kate. Whitney Appleton is a dear old
friend, my sometime lover, too, and he is delighted I'm free
Sunday and need a little sun. He will send a seaplane to
fetch me to the Appletons' huge Victorian beach house on
Fire Island at Point O' Woods. "The house is full of kids,"
he warns, "but we have some amusing houseguests and I
would love a chance to sound you out on some movie
deals."

I'm on my way.

Whit is the big bridge-building genius who sold his
company to a British conglomerate and dabbles in financ-

ing films. He is married to one of the Gilbey sisters, Laura, the beauty, languorous and unsexed. Or so Whit has confided.

"My fantasy is to have a voluptuous, perennially sexy woman no more than a block or two from my house so I can tell Laura I'm going out for a walk. No courtship. No dinners in pitch-black cheater's hideaways. I don't even want to talk to her. Just arrive, walk in and she'll be ready."

"Well, Whit," says Kate with a sigh of exaggerated regret. "I guess there is no future for me. I live four blocks too far away."

Whit is waiting on the beach. No sign of "amusing houseguests." Is it possible I can actually smell bacon drifting across the sand from the leaning Appleton castle on top of the dune? Whit's fourteen-year-old daughter Liza by ex-wife number two sits stretched along the surf line, ethereal in a gauzy caftan bedraggled by the sea, playing with a squeaky handful of spectacularly disheveled puppy.

Whit wades toward me, grabbing my carpetbag and the canvas sling on my shoulder, whispering: "You're golden, Kate. That tan looks so good on you."

Inside the grey bleached Victorian house the Appletons' Dominican cook is screaming at the little boys snatching bacon as fast as she cooks and drains it. "Carter. Barnes." Grinning mouths stuffed with bacon. "Shake hands with Mrs. Alexander," says Whit. "And this is Amadea, Kate." He drops my things on a bed in a turreted guest room overlooking the ocean. "Isn't that Amadea something? She's had her hair in curlers for two weeks. We've decided she's curling it for the day she goes home. Laura is playing tennis. Amadea's been serving breakfast all morning. I think we're the last. Let's have coffee."

No sign of the Cowboy.

"Kate, could you snip my frizzies?" Liza drifts toward us on the long stretch of screened-in porch, little convex tits bouncing inside the crinkled caftan. She has a tiny manicure scissors in her hand. "My frizzies are taking over. It's a never-ending struggle against the perversions of nature."

"Not now, Liza. Kate and I are talking." Liza melts mutely away pouting, collapsing in a heap against the porch wall hypnotically examining the ends of her pale red hair, snipping away.

Kate is braced, painfully tense, ready to assume the desired pose of nonchalance at his entrance, not yet ready to inquire. Whit is talking.

"Malnutrition?"

"Hey they sent her home from school because of malnutrition. Can you imagine? The shrink calls it anorexia. Self-induced starvation, not unusual in teenage girls, having to do with a fear of their own sexuality. Don't tell me divorce doesn't mess up their heads. People should be required to get a license before they have children." He pours himself a tall Bloody Mary. "I certainly wouldn't have passed a written exam."

Amadea brings a tray with toasted English muffins, bagels, cheese, croissants and marmalade in an ironstone jam pot. "That's Philadelphia cream and that's Boursin with garlic and herbs," Whit points out. "Bet you never thought you'd run into a bagel in Point O' Woods, eh? Oh yes, the Great American Wasp is breaking out. My new movement, have I told you? Anglo-Saxon lib. Laura is organizing a benefit. That's a joke, but why not? We're the last great maligned minority. How's business, Kate? When are we going to do a movie together?"

"I have a script, Whit. I'll get Harry to send it to you."

"What do you think of Gillian Hackman? Be brutally frank, Kate."

I'm so nervous, I'm eating everything in sight. Damn, that was garlic.

"She wants me to finance a documentary on women

in China. You know, Kate, I'm not in film strictly for philanthropy."

"Gillian is brilliant. I love her poetry. But she's crazy, Whit." I'm so nervous I need two hands to steady the cup.

"Yeh. Crazy. I threw up in her hotel room at the Beverly Wilshire. She made me take her for Mexican food. Then insisted we stop for milkshakes. I threw up in her bathroom. Well, at least I made it to the bathroom." He sighs. "She's very sexy."

"I think I'll walk on the beach for a while, Whit."

Where is he? Kate wraps herself in a filmy white burnoose, layering hands and feet and face with thick sun creams. Too many summers growing up on Lake Michigan beaches blistering in the sun . . . how cavalier I was. Now I am golden, yes, cunning late-blooming siren. I treat Kate's epidermis as if it were antique silk. Never more than twenty minutes of sun at a time, hooded even against the glare from the sand. I love the beach. I love the sound, the variation of the surf, the random lap and whirl, the pull of the sand as it gives way wet or builds, today set with shell jewels, tomorrow a shambles of seaweed. The smell of sun on skin, the heat of a light sunburn on cheeks and shoulders, the sun's erotic touch. The beach, primal and intimate with that dark inescapable power unleashed in hurricanes. I don't see him anywhere.

I stoop to pick up a piece of bright blue seaglass, feeling as if I have been sloughing through the sands for days. My hood fallen low over my face. Katherine of Arabia.

Suddenly Kate is surrounded by white-robed Arabs on horseback. She recognizes their faces. Joe Namath. Burt Reynolds. Hugh Hefner. Warren Beatty. Mick Jagger. They are going to rape her. Hefner rips open her burnoose. "Not exactly your typical girl-next-door," he says.

"Actually I happen to prefer older women," Reynolds says, pushing Hefner aside.

"What are we waiting for?" Namath wants to know.
"Anthony Quinn," says Hefner.
"And Rin Tin Tin," Jagger says.
"I'm not waiting for anyone," Reynolds is naked, re-
clining on a bearskin rug. He reaches for Kate.
"I thought Rin Tin Tin was dead," says Kate.

The Cowboy is not on the beach. Kate stands at the
water's edge. The undertow looks fierce. I drop my robe on
a sand ridge. Throw myself under the next wave, shocked
and shivering in the icy shallows. Need to cool off.

"You? Kate Alexander. What are you doing here?"
He seems pleased. I feign surprise, suddenly weak. The
Cowboy is stretched out at the farthest corner of the
Appleton sun porch with a narrow band of towel draped
across his groin. He'd fallen asleep over the *Times* finan-
cial section. There are three peach pits lined up on the
porch rail. His skin is darker than the sun-streaked, grey-
streaked hair, longer than I remembered it. The hair on
his arms is bleached silver and the lean muscled stomach
is beet-red from a virgin exposure to the sun.

"You're here because you knew I would be here,"
says Kate, a pure Scarlett line if I ever heard one. I hope
she doesn't break into a Southern drawl.

"Well, not exactly," he admits, "but what a wonderful
surprise."

"So close and you didn't call." Oops. That's not very
Scarlett, Miz Kate.

"But I have been thinking about you. I thought about
you three times—coming into Kennedy, at lunch Friday,
on Fifth Avenue after, all the smart-looking women . . ."

Kate touches the red plain of stomach with an ice-
cooled glass of lemonade. "That's going to hurt."

He takes my hand, the hand with the glass, arresting
it, not polite or affectionate but defensive. "I guess everyone must be down on the beach."

"That's probably going to blister."

He stares down at his crimson stomach. "Yes, that will smart."

"Iced tea is very soothing."

"I don't drink tea."

"No, I mean, you just smooth it on. Cold compresses. It actually brings down the temperature of the skin."

"All right. Do something."

He shrugs into a blue terrycloth robe and follows me into the kitchen. I can hear Amadea in her room beyond the kitchen, talking back to the television set. "I think water ought to do as well as tea. It's the cold that counts. It lowers the temperature of the burn." I fill a big pot with water and ice cubes. "How do you know the Appletons, Jason?" His nakedness inside that robe makes me nervous.

"We met them at Ryder's ski place in Vail. And we may do business . . . a big real estate resort project in Colorado. Whit wants to buy himself a politician. I've been telling him Watergate killed politics. I'm trying to persuade him to put the money into real estate and avoid a lot of aggravation and disappointment. What's that?"

"A towel, so we won't get the sofa wet. Lie down." There is his robe tied loosely around his waist. For a moment it immobilizes us both. I reach to untie it. He reaches too. Lets it fall loose across his thighs, exposing the flaming band of stomach, a trail of light pubic hair, casually covering the rest.

"God damned blue ball bitch. That is cold, lady."

"It's going to feel so good in a minute."

"Hmmm. Yes, it feels better already."

"I have to make it ice-cold again. Here, I'll just pat it on."

"That feels so good." He closes his eyes and sighs. "I thought about calling you when I got to New York but I decided to avoid that . . ."

"That what?" I could easily hate that face. The eyes

too easily turn into unoccupied crystal. The mouth with
that full soft lower lip, sulky, arrogant, reminding me of
that lazy enveloping good-bye kiss weeks ago in Paris.

"You ought to be an actor," says Kate. "When I saw
you that first time in the Plaza-Athénée, I thought to myself
that man is probably a second-rate actor. Not enough drive
to be first-rate. Those teeth. You have such perfect teeth.
Movie star teeth."

"You like my teeth." He bares them in a pleased
clowning grin. "My mother's brother is an orthodontist.
Movie star teeth are a family legacy."

"And your eyes are extraordinary for technicolor."

"Acting is no work for a man. You should know that.
Acting is fine for women and fags. That's why real men
are so uncomfortable acting. Why they all want to produce and direct."

He shudders at a freshly icy touch.

"Am I hurting you?"

"It's your hands. Your touching me. I am thinking
what you would be like in bed. How sensuous you are.
Touching me. I have an erection. I know what I could
do to you in bed. I know exactly how it would be, your
face, all distorted, no mask, no veneers, the makeup rubbed
off, everything exposed." He groans. "But I have no intention of disturbing the equilibrium of my life."

"Monogamy is a bore, don't you think?"

"Oh Kate, I would have thought you'd be more
subtle."

"Well, I don't have time for subtlety. It's Sunday noon.
You could come back to the city with me."

Silence. He is staring at me, rubbing an ice cube
across his stomach. "It really does work. You were right.
Cools everything. Kate"—he pauses. "My woman is here
with me. Diane. You'll meet her. And I am monogamous.
I told you. I like being monogamous. I had ten years of
fucking around, balling everything in sight. So now there is

someone in my life and a sense of equanimity. A balance . . . something obviously missing from your life. I sense you fumbling around, searching. But I have it. I love Diane. She was just a small-town girl, a naked mind, a naïve twenty-five-year-old girl and I opened her mind. I exposed her to the world. She knew nothing. I created her tastes, her appetites. She's growing . . ." He sighs. "Oh, there are problems. But I'm making this work. I expect we'll get married. I still want a family. Children. How many years do you have invested in your marriage?"

"Look, I don't want to talk about me and Jamie. My marriage has nothing to do with you . . . what I want to do with you."

"Oh, but it does. How old are you, Mrs. Alexander? You're going to be forty soon. You better get on or off the pot. If you love your husband, stop screwing around, stop dividing yourself. If it isn't working, get out. Start over. The freedom to fuck around is no freedom at all."

"You have the mistaken idea I'm trying to prove something. Oh shit. I want something to eat. There was egg salad in the refrigerator."

"You shouldn't eat so much either. At your age you need to be thin."

"Listen, Cowboy. That's enough. I don't want any more advice from you. If I need help, I'll write Ann Landers. I'm going down to the beach."

"I'll walk with you." He puts an arm across my shoulders.

I feel so sad. "Naked?"

"I'm not going to be able to zip up my pants for a week." He slips back into the blue terrycloth robe.

"Kate, oh Kate." It's Laura, wandering into the kitchen. "I'm bringing sangria and egg salad sandwiches down to the beach. You two have met. Oh, Kate. You've done something incredible to your face. You look twelve years old." Laura is swathed in chiffon, her big black nembutalized pupils hidden under a crosshatch sweep of an outsize straw hat.

"It's my same old face, Laura."

"No. It can't be. You haven't got a wrinkle." She sweeps paper plates and plastic forks into a wicker basket. "Amadea," she cries. *"Vaya con me, por favor.* Your color is divine, Kate. You must tell me what you've been doing to your face. Jason, we're all committed to cocktails and dinner at the Graysons' tonight. It's his birthday. The divorce is final but she insists on celebrating his fortieth anyway."

"I think I'll need a nap, Laura." Kate backs away. I need a booster of strength to meet Diane, I'm afraid.

Jason is filling a polyurethane hamper with ice. "Let me help you with the sangria, Laura," he says. "See you later then, Kate."

I cannot answer.

The Cowboy's girl is a beauty. I might have guessed. And a bit shrewish. He didn't mention that. She is tall, slender, with long perfect legs and full high breasts moving free inside a pale peach matte jersey gown, much too sexy for Point O' Woods but that fine wholesome American girl face dilutes the shock of fabric clinging to nipple. She is baiting him for not drinking, mocking his sunburn pain, criticizing his knotted work shirt.

"Who do you think you are? Harry Belafonte?"

Whit is getting us drunk enough to make it through the night, he says. "You'll know what I mean when you meet the Graysons." The fourth houseguest is Fuller Williams, a young pale Social Register Wall Street lawyer quite obviously dipsy over Laura.

"These Margaritas are totally wicked, Whit," says Kate, dark and mysterious in a black jersey slashed to the waist, with deep temple sleeves. Not very Point O' Woods either, and deliberately.

The Cowboy is quiet, pretending to read the *Times* Sunday Magazine.

The Graysons' porch is strung with paper lanterns. The men seem drained, paunchy in bright red and green golf pants, pale beside their horsey tanned women. There is a one-man band, almost green from the exertion of handling guitar, harmonica and portable organ, playing haunting melodies from Lester Lanin debutante days. A covey of teenaged girls with long bleached-out hair sigh and whisper on the edge of the porch, snatching barbecued spare ribs and miniature egg rolls from a chafing dish. There is one fat little boy eunuch gobbling fried chicken wings among all those pre-Raphaelite sprites. As if these men are too weak even to father males.

"I want you to meet my late husband," says a pretty young brunette I know from somewhere in the movie business. "Darling, say hello to Kate Alexander and bring your bereaved widow a drink."

The little man is very dapper. He bristles. "I'll miss being here to see the widow's face when they read the will."

I am wondering if cowboys dance.

"He's so tight he'll figure out a way to hang around and make sure we don't overspend on the funeral." The brunette sighs. "Darling. Drink. Drink. D-r-i-n-k. Do something about your widow's drink."

There is an arm around my waist. I turn. Disappointed. It's Whit. "Are you ready for a great Lindy?" He has the footwork, the style, even the expression of chewing-gum fifties innocence. Impossible to forget that rhythm, the bounce, the toe-heel repeat, the bunny hop . . . it's a part of a long-ago me. Whit is transported. Panting, flushed, he falls into a chair. Laura hugs him, passes a sip of her drink.

"What an incestuous crowd we are," she says. "Do you

know Tim Grayson is planning to marry Ginny Holland and Tom Holland has run off to Cozumel with Lilah Stone."

"That leaves Irene Grayson and Conrad Stone," observes Whit.

"That *would* be a neat package," Laura agrees, caressing her neat fleshless midriff. "Unfortunately, Irene and Conrad loathe each other."

"I've heard of great marriages built on less than that," says Whit. "Do you realize that half the women here are getting laid by Nelson Browning?" He gestures toward a slim, bearded man in a Filipino wedding shirt. "He's the greatest womanizer I know. Now how does he do it? He's a pharmacist. Does he fuck them on a stretcher behind the scenes between prescriptions? Does he fuck them in the drugstore john standing up? Nobody knows how many of the women here are seeing him. But apparently the action in White Plains is terrific. That's a long commute though for you, Laura, isn't it?"

She glares at him. "It's sad, isn't it, Kate. They must meet each other driving in and out of Westchester motels."

Diane is dancing with the Wall Street lawyer, laughing too noisily. Her voice is sharp. The one-man band is doing an old Beatles song, destroying it. The Cowboy takes my hand.

We are dancing, slow and close, in a darkened corner at the back ell of the porch. Twenty feet away three wraith-like girls whisper on the creaking porch swing.

"Have you ever been to Texas?" Jason asks.

Kate cannot quite make words. What a maniac. His skin touching mine burns. I imagine that projection inside his pants is swollen, steel.

"I have been in the West. I've been on location in Arizona, Utah, Mexico. Is that close?"

"That's all very fancy. I was thinking of the real West. You'd probably hate it, find it boring, primitive." His head is slow, cheek against mine. I am uncomfortable, aware of the body that can do without me. "You're such a city person," he says.

"I do love cities, yes, but I'm a beach person too. I've slept in tents and climbed modest mountains. I sail. You're quite a bigot actually."

He moves his hand inside my sleeve up my arm, pressing his hand against my upper arm, against my breast. I don't think I can stand that hand, this painful tease.

"All that time in New York and you didn't call. You must be some strange breed of subhuman."

"I didn't want to put myself in the position I seem to be in . . . rejecting you. I would like to be friends. You can't seem to handle anything but a fuck-me-in-passing arrangement. I like you, Kate. I admire you, your work. I would wish we could be friends."

"I don't want to be friends, Mr. O'Neill. Unless you're talking about lover-friends. I have more friends than I have time for. I want us to go to bed. Anything else between us would be perverse. I've known that since Paris. If you don't feel what I feel, let's just forget it."

He laughs, pulls me closer, grinding me into himself. I am kissing him, eating his mouth, touching the corners of his lips with my fingers.

"I love to kiss standing up."

"Do you know why?" He kisses my neck. "Because it's like the movies. So you see," he steps back. "There is life beyond the horizontal."

"You are tough, aren't you?"

"I feel everything, lady. Don't be mistaken. And I *am* tough. Everybody grows up tough in the Bronx." He lowers himself carefully into a wide wicker chair.

"I don't believe it."

"Oh yes, Bainbridge Avenue. When I was nine my dad lost his job but he had a few thousand dollars saved and he decided to see what the rest of the country looked like. So he packed us all into a brand-new Dodge. I remember how proud he was of the whitewall tires and I remember listening to soap opera driving west. He was a CPA, my dad, fell in with some cattlemen, invested their money, did a lot of fancy tax work, sometimes got paid in land."

"Oh there you are, Jason." Diane comes around the corner with the irresistible pharmacist in the Filipino wedding shirt. "We're all going for a swim. It's such a delicious night. Grab some towels, darling." She whispers something in his ear.

He smiles. "C'mon, Kate." Taking my hand.

But Kate has had enough of walking on live coals. She downs another glass of champagne, finds that sweet tipsy buzz, lets Whitney Appleton put his hand inside her dress, lets Whitney Appleton take her home and up to the turret room, says, "Oh Whit, if only . . . not here. Oh Whit. You're crazy. Don't be crazy. Whit, if you don't leave, I'll scream. I'm not kidding, Whit. Oh, all right. Just that. Just that, Whit. No Whit, not that. Please, Whit."

Oh shit.

Whit is nowhere to be seen at seven the next morning. Laura, rosy-checked and Panama-hatted already—so deceptively alive for a Nembutal addict—walks us to the bay to board the Fire Island seaplane.

Diane looks cross and hung over. The Cowboy is quiet, distant. No one speaks except Laura, breathy and irrelevant. Everyone else, even the pilot, mutely respects the fragility of the morning.

At the foot of Wall Street there are two limousines waiting. Elegant Laura. I am planning to say something to the Cowboy. Something clever, provocative . . . something vulnerable, memorable, seductive, I'm not quite sure. What I say is: "Such fun to have met you, Diane. See you soon. Good-bye." No kisses, no cheeks grazing. I cannot, will not, bear even his hand in mine.

A low yellow haze hangs over the city. The muffling

grey shag carpet inside the car reminds me of the limousine at Daddy's funeral. How safe it could be letting myself be absorbed into the strength of a man like the Cowboy. Abdicate myself. Rest.

Jamie is right. Fate is a cunt like all the rest.

XIII

WHAT HAVE I got myself into now? Here I am committed to spending the weekend working somewhere in the Mexican desert. But I cannot resist being SuperKate, loyal friend . . . Miz Wonderful. Larry Owens' voice sounded so desperate. He begged me to come. Bountiful Lady Kate. I need too much to be loved. The air is hot and thick. There is a steel-grey limousine waiting for me at the airport in Mexico City.

Larry Owens was so long ago in my life, young, hopeful, intense, I am not really anxious to see him, not close up. Something cruel happens to the golden boy wonders of our childhood. They grow up. Larry's unwilling middle-age decline will be a cruel mirror of Kate's, I fear. Larry has never been as good as he was in *Show Me the Way*. The film he still thinks (mistakenly) I wrote just for him. His sexpot aura lingers and he's made money in a bunch of dumb Westerns but the formula is stretched thin. I'm fighting windmills but I'm here. We were young together and good together so I owe him.

Anyway Larry is nowhere in sight. That is Murray Metesky the other side of customs oiling the way with crumpled pesetas. Murray the fashionplate is Larry's almost anything: buffer, agent, champion, mouthpiece, nursemaid, procurer, banker, beard.

"You look terrific, Kate," says Murray not even looking at me, taking my bags and passing them quickly to the driver, briskly brushing off his perfectly manicured hands. "Terrific." He looks at me now for the first time. "Terrific." You've done something wonderful to your face."

Why is everyone so fascinated with my face? "Same old face, Murray."

"Can't fool old M&M, love. Dare I ask?"

I can feel my allegedly near-invisible eye-tuck scars burning. "Will it make you feel better, darling, if I confess I had the whole thing redone in Switzerland this year. Sorry, love, it's the same old face, a few years older. Maybe it's my hair. I wear it longer. Or my new makeup. George Masters taught me all these things to do with cheekbones. That's it, Murray, cheekbones. Now, tell me what was so critical here for Larry it couldn't wait till I got back from Cannes."

Murray shakes his head and reaches into a drop-open bar built into the limousine. "We looked everywhere for Roederer Cristal champagne, Kate. But the best we could do is Dom Pérignon." He untwists the wire and works the cork free with both thumbs. Murray remembers everything. He has things like that written down on three-by-five file cards. Champagne is the last thing I need to quiet the strange nervousness in my tummy. But he's already poured.

"Shall I be frank, Kate?"

"I doubt that you can be, Murray, but I wish you would try."

"The script stinks."

"The last five films Larry's done stank. I hear. I wasn't masochistic enough to see them all."

"That's what he's getting these days. Stinking Westerns. And that one dog of a detective yarn, don't remind me. Larry is . . . edgy. Maybe he's just whacked out. He went right from location in Almería to this, no time off. He's bored with this dumb broad he brought along but he doesn't want to ship her off, says his tolerance for pain is gone. Sylvia hanging around drives him crazy. The producer is somebody's cretin nephew. Larry's favorite makeup man had another commitment. They promised to spring him and they couldn't. What's to be happy about, I ask you?"

"You need more than a script doctor, Murray. You need one of your high-class miracles."

"And I am going to be brutally frank with you, Kate. It ain't an Alexander-type script. I don't see how you—or anyone, frankly—can save it this far along."

"But Larry thinks I'm lucky for him."

"Oh yeah. Here's the killer part. Larry's gotten hooked on astrology. Got his own personal astrologer down here. Guy plots Larry's chart daily. Altoona, he's the guy with a direct line to the heavens, tells Larry an Aquarian can save the day. So Murray is instructed to go through his little file cards, isolate the Aquarians, and, *fantastico,* there it is. The Aquarian is you. I don't suppose you believe in that astrological crap?"

"Aquarians are natural-born skeptics."

The car lurches around hairpin curves, a frosted-air fortress driving through dry, forlorn little towns. "They're shooting in the middle of the desert. It's probably a hundred and six in the shade. If there were any shade."

"Better tell me Larry's sign so I can know what I'm dealing with."

"Pisces. Dreamy, vague, indecisive, restless, helpless. Pisces is a spiritual panhandler."

"That's it? Not a single saving grace, Murray?"

"Oh sure. Ah. Yes, Pisces is tender, romantic. By me that's not necessarily a grace. Kate, the stars do muck up."

Dusty mud hovels line the road. Barefoot children in rags scatter before us. We pass under an arch of purple juniatica and then suddenly through a stone wall into a moist green garden, pulling up outside a low handsome stucco inn. "This is Toyoca," says Murray. "In season it's a high-class resort for rich people from Mexico City. At the moment, it's mostly us here. Larry has a house next to the golf course. The director is in one of those little villas behind the inn itself. Your villa is hidden around the corner from the pool. Nice cool spot." The driver and a maid are disappearing with my bags across a cool expanse of terra cotta tile. "Larry wants me to give you the script and get you settled, make sure you have everything you need—"

There are flowers on an old Rennaissance table, a basket of fruit, bottled water and more champagne in an ice bucket. "The candy is from Larry," says Murray. "My secretary spent four hours in Mexico City yesterday making sure it had mints and caramels." More personal nuances gathered from my three-by-five file card. "Watch out for the fruit," Murray warns. "Peel it or you'll get the runs."

The script is on the table too beside a chocolate éclair and a note: "My friend the poet, A. Kenneth, says: 'Next time you make love try some fellatio or cunnilingus. It's like having your cake and eating it too.' Kisses from Larry."

Hell, do you think Murray got that off a three-by-five file card too?

Concentrating on the script is difficult. My mind is elsewhere and I'm tired. The script is moody, a Western Gothic, rather simplistic with a nicely complex characterization in the female lead. (I wonder how that happened when my friends in Hollywood seem so hopelessly fixated on the joys of male-bonding.) No depth at all in Larry's character. A great part for Clint Eastwood, not right for Larry. Thin, spare script. Everything depends on pace, direction and cutting. Neal Cochran has never directed a big-budget movie before but he's been hot in the best days of television and done some impressive work on "B" thrillers and Sci Fi. I feel disoriented, caught up in a long exquisite fantasy foreplay with the Cowboy, rudely interrupted. If I don't stand up, I may fall asleep.

The pool is cut from stone, half in shadow, half in sun, with a waterfall and twisting tropical vines winding round stone arches. No one here but me doing my Esther Williams number from shadow to sun. Wet and cool, I fall asleep on the hammock in the tiny hidden garden behind my room.

The Cowboy is masked. I am naked. He is dressed all in black with shiny high-heeled SS man boots. Slave girls in silver-studded black leather miniskirts bathe me in a shallow tile pool fed by powerful jets of water. They turn me and hold my breasts to receive the teasing force of a distant jet. They spread my legs and pull me closer to take the full shock of a fierce jet against my clit. He watches silently, teeth bared, no smile, unzips a diagonal of zippers releasing, Kate shudders, enormous cock, gleaming, black satin.

"Kate. Katie. Hey." The sun is setting in my eyes. I recognize that voice, Larry, throaty and intimate. He is standing at the door to my villa, stained and dusty, scratching at a stubby beard, easing out of his rotting sneakers with that little-boy smile I remember. "You came. K-K-Katie. Hug me." He has that strong work smell I'd forgotten. And he is smaller than I remember. He photographs so big and he is broad but no taller than me.
"I need a shower," he apologizes.
"You always did."

"Don't eat the fruit unless you peel it."

"That's the first thing anyone says to you here. Don't eat the fruit."

"Everyone's got the runs. May I use the shower?" He peels off his shirt and drops his pants, unself-consciously as if we've always been together and not virtual strangers for more than a decade.

"You were sweet to remember the champagne, Larry."

"I wish it were me. That's Murray's magical three by-five memory." He emerges from the shower in a towel and collapses on the bed. "The beard doesn't wash off. I look like shit in a beard, don't I?"

"It's not exactly decorative."

We are studying each other, tenderly it seems to me. I have watched that mischievous choirboy face age on the screen. Still there is a shock seeing the coarse thickened skin, the wrinkled neck and that little paunch, so sad. I feel naked in his gaze but then I realize Larry is only being polite. He doesn't see me at all. He is only waiting for me to save him.

"Remember Sixth Avenue, Katie. Remember how hungry I always was. Remember that first Shakespeare in the Park?" He takes two fat rolled joints out of a cigarette pack, lights one, passes it to me. Kate shakes her head no.

Larry came for dinner and stayed, a hundred years ago. But affairs with Larry never lasted long. The first night is always the best for him . . . from that moment, passion drains, meaning diminishes. He left me for a blond boy in an orange romper suit who liked to pretend he was Marilyn Monroe. Larry came back into my life as Goober in *Show Me The Way*. There is a bond I still feel. I've been curious why he married Sylvia, how they survive his wanderings, why they hang on to each other.

That is Sylvia on the phone. "Is he there, Kate?"

"Tell her you haven't seen me," Larry coaches in a voice calculated to carry.

"I hear him," says Sylvia. "I don't give a damn where he is. I just want to know what he's planning for dinner."

"Tell her I've invited a trio of cannibals to eat her plus all the sangria they can drink."

"Sylvia," I say, "he's a little stoned now but he's going to nap while I work on the script and have dinner here with me."

"Kisses, love. I have a few cannibals of my own to amuse."

The phone again. "Neal Cochran hopes you'll take time to see the rushes," says Murray. "It wouldn't hurt The Star to join us either."

"Rushes, Larry."

"I'll make my own rushes."

"C'mon, Larry."

"Please no, don't make me, Kate." He has put his face into the pillow and he's sobbing. Maybe it's an act. Maybe not. I can only hold him. "Tighter, Katie. Hold me tighter. Oh, I'm whipped. I'm beat. Kate, you go. When you come back I want you to meet the most extraordinary man. He calls himself Altoona."

"All right, Larry. Later. Sleep."

"Fix it, promise, Kate. Katie's gonna fix everything."

Damn. I'm promising.

Larry's co-star Lola Riojas is plumper, looks good on her. She is positively aglow watching herself in the rushes. Staggering across a river. Once, twice, closeup, reaction shot. And Larry does look strange, angry, apelike.

"Something's wrong with his face," I whisper to Neal Cochran.

"Your being here is a mixed blessing, Kate," Cochran confesses as the lights come back on. "I can't say I'm over-joyed. We're three weeks into this already and there is no give in the budget to reshoot anything major. Larry's smoking too much. Maybe he's into something else, acid, coke. He needs to lose ten pounds. Too late for that now. He's just plodding through his scenes. If you can somehow psych him out of it, well six million dollars will be eternally grateful."

"It's his face, I think. Something's wrong with his face. What is it?" I am searching. "He's wearing his hairpiece too low."

Cochran groans.

"That's why he looks like an ape. Give him an inch more forehead, I bet you'll see an incredible difference."

"Shit," Cochran says, smashing a fist into the arm of his sofa. "You're telling me we have to reshoot everything with his face in it. Damn."

"Is it really that much footage, Neal?" Murray slithers in to soothe him.

The waiter emerges from my villa, bows, smiling an embarrassed leer. Acrid scent of grass. Larry is sitting up in bed, straight upright, back against the headboard, feet straight out, a stone. Our dinner is set on a small low table. "Here, Katie, let me pour. I've got to put my head down for a few minutes on this pillow. You work, Kate. Do something, do some of your Aquarian magic."

"Can you sleep while I type?"

"Didn't I always, Katie?"

I'm not going to remind him that was fifteen years ago. "Well, sleep, sweetheart." I am high myself. Isn't often I get to drink all of a bottle of earthy Margaux. I am about to call for coffee when a waiter appears at the door with a carafe. Espresso, of course. Strong and thick. Murray knows.

The script run through, a few lines inserted, a phrase or two to establish some complexity of character for Larry. Here Larry finds Lola after the rape. That scene can be crucial. As it stands, it established Larry as an unfeeling gun-for-hire—the same dumb amoral anti-hero I think movie audiences must be bored stiff with. I can't actually transform Larry into an Albert Schweitzer of the range but he needs to be softer, more vulnerable, a few humanoid characteristics, please. I will change some dialogue and persuade Cochran to reshoot that hanging scene. Writing is infinitely easier when it isn't your own script. You just cut and slash and throw in a little this or that, not quite enough to get it sent to the Writer's Guild for credit arbitration. If it doesn't quite jell, the original screenwriter will get the blame. If I press, I can have the pages ready for Cochran at breakfast. At lunch I can argue and cajole and there's time enough to work them into his blocking.

Larry snores. Ever amiable Jamie never snores. I wonder if the Cowboy snores. Or grinds his teeth. I am wide-awake now, over-coffeed and restless, eager to finish and get out of here.

"Katie."
I'd fallen asleep in my chair.
"Katie, come lie with me."
"Oh Larry."
"Not that, Katie. I just want to smell you. We'll just lie here and you'll hug me like you used to."
"Larry, that was a hundred years ago."
"K-K-K-Katie. Please."
I lie down next to him fitting my knees into the backs of his.
"I can't feel you, Katie."
"Larry, it's too long ago."
"Don't talk like that. We're friends forever, aren't we? You promised."
The sheet is between us. I slide inside it, closer.
"You're wearing something, Katie."
"Yes, Larry."
"Just touch me, Katie."
"Oh Larry."
"Just put your hand there for a minute."

"Larry, you asked me to fly down here to do something with a shitty script. Please, what are you trying to do to me?"

He puts my hand on his cock. Soft cock.

"It isn't there, Katie. I'm really scared. Everyone is pulling at me all the goddamned time. Be taller, Larry. Be thinner. Be tough. Fuck me again, Larry baby, make me come a few more times, Larry. What do they want from me? Maybe it's all a fraud, Kate. Was I ever a good actor? I was, wasn't I? I was brilliant as Richard. And your movie . . . I made it all work. I'll never forget what Bosley Crowther wrote about my Goober. 'Haunting.' That part was written for me, wasn't it, Katie?"

If you hold on to an illusion long enough, it might turn into truth. "Yes, Larry."

"Jesus, Kate. I'm thirty-eight. That means you're forty. I don't know how you stand it."

"I don't talk about it for one thing."

"Maybe I'm more sensitive than you. Pisces are hurt very easily."

"Larry, I'm lying here in bed with you, against my wishes, with my hand on your penis after a five-hour plane flight and an hour drive to spend I don't know what time it is now . . . working on your script. Please don't question my sensitivity."

"Oh Katie. I'm not worth it. The picture isn't worth it. You're too good to be piddling around with this garbage. I have no right even to ask . . . hold me, Katie. We'll just lie here like this and maybe I'll sleep."

Well, Larry is asleep. I am lying here, wide-awake, my knees sticking to the backs of his sweaty knees. Maybe one of these days Kate will grow up enough to stop trying to get everyone to love her. Do I really need to harvest the hearts of the world? Surely a dozen or so devoted slaves and disciples ought to be enough to reassure your average everyday emotionally deprived waif.

XIV

HARRY HINKENSTADT hands me the phone.

"Hello." I recognize the self-pleased voice of Jason O'Neill. "You were looking for me," says the Cowboy. "There is a trail of clues to prove that you've been looking for me. Well, I'm here."

"How did you find me at my agent's?"

"A very fey young lady answered your phone. She was sponging the plants with milk, she said, and waiting for the decorator to stop by with Babe Paley's house painter, whatever that means."

"Holly told you all that?" I am signaling Harry Hinkenstadt. He makes a face and leaves me alone. "Holly is always so paranoid and closemouthed."

"I seem to have a way with women."

"Oh yes. I'd forgotten." My hand is shaking. Harry was asking me to make a decision. I can't remember what I was going to say.

"Do you have time to meet me for a drink?"

"Tell me where you are and I'll think of a place."

He is 85 floors up in the Empire State Building. My mind refuses to function. I can't think of a place. All I can think of is The Plaza. I can't see him in the Palm Court. The Oak Room, yes. But even better . . . Trader Vic's. I can probably get him drunk there on their rum-spiked liquid fruit salad. Besides there is something leering and naughty about the bar at Trader Vic's. In the half light I can be outrageous and it won't seem all that blatant.

The Cowboy is too big for the banquette. But he is already drinking a mai tai as if it were pineapple juice by the time I arrive. "You're really something in pink with half your left breast showing," he says. "Don't act surprised. You must know very well what's going on down there."

"I like to see them myself."

"I find that healthy." He orders a scorpion for me. I will pin the gardenia in my hair. "Tell me about your life. Have you straightened it out since the Appletons'?"

"My life is not going to get straightened out. It just gets more complicated. I finish one script and then there are two or three on the fire. I'm leaving for the Cannes Film Festival next week. It's late this year."

"And lovers?"

"And lovers, the same."

"I saw a poem you wrote in *Vogue* of all places."

"God, you are some effete cowboy."

"You really can write. That was Alexander at her best. I felt like I was crawling into your flesh. Not just your head which I already find attractive, but into your viscera."

"My pancreas and me."

"You should learn to take a compliment. I see you have more confidence in your cleavage than in your work."

He can be very annoying. To the point like a panther. I wonder if my chest is mottled the way it used to get at proms. I feel warm and sticky, exerting all will to seem calm and cool. "The message of cleavage is clear, rarely misunderstood. But a poem is different . . . I'm not always sure what I meant or what people will read into it. Why are you here, Jason? What brings you to New York again?"

"I don't really like this drink."

"Well, actually that's my drink. Try piña colada . . . pineapple and coconut. Virtually a health food item."

He nods to the waiter. "Piña colada, I taught a little class down on Wall Street this morning to some investment counselors and a few tax men. Everybody wants to know about cows as a tax shelter. If I lose their money they don't mind that much. If I make money for them, it's an amusing little dividend. Diane has gone. She's left me." He says that in a flip aside, sips his drink and smiles. "I'm a wounded man." He grins. I sense he is very close to tears.

"You said it was going so well. You seemed really content, confident, so proud . . . I envied you."

"Well, I lied. I exaggerated. I thought it was good. For a long while, yes, it was good. She is young, you know. She was an innocent when she came into my life. I exposed her to the world, to luxuries, to books, ideas. My tastes, appetites, she got everything from me. Now she resents it. She needs time away from me, she says. She's itchy. Women everywhere seem to be too goddamned fucking itchy. Now I find out she'd been cheating on me for more than a year, fucking her best friend's husband, my lawyer for Christ's sake. She's leaving this weekend with some twenty-three-year-old disc jockey who's just got a job in Carmel."

"What will you do?" His rage distorts his face and I can see how hurt he is. I can scarcely hide my excitement. I am like some heartless unweeping heiress forced to mourn at the bier before I can cash in the insurance check.

"She says I'm domineering and tyrannical. Didactic. I am not didactic. She seems to have the mistaken idea I have no respect for her needs, her privacy, her growth.

Well, I'm forty-one years old. I like the way I am. I'm not going to change."

"You're not domineering?"

"Oh, do you think I'm domineering? In what way?"

"Well, you do . . . forge right in. You have very strong opinions. You don't let me get away with just saying something without thinking. You make me defend what I say."

"You don't like that?" His voice is ice.

"Yes. Yes, I love that."

"I don't consider myself domineering. Or didactic. Or difficult." The snarl closes his face. I wish I could start this conversation over at the beginning.

"I used the wrong word. Domineering is the wrong word. I mean strong. Powerful . . . in a healthy attractive way."

Body language talks. Now he is leaning toward me again. "So many women seem to be going through this kind of . . . wrenching identity crisis. I see it all around me." His hands, clenched together angrily, open up and surround my hand. My hand in his spread open now as if he intends to read my palm. His other thumb and forefinger encircling my wrist, moving up the inside soft skin pale against his dark tanned hand. Brutal hands, big, scarred, the fingers square, broad, almost swollen. A sudden memory makes me weak: the college girl myth: that their fingers reflect the size and shape of the thing between their legs. His hands are a monster version of my father's hands. Broad and square, both, neat closely trimmed nails. Daddy's clean hands to hold the back of your bicycle seat as you ride first time two-wheeler corner and back, immaculate hands to roll back the eyelid and find the elusive lost lash, strong hand that seizes you caught you necking in a jalopy without taillights, starts to choke, pushes you away: "I promise I'll never touch you again."

"Jason, I don't know what to say. I'm so sorry. She's put you through hell, hasn't she? You're suffering. I want to make the world look good again. Do magic for you. I know. I know exactly what you should do. You should escape, get away, do something wonderful for yourself. Come with me to France. Yes, you must."

He is smiling at me, wry and bemused. "I really should, shouldn't I?"

"Oh you must. Come with me to Paris. I'll show you Paris. We'll get in a car and drive through France, eat all the good things, taste beautiful wines, walk in magic places. Come with me to Cannes. The Festival can be insane but we needn't get too involved with that. I know wonderful little inns. Say you'll come."

"When?"

Details. Dates. All the mundane complications will be smoothed away. And even as we count the days, the deadlines, his business obligations, I am thinking now, today, tonight. Now we are going to bed together.

"Are you free for dinner?" he asks.

"Yes."

"I'll cancel my plane flight. Make it tomorrow."

"Yes." Then. "Damn. I'm not free. I forgot. Jamie is in a panel discussion tonight at the Harvard Club. There is no way I can miss it."

The Cowboy laughs. "We do have rotten timing, don't we?"

But there is time. I am thinking of his room at The Regency. "There's time," I say.

"Take me somewhere for great hot and sour soup," he says. The disappointment must show in my face. He has both hands on my thigh, pressing gently. "I want to wait. I don't want just two hours with you. I want time." That tone in his voice. His hands. That aching tickle inside me is a painful twist. Remember that silly expression. You curl my toes. There is a kind of geometry in this sexual longing. Today will be dedicated to the Society for the Advancement of Prolonged Foreplay.

The Flower Drum is deserted except for a small cocktail crowd at the bar and Mr. Lee is free to orchestrate an elegant feast. There are crisp dumplings in handsome ceramic ramekins, tangy thick soup with dark mysterious cloud ears and knotted golden needles. The Cowboy is pleased. I grab his hand to snatch a lethal black pepper pod from his chopsticks.

"Chopsticks. You are a singularly civilized cowboy."

I am too sexually excited to eat. I am watching his mouth, his tongue, those perfect movie star teeth.

"It could be a disaster, you know," says Kate. "Traveling through France with an absolute stranger."

He nods thoughtfully. "Yes. It could. But I doubt it."

"You know. You're so positive. How do you know?"

"Oh." Throws back his head. Diabolical confidence. Flash of dimple, a warning. "We like all the same things."

"You don't know me at all."

"Enough. I know you enough."

"Would you believe I'm so excited I'm having trouble breathing?"

"The sophisticated worldly unflappable Katherine Alexander." With the tips of his fingers he outlines all the V's of my fingers, a calculated eroticism assaulting me like a charge of electricity.

I cannot remember getting up, Mr. Lee bobbing in the background, paying, moving through the Flower Drum toward Second Avenue. Remember only the rough fabric of his sleeve, Kate stepping into the phone booth, his fingers on my mouth, lips, a shudder, an aching weakness. "I'll leave you here." And then dark into empty sunlight. Kate in a taxi, suddenly unable to remember the address of the Harvard Club.

"Your husband is brilliant," says the ruffled toad-lady sitting next to me. "Not just his work which my husband admires, but—" She touches my arms. "How witty he is."

I suppose he is. I haven't heard a word.

Jamie frowns when he sees me and realizes I am wearing my bosom-baring Blanche Dubois dress. But the frown fades as he notices I've managed a measure of modesty with the help of my Buccellati diamond-studded butterfly.

All that week—near-manic highs. Giggles for no reason at all. Incredibly tingling expectancy. Shopping for France and adventure. A rampage through Altman's lingerie department, rejecting lacy black nighties. No, it must be sheer, simple and see-through. Spending an absolutely unprecedented seventy-five dollars for a pale blue nightgown by Dior, cut square and low. Buying a dozen pairs of bikini panties and all-lace bras, and rosy satin deshabille slit right up to here, fantasizing rose satin lifting, lace-wrapped breasts being bared, Frederick's of Hollywood bikinis being ripped away. Turned on hot and creaming in a spartan Altman's fitting room, behind the green door. Biting my lip with a commendable pang of conscience when it comes time to sign the sales check, Mrs. James Alexander. Well, it isn't actually a crime. Jamie will adore Dior'd titties too. Jason. Jamie. How convenient. If in a moment of blurred consciousness, I say Ja . . . I have a second or two to find the next syllable.

Glass calls, his once-a-month libido alert. "I was thinking I might take Tuesday off for a meeting with some money people and if you're going to be around, maybe we could get together, chew the fat."

"Ugh."

"You know what I mean. A little exercise."

I'm busy, Glass. I'm free of your fickle tyranny. I can't even imagine Kate in bed for your athletic workout fuck. No. I don't want to be with anyone. I'm too caught up in fantasies of Jason. Specific fantasies are impossible. My head is filled with hands, his mouth, blurs of bodies touching. I can't even stand to touch myself. I don't want anyone inside me. Not even Jamie. And Jamie, strangely sad, distracted, wants me. We make love finally. How can I say no? Slow motion, gears never quite meshing. "I'm just back and now you're going," says Jamie. "Perhaps I can steal some time away to meet you."

Kate bites her lip. "That would be fabulous, Jamie. But you know how you hate that whole Festival scene."

"Jason O'Neill," says Holly. I take the phone. Heart pounding. The trip is off. He can't come. Sorry.

"I have my ticket," he says. "I can't wait to be with you. I lie in bed at night thinking about you, thinking what I'm going to do with you. Say something. Don't let me say it all."

"I . . . can't wait. I'm like a fourteen-year-old."

Holly looks at me and leaves the room, closing the door.

"You'll be in Paris a week before I get there, so I want you to find some place romantic for us. Call me with the address. An old-fashioned hotel with a courtyard overlooking a park or the Seine. A room with lots of velvet and a big bed."

"Yes."

"Are you frightened?"

"I am imagining myself between your legs."

"Don't—"

"Soon, then."

I have to lock myself into the bedroom for a few minutes. Limp, wet, drained . . . I cannot speak to Holly until I catch my breath.

X V

JAMIE LOOKS ALMOST COLLEGIATE in his jeans and smoky faded blue shirt with a baggy old denim jacket from the Year One, held by two fingers over his shoulder. He is lightly tan, the grey hair looking almost all ashy blond, lugging my baggage with so much grace and energy. But he registers shock looking at me: "You're so chic. You look like the front page of *Women's Wear Daily*."

"I'm flying first-class to Paris, sweetheart, I thought I ought to look the part. I have a feeling the way you're looking at me, chic is not good."

"Well, it's . . . formidable. Very glamorous. Terribly grown-up. It's not the way I see you. I see you at the beach in my old stretched-out sweater or the way you are here at your typewriter in that old pink shirt, hair flying, barefoot."

In the taxi, Jamie takes my hand, twisting the wedding band. "You remember what it says inside here?" he asks.

"I remember." Silly. Could I not remember? Jamie
found the ring in a dusty little antique shop on a sidestreet
off Third Avenue. A graceful band of Victorian gold etched
with precise perfect tulips. He had it engraved, "Love forever." Jamie kisses the tips of my fingers.

"You two honeymooners?" asks the cabdriver.

Jamie smiles. He likes that. "Not exactly," he says.

"I would have guessed honeymooners," says the driver.
Nathan Herschel. Medallion number 564G. Fat man in a
blue shirt. "It's good to have love in a family. My family
is devoted to each other. All my kids love me. Weekends
they all come to our place for dinner with their husbands
and kids, got to be with Pop."

Jamie murmurs approval.

"Course my wife is a great cook. Maybe you noticed
I could do with a few less pounds here and there. My wife
is Italian but she makes sensational matzoh balls."

I am staring out the window at the ghost of the World's
Fair at Flushing.

"You want to know the secret of making really good
matzoh balls? It's seltzer."

"Seltzer," says Jamie.

"Yes, instead of chicken soup in your batter, you
know, you add seltzer. That's the whole thing."

"Seltzer," says Jamie.

Suddenly I find my eyes filling, my mouth quivers and
I am crying. Remembering Maggy and me sick in bed with
some long-ago terrible flu and Jamie making chicken soup,
climbing into bed beside me, both of us eating it together.
Maggy wouldn't touch Jamie's soup. She wanted bananas.
She would only eat bananas. How can I lie to Jamie like
this? And I don't even feel guilty, not guilty enough ever
to turn in my scarlet *A*. Here I am again, holding his hand,
saying good-bye to this loving man, loving him so much,
knowing I'm going to be in bed fucking myself crazy with
Jason, almost a stranger, a week from now. Traveling to all

of Jamie's favorite places, exploring all the magic places Jamie and I discovered together. I have never heard of anything quite so immoral.

What makes you think you're entitled, Kate? Who said, Kate Alexander, it's all yours? Don't let anything pass you by.

"Tell me why you're crying, Rabbit?" says Jamie holding me close.

"I don't know."

"Yes, you know."

"I don't know."

"Perhaps you just would rather not say."

"I miss you already, Jamie."

XVI

THE PINCHED INDIFFERENCE of this hotel room tells me precisely where I stand with the crown prince of Cosmic Communications, E. Jay Eskins. I am small change. But precious small change. Tiny corner room, endless trek from the *ascenseur,* prim single bed . . . not exactly your narrow virgin cot but definitely a cradle for celibacy even in its red velvet Empire disguise. Not a room to woo Doc Simon to contract. But still, it's the George V after all, and $120 a day. There are roses (eleven . . . is that some subtle new economy?), champagne on ice (nonvintage, of course) and a modest basket of less than aristocratic fruit. E. Jay loves my new script about the mousy scientist. He likes it even more because the fifth hottest director in America loves it too. But there are a few little things to discuss . . . the usual. I am here. They are not. E. Jay's Parisian secretary stutters, pitiful liar, poor dear. The story is they've flown off to Brittany to approve some locations. Could even be true. Anyway, I'm grateful. Time to nap away jet lag.

Stretched out under aging red velvet. Both hands between my legs. Not actually rubbing, just pressed close, so Kate feels warm and protected, good to have two fond friends cuddling there. Kate is saving herself for the Cowboy. These weeks of telephone foreplay have left her weak and wet, wet all the time and pleasantly aching. Oh, there are dozens of men I can call, ex-husbands of supposed friends and transient lovers, scoundrels, a saint, legendary studs. Names and phone numbers lined up in Holly's amazing microscopic print are here in my little black book (overseas supplement) which is actually brown . . . what subtlety. But I'm saving it all. A kind of revirgination is building here. Not even masturbation is permitted. Even fantasy has become too painful but switching off the porno projector in my head is difficult.

The phone. Long distance. Jamie. I itch all over with . . . what? Guilt, can it be? Sweet considerate loving Jamie, whispering miss you's, love you's, with messages from Maggy and Holly and even a catty little item from *Women's Wear* about one of my favorite enemies, Rosemarie de Groot, being tossed out of Elaine's. "She was a dog," Elaine is quoted. "Imagine, licking David Halberstam's hand like that."

Drifting back to the jets in my fantasy swimming pool again. The phone. Tex-ass calling, the operator says. My pulse pounds. He's not coming. It's cancelled.

"Did I wake you? I won't ask if you're alone. Masochism is not my strong hand. I have my plane ticket. You're still expecting me?"

"You're still coming?"

"Well, there's one small problem."

"I was afraid of that."

"I have to be in Geneva Friday but I still plan to arrive in Paris eight A.M. Thursday. Don't meet me at the airport. I want you waiting for me in that hotel room overlooking the Seine."

"It's not a hotel. I have the apartment of a friend." I give him the address. "Oh Jason, it's crazy. Can't you go directly to Geneva? Then we'll meet here."

"Impossible. If I wait any longer to be with you, I'm going to explode."

"Oh."

"There is a picture of you in *New York* magazine this week, about to bite into an apple. You're wearing the same rings you wore that afternoon at the Chinese restaurant. Just seeing that hand gave me a hard-on."

Hot chills. Is that possible? That line delivers hot chills.

"I'm not seeing anyone, Jason, I'm not even playing with myself."

"Do you play with yourself a lot?"

"Oh yes. Yes. Masturbation is just another wonderful invention."

"Touch yourself."

"No."

"Yes. Just one finger."

"I'm saving all that for you. Jason. For Thursday."

"Nobody has ever done the things I'm going to do to you."

"You're sure?"

"You'll see."

"This conversation is mad. At thirteen dollars for every three minutes."

"I wouldn't have thought you'd worry about things like that."

"Oh, you don't know everything about me."

"Enough."

"Hurry."
"Soon, Kate. Soon."

What I love about Matthieu Theroux's apartment is
the way the floor sags, worn to a splendid patina by cen-
turies of bare feet. The way the ceiling angles and drops,
the dormers, the beams. The Seine like a goddamned forty-
franc tinted postcard below. And this spectacular view
across the water, into the Tour d'Argent. Matthieu keeps
his high-powered spyglass looped over the lion finial of an
outsize hall porter's chair. I can see what the tourists are
wearing to dinner tonight. There go the Tour d'Argent
lights dimming, the better to give mellowed gluttons and
sweet awed innocents the full dazzle of Notre Dame in
lumière. I wonder if they have binoculars over there. Who's
peeking at me, naked lady, watching Grace Kelly sneak
up behind Claude Terrail and strike him from behind with
a frozen duck? They've got Grace's head in a duck press.
Claude's cornflower boutonniere drops to the floor in the
struggle. I am the only witness. Jimmy Stewart will be here
any minute, his leg in a cast . . . oops, wrong reel. I
mustn't turn simple voyeurism into a major plot diversion.
And Jason is hardly Jimmy Stewart. Who would we cast
in the movie as the Cowboy? McQueen. Paul Newman,
maybe. If only Eastwood were more urbane. Robert Redford is too handsome. Maybe Jack Nicholson . . . with
hair.

I must give myself the Loretta Young beauty facial:
ten hours of deep sleep. The Cowboy will be here in the
morning. I've done 10,000 leg lifts and situps and touch
toes in anticipation. I've pumiced and plucked and waxed
and buffed and creamed so much superrich moisturizer into
my hands that I have indeed developed a rash from elbow
to fingertips. Halfway through my conference with E. Jay

Eskins and the fifth hottest director in America, they had
to rush me off to intensive care. Scratch, scratch, scratch.
A French dermatologist reluctantly gave me steroids. If
I'm not cured by tomorrow, it's suicide. E. Jay was unreasonable but not unreasonably so. He thinks my mousy
little thirtyish spinster scientist could be Liza Minnelli. He
definitely wants to shoot on location in New York. At
Maxwell's Plum, on a singles' cruise, at a rock concert in
Central Park, perhaps even a mating weekend at Gros-
singer's or an awareness marathon as Liza the wallflower
struggles to juggle the men flocking to Liza the femme
fatale. But E. Jay thinks my script is a little too sentimental,
too video sitcom. He wants more adventure, maybe an
element of danger . . . can I introduce Interpol or the
CIA or even the Red Chinese?

"NOW would be a wonderfully contemporary villain,"
I suggest.

"Now?" puzzles the fifth-hottest director in America.

"NOW. The National Organization for Women," I
explain. E. Jay is not *that* naïve. We will not offend mi-
norities . . . and we will definitely not offend majorities.

He is calling it *Queen Bee*. I am to get him a rewrite
fast as I can.

"Madame, monsieur le cowboy est arrivé."
Who am I now? Certainly not Camille, not at all sickly
yet definitely horizontal, demi-demure in my pale grey chiffon see-through shorty nightshirt, covers tossed artfully over
most of one breast and just a third of the other. Pretending
the noise has awakened me when, cunning adventuress that
I am, I have been up since 6:45 to bathe and cream and
perfume, to erase the shadows and paint the hollows and
blush the cheekbones and tease my hair into studied nocturnal disarray. Sick with anxiety and lust. Whipping
through my movieola desperate for a cinematic precedent.
Crawford. Too earnest, too sincere. I cannot see myself as

Crawford. Young Katharine Hepburn. I can't be that crisp.
"Oh God, you're here," he says. As if he can't quite
believe it.

How would Lombard handle this? Each time I see him,
it's a shock. I forget how tall he is. Curly hair greyer than
I remembered, skin tanned and coarse, he's older than I
remembered. Suddenly there is a total stranger in this room.
A strange man I don't know at all. A man I kissed in a
phone booth is sitting on the edge of the bed beside a nearly
naked woman, me. Buttons pressing into me as we kiss. A
man with an unknown smell, no smell at all, no Jamie smells
or Glass smells, no Tweed or Brut, just a faint smell of soap.

Anik sets a small scarred suitcase in one corner, and
disappears. "Come see the view." I take his hand, pulling
him toward the window. "Romantic, you said. The Seine.
What do you think?" Anik troops back with Norbert, the
handyman. And I am standing here naked as a loony in my
wisp of nothing trying to pull the curtain across my ass.
Preposterous. Never could happen to Lombard.

They are shouting at each other behind me, the Cowboy and Anik. She doesn't speak a word of English. His
French is near nonexistent. Yet he directs her and she scur-
ries about, apparently comprehending everything from the
timbre of his voice, hanging a Valpak in the creaking armoire, tucking the battered valise underneath, disappearing
with his beige suede stetson to see what can be done about
the streak of grime across the brim.

I should be dressed. I realize that now. I'm too naked
too quickly. There is no gentle ambiguity, nowhere to go
but bed. Weak in the knees even . . . that's more Carol
Burnett than Lombard. What happens next? I have not
dared to block out the action. Now we are alone. The room
suddenly seems crowded.

Hands. Skin. Teeth. Hands on silk chiffoned flesh,
mouth on cloth and skin. There is so much of his mouth,
so much softness and pressure, so much insistence of tongue.

I cannot remember how we got across the room to the bed, how he got out of his clothes. Did he fold them, hang them neatly, throw them? I don't remember. His legs are thin and paler than his back. There's a scar on the back of his neck. I feel it under thick curls of hair. The hair on his chest is curly too and flecked with grey. It grows in a line down his stomach, dark blond, brown and grey. Submission fantasy cock, enormous, feel the hardness pressed against my thigh. Tongue and mouth everywhere, teasing, biting, sucking, insisting. His hands kneading, pressing, hands that hurt, soothe, caress, hurt again, using my breasts in some new merciless pattern of pleasure and pain. Fingers playing me. And Kate, a simple predictable instrument, tuned to pure erotic response. Writhing, pulled towards, pulling away from, shock, coming apart under his fingers. Fingers inside me, twisting and pressing, rude violations so good. Put it in, Jason. Why doesn't he give it to me, put it inside? Now.

"Now, Jason. Now."

No, he will be deliberate and slow. He wants to do everything to me. "We have time." He blurts it. Won't let me move, holds me down, wants to kiss, pinch, rub, lick every part of me. It feels like I've been burning for a hundred years already and he is only just now putting his mouth between my legs. Mouth, gentle, loving and playful. Mouth, biting and mean, sucking, celebration of cunt, I don't know, don't even know anymore where I am, who he is, what's happening, gone. Nowhere. Gone, gone. Floating, tumbling, exploding, coming apart again. And then back, Kate so brave, opening both eyes. He has stopped. He rests his face against my thigh, face red and wet, mouth blurred with all our mixed juices, watching me. Kate giggles. He reaches one finger to a nipple. The shock cuts right through me.

"Please, please." I'm begging. "Put it inside me."

He kneels in front of me, low, thighs wide, around me, under me, raising me. Rubs the head of his cock against burning pussy, into the wet, rubs it against the magic button, down, rubs it across the mouth, back and forth, a new exquisite unbearable tension, sticky wet I can hear it. Then into me, filling me like a blow to the solar plexus, I'm gasping for breath, never been so full, never felt so much pressure. He's deep into me, tearing right through into my throat. I'm gone into blackness, out of my mind again. Nothing is me, only cunt.

How many comes? Hours. Too many comes later, my pussy is raw and burning and swollen. My throat is raw. And his cock is still steel battering into me, against me, inside me. I want him to come. I'll do anything just please come. It's too much. Scratching, hitting his shoulders with my fists, begging him to . . . please Jason, come.

"Come . . . with . . . me"."

I can't. There is no more. Just a screaming package of pain and raw nerve. He kneels again, pulls me forward, shoves my knees back, driving into me fast deep deeper than before, a new pain growing sweet, insane, into breathless shuddering. Come. His climax is violent. Body jerking, eyes rolled back, rhythmic groans. Scary, I fight back a giggle. He collapses beside me, his face in the pillow, one thigh fallen over my thigh.

I'm lying here, definitely here, watching us through the camera eye, studying that self-conscious moment of coming back from a twilight zone of vulnerability and animal abandon on wet wrinkled sheets in a patch of come beside a total stranger. Kate's brain is seized by a clown, dispatching boffo one-liners. You oughta be in pictures. And now what do you do for an encore? Not tonight, dear, I have a headache.

He opens his eyes. "I knew that's how you would be," he says.

Kate giggles.

He pulls me close, kissing tear- and mascara-streaked

eyes. The clown in my head fades away. Kate, the sex bomb, late-blooming adventuress, what have you gotten us into? Thank God for jet lag, he sleeps. Kate sleeps too.

Awake to the feel of his cock hard against my hip. Grey day, pale blue-grey light from the window. Grey sky. He is looking at me. Did I wake him? Did he wake me? My mouth surrounds his cock. I like the taste of myself, the taste of his come and my wet, the smell of me, the faint milky smell of his balls in my hand, in my mouth. Exploring. What does he like? Teeth no teeth pressure lots of pressure just a little, sucking, teasing licks? What do I like? His excitement, how he watches me, kneeling between his legs my skin iridescent in the grey rain light. I want to look at it. I rest it against my hand, the mysterious magical instrument, thick, with my thumb and index finger I can barely encircle it, purple, ribboned with jagged distended veins. He is watching me, circling it under the head with my fingers, licking its tiny eye . . . he is obviously quite pleased with it. He smiles a self-satisfied grin. I have the shaft in my hand, the head in my mouth, gently then suddenly serious, a deep powerful suction, then taking all of it into my mouth. Deep into my throat. My little Linda Lovelace trick. He falls back on the pillow, no more the casual, curious spectator. Now this is just between the cock and me.

From a certain perspective, all this licking and sucking seems silly but from close up I find myself dedicated and uncritically sincere.

Afterward . . . his fingers on my cheek stick. There is come all over my face, come-tangles in my hair. They say come is great for the complexion. Why do I keep such trivia stored away?

"Am I different than you expected?" I ask, still inanely shy.

"No. You're exactly the way I thought you'd be."

"Oh." Disappointed. "Not even faintly more wonderful than you expected?" Silence. "You knew everything? *Every*thing."

"Yes. I knew you would be magnificently sensual. I knew that. I knew you would be very responsive."

"There must be something. Muscles. You didn't know I would have such wonderful muscles."

"That's true. Do you ride a bicycle? Those are exceptional muscles." Kate flexes and stretches one leg, toe toward the ceiling. He strokes it.

"I go to a gym. We do very difficult exercises against springs and weights, an hour a day."

"These little muscles aren't bad either."

"Oh yes. You like those. I trained those muscles myself. You can flex them anytime anywhere. I can make myself come flexing those."

"What a virtuoso. Also . . . I didn't know you'd be so noisy," he says.

"Am I noisy?"

"You scream. You don't know you scream?"

"Scream."

"And laugh. At first I was thrown by that. What is she laughing at, I wondered. A strange insane laugh."

"I laugh?"

"No one's ever told you about that laugh?"

I'm not answering. Yes, men tell me about that laugh. I never hear it but sometimes I can remember it.

"Why do you suppose you laugh?" He has my right breast in his hand, pressing it neatly, first this quadrant, then the inside quadrant, then the bottom . . . as if trying to arrange it into a more perfect Playmate erectness. Or as if he were examining me. Positive and impersonal, impersonally intimate.

"I'm happy. I feel good. I love everything that's happening. It's fun . . . funny too, fun."

"Am I different than you expected?"

"Oh yes. My expectations were not very specific. I didn't know how your skin would feel. How good you'd be. Your cock, what it would look like. It's . . . ah . . . very handsome."

"Dimpled?" he offers.

"Big."

"Ah."

"Fat."

"Does that please you?"

"Big isn't that important, actually."

"Oh? Most women of experience and candor tell me it is."

Damn it, this bed is getting crowded. All the men who tell me I laugh. All the women who love his big cock. It's an absolute orgy. We'll have to resurrect De Mille to get it on film.

"Jason, the sex manuals say it isn't size . . . it's knowing." Kate is trying. "Ordinary cocks can be wonderfully . . ."

"All those manuals are written by sex therapists with small cocks. That's why they write them."

Shit, how did I get into this? "I love to feel full, Jason. You fill me up. No one else has ever filled me so full. But it's really all the things you do. But you know that. You know everything. You're so . . . professional. I feel you're a scholar of . . . making love, that you've studied hundreds of women. I suppose it scares me."

"Hundreds? Thousands. I've covered the Eastern seaboard and I'm working my way west."

"Did I sound like I was complaining? I just meant you're unbelievable. Special. I'm scared. I'm not sure it has anything to do with me."

Gathering me into his hug. "I promise you it's real. It's you. You'll see."

That's scary too. Now why should that be?

"Are you hungry, Jason?"

"I'm going to sleep some more. It's the middle of the night for me. Come back. I want to hold you while I sleep."

His arm around me is tight, heavy, tighter than Jamie's, tight like a safety belt. For a moment I feel claustrophobic, unable to take a deep breath. He sighs and moves his hand down between my legs, both hands down there cupping my steamy pussy. Kate moans.

"I'm just protecting it for later," he says.

He sleeps on his back, straight, trusting, neat. I've never slept with anyone who sleeps on his back. You need great confidence to be so . . . open. Jamie burrows into the pillow, protecting his tummy, knees up. Glass bends one leg up, second leg straight out to stretch his vulnerable back.

I need to get up. I'm too weak to stand. He wakes, pulls me upright, stands there holding me. "I feel so silly. My knees. And I'm starved, aren't you starved? Shouldn't we go out, go somewhere wonderful to eat?"

Very discreetly he leaves me at the door to the W C. Even peeing hurts. "I promised to show you Paris."

"I want to see Paris with you," he says. He picks me up at the john door. Sits on the edge of the bed, me on his lap. "But I'd rather eat here. How do you say raspberries in French? We'll send what's-her-name for groceries."

"Framboises."

Anik is beaming. She loves this. She loves love. She has confessed to me that her man is a sailor. When he comes home on shore leave she cannot walk for a day.

"Framboises, s'il vous plaît," he says. "And cheese. I don't like smelly cheeses."

"Sausage?"

"Good. Garlic," he says.

No smelly cheese, yes smelly sausage. "And pâté?" There is just time for Anik to make the shops before the midday closing. "And a long crusty baguette, Anik *bien cuite,* well done."

"Fruit," he says, *"Framboises.* Apricots."

"Abricots, Anik."

She is gone. "How did you find this place?" he asks.

"Matthieu Theroux is an old friend. He and Denise have another house not far from Cannes."

"Will she be long, Anik?"

"Oh yes, she'll be long. You can't shop fast in France."

"Then I'll just do this a little while. Is that nice? Do you like that?"

"Yes. Everything."

Anik is back with a tray and a basket of fruit on her arm.

"Do we really want to eat all that in bed," he says.

Don't we? Well, he doesn't. He is not Jamie. He wants to brush his teeth. He wants to sit at a table. Anik can pull the desk up to the window. But the dining room is even brighter and more comfortable, he reports from an exploratory expedition. "Or would you rather not leave this room?" he asks.

"And break the spell? No, the dining room is fine."

He prefers white wine, very cold, not too dry. And sweet innocent white cheese. Or gruyère. The familiar. He wants to eat his sausage with a fork. He watches me tear off a hunk of the bread. He asks for a bread knife. He has so much to learn. Kate smiles.

"You *are* tired." He's brought two apricots back to the bedroom. He is naked inside a short Japanese kimono, so short it reveals an inch of his ass. Japanese kimono does not mesh with my Hollywood cowboy images, but that's a beautiful ass. Neat, tight, with muscled hollows, indentations to make an ass-fancier weep. "Let me give you a massage," he says. Lazy, wine mellow, I give my body to his stretching, kneading, pressing, anesthetizing, then very subtly almost imperceptibly, shifting inflection. Fingers teasing, drawing circles, finding free-lance erogenous zones between fingers and toes, behind knees, inside thighs, fingers accidentally brushing against cunt. He turns me over. Deliberate now, stroking breasts, underarms, stomach, inner thighs, pussy . . . blowing on skin, fingertips barely touching, tapping a pattern with the tip of his tongue. Making Kate wiggle and purr, low guttural sounds talking back to fingers.

Everything blacks out, swallowed into hot pink sensation. Enough. Enough. She is trying to escape from his fingers. Enough. Too much feeling is too much feel . . . ing. He turns her over again. He lifts her ass. "No." She pulls away. "No. No." He lifts her ass again, pulls it toward him, pulls her onto her knees, dips his cock into all that stickiness, shoves it in cunt from behind, holding her ass, seeking the angle that makes her cry out, ramming it in. "Too deep, Jason. Too deep."

He stops.

"Don't stop."

Driving it harder, faster, gasping, he comes, falling with all his weight on top of her. Sobs. Her own.

"Oh baby." He touches her arm very gently. "Is something wrong?"

Silence. Great rasping sobs. And then silence.

"Please baby, tell me."

"It's nothing. Just sometimes, everything lets go."

Wild timeless afternoon. So much tenderness. So much talk. Endless fucking. Finally too raw to bear one more stroke, I push him away. "Have to sleep just a little while."

Kate is standing at the edge of a diving board a thousand feet above a giant swimming pool. A chorus of bathing beauties cuts intricate patterns in the water. There is a circle of flames. She is poised for the dive. She feels the

chill air on her arms as she raises them above her tiara,
feels pride in her virtuoso jackknife, twist, somersault and
plummet.
    "Oh, my God, it's not Esther Williams. It's me, Kate.
I can't swim."

I wake to see Jason standing at the window, dark now
and still raining. I come up behind him. "Do you think
you're going to be too much for me?"
    He laughs.

Jason wants a glorious truly elegant dinner. He consults his notebook. He has collected pages of research from
all the Marco Polos of the cattle world and Hollywood.
Where to find the best onion soup. Where to buy copper
pots. Where to get perfume at the cheapest prices. He has
shopping lists: Joy for his sister, Replique for his mother,
anything by Dior for the foreman's wife, Zizanie for the
foreman. Zizanie for the foreman? Oh, yes. Texas has
changed some since *Giant,* my love. So for dinner tonight,
it must be Lasserre where the ceiling opens to display the
Paris sky and he has been instructed to order truffle, a
whole truffle *en feuilletage.*

I feel as if my skin has been tattooed with fire. We are
both outlined in neon. How can it be that no one seems to
feel the heat rays? I am sure it must show. I am sure I can
smell it. And yet we both look remarkably circumspect,
very proper, seated here in the lobby of Lasserre, waiting
to ride the velvet-lined elevator to the gilded splendor of
the dining room. I am covered primly to the neck in my
black crepe cheongsam—not actually bruised but feeling
bruised, still raw. The Cowboy's hand is boldly clasped
around one elegant arch and instep exposed by a provocative arrangement of suede and strap, what Jamie calls my
Joan-Crawford-fuck-me-shoes. The intimacy is incredibly

erotic, almost unbearable. I cannot remember feeling so possessed as by this man's hand holding my foot. A few feet away another couple wait too. She is fiftyish and cute, a Southern pixie. I hear her whispered drawl. She is trying hard not to stare at Jason's hand on my foot. Look at her wiggle. She's getting it too.

He is really going to Geneva. How cool and collected that he can just pull himself together, a vision of the contemporary cattleman in beige linen with a brown bandana hankie in his breast pocket. Brown bandana, the man has style. It's all wonderfully Henri Bendel. Stunning. I never quite understood that word before. The man's beauty truly stuns me. I'm mush. Well, I'm numb anyway, propped against the pillows feeling hollow, too fragile to move.

"Must you go?"

"You're so throaty this morning," he says. "That voice. You should scream a few hours every day just to keep that voice."

So that is why I'm hoarse this morning. I thought it might be a virus. Apparently I screamed some. He sees I can't quite comprehend his capacity to leave and he explains. Very convincingly. Geneva is important. And it makes our whole frivolous jaunt tax-deductible for him. In my bracket, I should appreciate that. He will miss me. He will be true. He will meet me at the Avis desk at Orly tomorrow morning at, he consults his schedule, 9:45. Promise to be there. Is the man crazy? Solemnly, I promise. He hugs me, and one of those soft full-lipped kisses surrounds my mouth. Then with movie star eyes masked behind pale blue movie star shades and a hand through the wild shock of hair, he grabs the refurbished stetson, is gone.

Oh yes, the fever. And that ominous little cough. I am Kate, the doomed lady of the camellias. I am brave. Hear my famous haunting broken laugh. See the intimation of tragic desolation in my eyes. And the droop of my beautiful bared shoulders says it all. At any moment I may fall into a tubercular swoon.

Armand embraces me. I throw back head, my exquisite Garbo-like profile brave, beseeching . . . doomed. I hold him. I push him away. I pull him to me. I cover his face with my tragic doomed kisses. I kiss him on the mouth. And then with my mysterious pained ironic smile, I send him away and holding tight to my dearly beloved pillbox, I collapse in a languorous swoon.

These are the heartrending moments that Geritol and vitamin-enriched cereals have stolen from our repertoire.

Can't remember feeling so . . . used. My pussy feels as if we've made love without stopping for a week. Impossible to believe we were together just twenty-four hours. I know we made love last night and I'm sure sometime before dawn (unless I dreamed it) and somehow, what gluttons . . . Kate the masochist . . . again this morning, very slow, gentle, full of wonder.

XVII

I PROMISED a few days ago to meet Caroline Everly for lunch just down the Quai but I am too shaky to make the stairs. Though I see Caroline only once or twice a year, we are what our grandmothers would have called . . . soul mates. What I mean is our glands must have been formed from the same essential mass of protoplasm. I didn't know Caroline when we were caught together in Utah in one of those isolated movie locations that breed instant and short-lived intimacy.

Caroline is ready to jump from the top of the tallest building. "You're safe," I say. "The tallest building within one hundred twelve miles of Mobi, Utah, is fourteen feet high." The problem is a man, of course. Around the corner in his dressing room with a feisty little redhead stunt girl he's taken under wing is Caroline's off-and-on-again lover exercising his independence.

* * *

Caroline arrives with fresh mint for tea and oil of jasmine and liquid Vitamin C in homeopathic response to my hoarse lady-of-the-camellia voice on the telephone. Anik leads her into the gabled bedroom.

"Where does it hurt?" Caroline asks, handing the mint to Anik with brewing instructions.

"All over, Caroline."

"But especially between the legs. Lucky you. Can I see?"

"Caroline, for God's sake."

"Now when did you get shy?"

"This is super grass," says Caroline, that Sunday night in Mobi. "Just one drag will get you flying. I've got half a coffee tin left of this unbelievable stuff."

"I get too horny when I smoke, Caroline," says Kate mournfully. "Then if I haven't got a man handy, I get sad." Caroline lies anesthetized on the sofa in front of the fireplace. "Besides, maybe I'll still try to work later. Is this really all we're eating for dinner tonight? Just yoghurt. Caroline, you have such commendable moral fiber."

"Take one drag, Katie. It's sooo good. Shit, what irony. To think that all I have to show for seven months of aggravation with that bastard is half a coffee tin of grass. Nothing else. Not even a souvenir T-shirt. 'Welcome to Mobi. Fuck a movie star.' Do you know how to get a man to give presents, Kate? I'm lousy at that. I have a friend, Roberta . . . she's got the knack. Roberta always says, 'You keep one hand on his cock and the other pointed toward Cartier's.' You should see her souvenirs."

"This is great grass." I'm lying with my head on a pillow in front of a faltering fire.

"Are you getting horny, Kate? Remember, we have each other. Vinnie wanted me to get you to go to bed with us, the bastard. Would you have liked that, Kate?"

Not too stoned to be stirred by old fantasies. "I don't

know, Caroline. I've thought about . . . you mean everyone making love to everyone?"

"Hmmm."

"I've thought about that. I love women's bodies. I'd
love to touch a woman's breasts." I am playing with my
own.

Caroline rolls off the sofa and kneels beside me. "Here.
Touch mine."

Kate doesn't move.

Caroline presses her fingers between mine against the
tips of my breasts. Through wool and nylon I feel the chill
making nipples hard. "Wow. That's so beautiful," says
Caroline. "No wonder men love our bodies. We feel so
fucking beautiful." She is braless inside a clingy black shirt.
Kate reaches inside. The skin is silk. Her breasts are small
and firm. She tugs at my sweater. I pull it over my head,
taking my bra with it. She catches both breasts in her hands,
kissing and sucking. She is naked, undressing me.

"Oh Kate, your ass is so smooth. Your skin." She has
one hand between my legs, gentle. Her fingers open me up.
"Oh damn. I can't find it. Now I know why guys have so
much trouble finding it."

Kate giggling.

"I know it's got to be here somewhere," says Caroline.

"Ohhh. You found it." Caroline knows all about eating pussy. Of course. She knows about friction and time,
tongue dartings and pressure.

"Oh Kate, you taste different from me. You taste so
good." She does something no man has ever done . . .
pinches the folds of my pussy across the clitoris, pinching,
pulling.

Amazed and self-conscious, Kate watches. But finally
the brain surrenders to pussy and I'm gone, hugging the
pillow over my mouth to muffle the sound. Later, kissing
her face wet with me.

*　　*　　*

Next morning at a corner table of the coffee shop, Caroline has hotcakes with blueberry syrup. "I don't care about calories this morning. Just this once. Oh Kate, I get bored with my supposedly admirable discipline. Hey"— she smiles. "Discipline. Discipline, Kate . . . have you ever tried discipline?" She stirs Sweet 'n Low into her tea. "Not interested, huh? I loved last night, didn't you? Women's bodies are just a whole other thing. I love the way you come, Kate."

"There's a but in your voice, Caroline."

"I guess there is. I guess I thought it would be . . . more exciting."

"Me too." So that's out. Caroline sighs. I feel infinitely more relaxed. Something was . . . not wrong . . . but less than spectacular. "I don't mean it didn't . . . everything you did felt wonderful, Caroline."

"You too. Going down on me. I wasn't too stoned. But—"

"Something was missing."

"A cock."

"Penetration."

"I have a vibrator," she offers.

"A vibrator isn't the same, Caroline. It's not warm flesh. I missed being filled up." Of course, this is not the best of news for certain splinters of the Movement.

"We're hopelessly old-fashioned," Caroline agrees. "Do you think Heidi fucked?"

"Heidi?"

"You know, Heidi of our childhood. What about Jo in *Little Women*?"

"Jo, yes. And probably Amy. Beth was too saintly. Do you think the Queen of England masturbates?"

"Oh, I hope so. What about Eleanor Roosevelt? Do you suppose she gave good head? With those teeth."

"Oh, God, Caroline."

Well, anyway. I love living my fantasies. Even when

they don't quite work. I can call it . . . research. My scientific findings are: We needed a catalyst, the cock.

Caroline instructs Anik to fill the tub with hot water but not too hot. *"Madame Alexander est un peu faible"* . . . just a little weak. "I'm sprinkling jasmine oil and Vitamin C extract in the water," she calls out. "Or is E the vitamin for genitalia? Well, we'll see."

She sits on the edge of the tub. "Frankly, Kate, I never thought I'd hear the expression 'too much' from you. So there is such a thing."

"That's not the miracle. I'm just thinking how cavalier I was. Assuming Jason would arrive, we'd meet and everything would work out. That this almost total stranger would walk in the door, unzip his pants and we would be immediately compatible and off we'd go."

"And so . . ." Caroline sips her vodka. "It is everything you naïvely hoped. And more. You make it sound like a problem."

"What is that book Truman Capote has been writing all these years. *Answered Prayers.* You know the saying . . . be careful what you wish, it might come true. Feel my forehead. It could be a virus."

"Kate, you're so dramatic. You've got a dose of the honeymoon disease. Too much fucking. Maybe we should toss a little bicarbonate of soda in the tub, too."

And now I am soaking my sweet burning little virus.

Wonder why neither of us has mentioned Jamie.

XVIII

ON THE ROAD. In my wildest and most narcissistic fantasy I did not imagine how it would be. He thinks Kate is wonderful. He thinks she is some goddamned raving beauty. He adores her body, this time-flawed painstakingly maintained and refurbished arrangement of skin and bones and flesh. He is so positive, so awed and admiring, even I, the great champion flaw-finder, am starting to believe. Suddenly my hair—well, I do have marvelous hair even if it drives M. Marc to despair because I will not cut it—my hair is now a national treasure, glorious, American. My skin is babysoft. I smell so good. Not just my perfume—Cabochard, he adores it—but all my woman smells, me. Adores them. My pussy smells like peaches only better. All his life every masturbatory fantasy has starred a woman with ass, hips, breasts precisely like mine. Cellulite . . . he doesn't see it. Tit-tuck scars, oblivious. My voice, ah my voice . . . still slightly husky. He has never heard a voice of such elegant sexiness.

* * *

In the airport, that morning, standing at the Avis desk, I watch his lazy loping stride across the floor, eyes searching, scowling, a goddamned knockout—a peacock—in faded blue denim, discreetly flared pants and battle jacket, precisely the same faded blue in his cotton turtleneck, that hat. And in my understated St. Laurent pants suit, I feel like a little brown wren. Then the grin. He has spotted me. "You're here." Hugs me. "I had an awful feeling you wouldn't come."

Silly. This All-American Cowboy peacock was worried I would stand him up. What a wonderfully ridiculous notion. As if there were such a Kate, an arrogant mankiller Kate. It was I who was worried he wouldn't be here. Bite your tongue. Don't say it. Don't spoil his wonderful illusion. Don't let him know the doubting Kate, the ugly duckling Kate, the self-mocking Kate. Don't let him see her and maybe she'll go away.

He is a morning person and a compulsive organizer. Every morning he maps out an itinerary for the day. Plots our path on his Michelin maps, tracing the proposed route with his Big Red felt tip pen. Consults his list of recommendations, restaurants worth the detour, châteaux and vineyards not to be missed, castles with stately bedrooms swathed in velvet and fireplaces big enough to cook a boar in . . . as if we'd ever be bored. He wants to wake at dawn for an early start. But I convince him nine o'clock is a virtuous compromise. Anyway he has his own internal wakeup device and it seems to be connected to his cock. I am not quite sure which wakes first. His brain or his sweet fat prick. I reach for it in my half-sleep waking with amazing grace for a fiercely non-morning person like me. Sometimes I wake to find him inside me. Part of my dream. I wake from a dream of fucking, creamy, always ready. At night we are adventurers, research scientists, sexual pioneers. Mornings we make love.

* * *

He is not a dawdler. He forces himself to be tolerant of my morning haze. He leaps out of bed instantly accelerated. He is not at all interested in breakfast in bed. The first morning on the road in a romantic inn hidden deep in a forest (recommended by his friend, the gourmet food buyer for Sakowitz) he watches me sip my black coffee and nibble at a croissant in bed as an anthropologist might study the amusing yet faintly disgusting customs of some aborigine tribe. He orders orange juice and hot chocolate with a plate of croissants, butter and jam—demanding salt for the butter—at a table looking out on a circle of formal garden. Next morning he informs me he prefers to take breakfast in the dining room.

He can't stop touching me. In the car, his hand on the back of my neck, at my throat . . . bringing my hand to his mouth. At dinner, his hand inside my skirt under the tablecloth. He will look up from his book as we lie reading in bed—he is a scholarly cowboy in his gold-rimmed aviator glasses. He is farsighted. That is how you know you are getting older, dear love. When all the beautiful boys who adore you are suddenly men cursing over the fine print on menus held at arm's length, cowboys in bed in bifocals.

I am lying here trying to work on the new script for E. Jay Eskins and he is adoring my hand. I cannot turn the page. Or he will touch my ass, examine the shape of each cheek in his palm, study my ear as if it were a poem in Braille . . . and my belly button. That tickles. I don't like that.

"I forgot your belly button is taboo," he says. "Good thing I'm not a belly button man."

He talks, talks endlessly. He has brought an envelope of treasures to show me—a big manila envelope with a flap and a ribbon tie. Short stories, one that he wrote, one of

mine, the funniest story he ever read, cut out of an old
Playboy magazine, a letter he wrote his father thirty-two
years ago, family snapshots, dirty limericks.

I had forgotten what falling in love is like. I am be-
coming an addict. How did I ever agree to give it up for
so long? Yes, yes, I know. You trade that roller coaster high
for something better, Jamie forever, to cherish and keep,
loving eyes open, loving what really is there, everything
you know. No more diving off cliffs into the arms of a
stranger never sure whether there are rocks below or
crocodiles or a man to catch you, love you. The dive worth
every risk. Does this sound like a Tarzan remake?

What do we talk about? Almost nothing else. Who
was the first? What was it like? How do I feel in your
mouth? Does my come taste different from other comes?
What do pussies taste like? What do you think when you're
eating me? Does it hurt? What did you think the first time
we made love? When did you know we would go to bed
together? If I had a cock, would you let me fuck you?
That last line is Kate, of course, wanting everything.

Evening, afternoon, I don't know, can't keep track.
The room is dark. After love. Me very shaky, body racked
with crazy kind of shock waves. He pulls me closer, makes
me still. Then he is kissing me, soft full lips and his tongue
in all the corners of my mouth. His fingers fold my lips
open for his tongue. What is he doing to my mouth? Oh
God, he is making a cunt of my mouth. My whole body
feels it. My mouth is a cunt and I'm coming.

"I don't believe you, Jason. What you did . . . to
my mouth."

"No, Kate. It's you. You're unbelievable. You knew."

He loves our rented Mercedes. He drives with his
head telescoped deep into his neck, fierce, competitive,

snarling obscenities at the suicidal French drivers, challenging them to insane drag starts, Russian roulette passing on two-lane roadways. He rides the Mercedes as if it were a horse, bucking in and out of traffic, reining in, letting loose. Streaking off onto side roads or onto the shoulder to examine a ruin or to stretch his back and legs and stare across long vistas.

"Oh, those poppies," I cry, knocked out by a field of red.

He screeches to a stop, slams out of the car, picks one and puts it into my mouth.

I can't keep my hands off him. I like to tuck my hand under his thigh. That's to stay just at the edge of his perception when he seems deep in thought. On his thigh inside pressing that wonderful muscle I've come to admire when I don't want to be ignored a minute longer. Reaching close after a perilous near-fatal pass on a curve to kiss his sideburn or his tough wrinkled sunburned neck. He smells of suede.

"Don't fall asleep," he begs me on a boring stretch outside Roanne.

"I'm here."

"Diane could never stay awake in a car. Texans are always driving two hundred miles at a clip."

"I wouldn't dream of wasting one minute." He puts my hand on his crotch. "Oh my, what have we here, Jason. How lovely. Have you ever been eaten on the highway between Chagny and Roanne?"

"Not to the best of my recollection."

Zip. Ah, how fresh and pink it is in my hand, how sweet with its tiny smile. Kate, suddenly shy (or possibly concerned about highway mortality): "May I?"

He pulls me closer.

I know what pleases him now. He does not want teeth, not even gentle teeth teasing. He wants to be surrounded by mouth. Fast, slow, pressure, tickles, he wants to be swallowed, to be milked between thighs, to slide between breasts. Sometimes Kate eating is cool, imperious and precise and sometimes her mouth leads her off into a feverish, wet, weeping, dribbling come-streaked frenzy. We are careening down the highway, groaning, laughing. I feel him braking the car, screeching off the road into a field. He throws open his door. "Get out of the car, you bitch." Coming around the car with that fiery red prong sticking out in front. I'm standing there laughing. He pulls down my pants, my panties, pushes me backwards over the fender, coming into me fast and rough, making me come with him, then collapsing into the scratch of grass.

Kate stands there in a muddle of knit and lace and a great ribbon of roadmap. Laughing. "Crazy. Crazy." I fall beside him. "Too chicken to come on the highway?"

"I wanted to share it with you."

"Am I all right? Do I do it all right?"

"You give great head, lady. Didn't you tell me that?"

"Did I? You're kidding. Did I really say that?"

"You think of yourself as modest, shy, unassuming but you're some kind of narcissistic nut, lady. Would you like to sit on that for a while?"

"Jason, you're unbelievable. Where did that come from?"

"I don't know. I amaze myself."

I'd forgotten how cozy cars used to be. With the sexual revolution I suppose kids don't have to make love in cars anymore. What a tragic loss to the culture. Making out in cars . . . I loved it. Steaming up the windows of Terry's old Dodge jalopy parked on the grass behind the high school tennis courts. Terry, the boy next door, can't remember the last name, slight with bunched-up muscles from running track. Kate the incurable cocktease, rubbing up against danger. Defending various Maginot Lines. Retreat. He sneaking under sweaters, trying to undo bra hooks, failing, lifting the whole stern white cotton quilted Maidenform fortress. Kate sitting there like a prisoner, bound with her own underwear. Van Johnson never did these animal things to June Allyson, you knew damn well.

Kate determined to recapture a measure of grace by unhooking, untangling and tossing everything into the backseat. Boldly naked for the second wave of attack. Below the waist. Fingers trying to get into crotch of white cotton panties, elastic snapping. Finally Kate with a great ungenerous sigh of submission, peeling everything off, fighting his mouth and his fingers, to reach a mute compromise. He may pull her onto his lap. They will rub against each other, not letting it in, that thing, keeping it a few millimeters away from that must-be-preserved hymen wherever it is if it is still intact after all that masturbation, falling off bicycles, riding lessons, playing doctor, one doesn't really know. Oh what a glorious struggle.

And then the cops with their flashlights. How sordid. Butterfield 8 but without the glamour. Terry beet-red. Kate, heart pounding to burst. "You can turn off the flashlights now, I believe, can't you?" she says.

The cop, recognizing Terry. "Not you again."

An innocent bath. That's how it begins. He helps me out of the tub, wraps me in a towel. I'm trying to pull him to the bed. He's choreographing the pace. He rubs me all over, rubs the towel between my legs. Pushes me into the bedroom and throws me across the back of a chair. I spread my legs obediently, hot, so hot . . . limp and obedient as a lifesize Raggedy Ann, waiting for that re-entry. Fingers open me up, then the cock, filling me full, driving hard into me. Epileptic climax for him, blackout for me, can't think where I am. Who. Am. I. Is. He.

He carries me to the bed. Even half-conscious I am

sure if I were wearing red shoes I could make myself as light as Fonteyn. He fluffs the pillow beneath my head and touches my cheek and pulls the sheet high, folding it back neatly. He takes my hand in his, between us, lying side by side in the dark. "I love you, Kate."

Yes, I heard that. I am not going to answer. Men say that, you know. I love you. It doesn't mean anything much. What it means perhaps is . . . at this moment I love you. Four seconds from now who knows. Farewell, toots. You're on your own. Kate is not like that. Perhaps it has to do with gender. I wonder if all women are like me. I don't just toss around idle I love you's. When I say it, watch out. It doesn't mean, thanks baby, that was a nice fuck. It means, I love you.

"This is really quite extraordinary. How we get along," he says. "You know that?"

It is a sunless day with a curious pale pink light filtering through peach gauze curtains. The French are very clever with their mirrors. By opening the armoire an inch or two, we can watch ourselves making love. There is always a mirror. In the middle of a wall for no reason at all. Over a bureau too low to paint a face in . . . just low enough to reflect myself to me stretched across the bed.

"How beautiful we look in this light," says Kate. We study ourselves in the mirror. Jason watches his hand tracing the outline of my body, cupping both breasts. "Do you think we could ever be normal everyday people together? Want to go to a movie. Be too tired to make love. Want to see people. Instead of fucking. Get up in the morning and get dressed . . . without making love."

"That would be strange," he says.

"That would be real."

"It will be different," he says, putting his cock between my legs from behind.

"Maybe we'll love it."

"Maybe we could always be like this."

"Give up making movies and raising cows," I say. "Just fuck all day."

"And read in between."

"Or write."

"See, your Puritan work ethic is incorruptible."

I guide him to the edge of the bed, so I can kneel on the floor between his legs, eating him at precisely the right angle for the mirror.

I'm getting used to the way he looks. I'm falling in love with his body. There is a thick raised white scar behind his left knee. And his ass is a constant joy, tight apple ass, with those muscled indentations I can press my fists into. He smells sweet, even his sweat is mildly sweet. His asshole tastes like apple cider. I love his balls, tight and round, a neat pleasing package. Sometimes I smell a faint perfume of milk. Or sunshine. I am soothing my hot little bottom in the lukewarm water of the bidet—dosing my overindulged pussy with lemon-scented splashings. He watches me. I cannot ever remember feeling quite so uninhibited with anyone. The light in this room is blinding white. I am naked, face naked too. And he is watching me. Fascinated by what I do to soothe and calm and sweeten my pussy.

"Aren't you jealous I can kiss it and you can't," he says. In bed again.

Never thought about that. But I'll humor him. No one would believe the time we spend marveling over all the assorted parts of our anatomies. "Yes, I guess I'm jealous. But I can eat your cock and you can't. Or can you?"

"I've tried a few times in moments of extreme loneliness. But you have to be double-jointed. How is my cock, I mean, compared to other cocks you have known?"

He knows damn well how is his cock. He is insufferably arrogant about his cock. I am sure women have been admiring the fat monster forever. I told him big made no difference. Now I know with a kind of rage—it matters. I'll spend a long time of my life wanting to be that full again.

I am playing the game, after all, it's my game. "I would say your cock is, among the cocks I have known, uniquely beautiful."

How solemn he looks as he rubs his cock up and down wetting it with my stickiness. "Pretty pussy," he says. "You should see it too."

I have seen pussies. Never really thought of pussies as beautiful. My friend Ariane the sculptress does exquisite erotic pink petals cast in Lucite. He hands me my evening bag from the bedside table.

"Your mirror," he says.

I open the compact. And, well, yes, I suppose it is mysterious and beautiful. He taps his cock against the clitoris, making shocks, down, dipping into the sticky cunt. I see it in my tiny mirror. Tight little curls of hair. The thick engorged rod with one throbbing dark vein burrowing into me, slipping into raw red fleshy pocket. For a few minutes I watch, fascinated. It could be boring like *Deep Throat* except the beautiful cock is Jason and the pink juicy mouth is me. Then he sits on me sideways, one leg under him, the other in his hand, my legs like a scissors. Goes into me so deep I'm forgetting everything. The compact drops. What a crazy angle. I didn't know it could feel like that. I hear lots of wild animal growls growing into sandpaper screams.

"You know why I love it when you do it that way?"
"Yes, I know."
"Jason, you don't know everything."
"You love it because you can't move. You're totally in my control."

"Oh, is that why? Hmm. I thought it was because you go so deep. So maybe I'm not a true masochist. Maybe I'm just an everyday old-fashioned woman hungering for submission. Show me again where the legs go. I want to learn how you do that."

"So you can teach my successor."

My smile freezes.

Are other women curious to see their own pussies? I wonder. My friend Carla Giannini confessed once to me and Jamie that she'd used a makeup mirror to look at herself a few days after her second baby was born. To her husband's extreme mortification. "Carla, please don't tell that story, not here in Lutèce, please.'

"I wanted to see the stitches," she explains ignoring him. By accident she'd used the magnifying side, terrifying herself.

I smile. Jamie grimaces. "Carla, I can't stand gynecological horror stories."

I never looked at my pussy before yesterday. Now I am studying the dear thing in repose. I'm getting rather to like it. There is a tiny freckle on my vulva. Imagine. I have been walking around the world with this freckle for who knows how many decades. Secret and uncharted.

XIX

SOMEWHERE BETWEEN ROANNE and Lyon we stop to picnic. I swore I would never eat again after the dizzying mad *bouffe* at the Restaurant Troisgros. But the Cowboy is starved. He runs amok in a village charcuterie buying 100 grams of this and 100 grams of that. Lots of Gallic clucking and oh la la's. He buys too much, of course. Then more hunger-panging impulse shopping at the cheese merchant, yes this, not that.

"Too crotchy," he says, rejecting a round of ripe reblochon.

Crotchy? I can't believe it. From a man whose diet is 60 percent pussy. What a mess of contradictions he is.

Where shall we picnic? I am watching for a tree in a meadow or a stream as he careens along the roadway. "There. Oh damn. It's perfect but there's barbed wire."

Barbed wire won't stop him.

So here we are, not a cliché is missing. There is a dark mirror pond, wild ducks honking, two horses feeding in the meadow beyond and cows grazing in the field. Shall we spread our goodies on my scarf or the Michelin map or the *Herald Tribune*. We need the map. And Jason hasn't read the *Trib* yet. So, it's my scarf. I hand him a slice of crusty brown baguette. He squirts a tube of mustard on his saucisson. It's a bucolic scene from a thousand Hollywood movies just before a crazed bull charges, too perfect. At any moment, three Marx Brothers should appear. Wild cyclamen in the grass, benign bees, the horses nuzzling. This incredibly beautiful man, all in blue again, faded blue sweater, bleached denim shirt, blue eyes, blue skies, the sun, cold white wine, high-flying Kate, wallflower Kate in her rich girl hair and a clingy brown T-shirt, collapsed on the grass, his head in my belly.

The Cowboy is far away. I'd like to know what he's thinking but perhaps it's wiser not to ask. I touch his hand.

"I was just thinking how I came to be here." He smiles a lazy lizard smile. "My life seemed . . . organized. With cattle you can't predict, of course, the market, the inflation, that boycott a few years ago, but in my personal life, I felt settled. I'd found a woman for my life. Even when she began getting restless, I figured, so what. She's growing. Then I found out she's balling every guy we know. She said it was just a phase she was going through, something she had to . . . 'explore' was the word she used. I knew an ultimatum would drive her away. I knew I didn't own her. I didn't want to. Finally I said, do what you have to do, but tell me. That way I won't feel excluded, abandoned. That was crazy, I know, but it seemed a way that might allow me to keep my dignity. Finally I realized she was *enjoying* the confessions, shocking me, maybe even getting as much pleasure out of shocking me as she got screwing around. And she'd lost all respect for me because I was letting her. Though she'd have lied or left me if I hadn't. It was a no-win war." He looks at me. "Did I tell you she was even balling Ryder Meade. She and him and a vibrator, all kinds of creepy shit with a vibrator. That isn't what I was thinking about." He takes my hand to his mouth. "I was thinking about being forty-one and starting all over again. How angry I am. This isn't where I meant to be at my age. I had everything all worked out. I thought we'd marry, have kids even. And now I'm starting to care too much about you. What if she comes back? Will I want her?"

"Oh, Jason. Aren't you teaching me to live in the present tense? We're here now. I'm not going to think about anything far ahead. Let's just eat and drink and fuck and laugh. It isn't just Diane, there's Jamie . . ."

"Fuck him. Stop talking about Jamie."

This is getting complicated. I came along for an innocent adventure. I got led into this by my pussy. I had no intention of ever falling in love with anyone, no chance, no way anyone can lure me from my warm Jamie nest. If the Marx Brothers don't pop out of that haystack in a few minutes, I may be in trouble.

"Be careful, Jason. You're spoiling me, you know. I might have to just stay with you indefinitely because, after you, no one else will be good enough."

"How do I spoil you?"

"You're so protective. You do everything. You yell at the porter. You decide what route to take. You tuck me in. You find extra blankets. You arrange my life. You just . . . take over, Jason, and everything is so easy. You make love to me, fill me up, open me up . . . hours and hours just pleasing me. You do things nobody ever did to me. Like, for instance, you're using my scarf at this very moment to wipe the grease off your face . . . Jason."

"Sorry."

"Sometimes I think . . . when I *can* think, in bed,

you're so unbelievable and I'm so . . . passive. I want to do something new and sense-shattering to you . . . for you."

"But you do, Kate. I don't know anyone who responds the way you do."

He has his hands between my legs in the garden of the Restaurant de la Pyramide in Vienne fourteen kilometers south of Lyon.

"You were so good last night in the middle of the night," I say. This is what we talk about at lunch and dinner. Italy could go Communist, New York default, Atlantis reappear off the Florida Keys, Prince Charles marry Chrissie Evert, we would sit here trading instant replays of last night in bed.

"Did you wake me, Kate, or did I wake you?"

"I woke up and saw you lying there watching me."

"You do come awake fast. Aren't you ever *not* in the mood?"

"Not yet."

"Do you think it's just sex between us?"

"It could be." Then noticing he seems annoyed. "Of course not, Jason. You can't be serious. It's everything. Maybe it's witchcraft, a magic spell. Probably we shouldn't examine it too closely."

"Kate, you are not a serious person."

"Oh, if you only knew . . . I am a very serious person."

"The truth is you don't know me at all," says Jason. "You know nothing about me. You don't know I'm a pretty fair artist. You've never heard me play the flute. I haven't even shown you my double-jointed thumb. We have no idea what we're like together out of bed."

"Jason, sweetheart. I'll go anywhere. We'll do whatever you say. Churches, châteaux. Tell me."

"I'm not sure I feel like going anywhere. What I want

is to fuck you till you're screaming, till we're both numb."

"Do it. Fuck me numb."

"Can you wait till I finish dessert? Kate, you're not eating."

Damn, he noticed. I cannot go on like this, eating lunch and dinner. This morning I couldn't button the waistband of my St. Laurent pants. But he doesn't want to miss anything on his list. If I order salad only, he's disappointed, feeds me foie gras and rich country terrines, silken ices, petits fours. "Jason, please," I beg.

"Eat," he says. "At least taste. If you obey I will do something to you later no one has ever done before."

"I'll be dead later, Jason. And you're right. Necrophilia is something I've never done before."

He is never too high, never too stoned from these outrageous eating binges to make love. Subdued at times, yes. Sometimes I watch him, withdrawn in thought or dazed from some memorable excess at table, stroking his still miraculously lean stomach as if to comfort it. Then just some small gesture . . . I stop in front of the mirror to brush my hair or open my robe to smooth cream on my legs and he responds, turned on in an instant. And he wants to make love. Fuck. Nothing discourages him. If I am asleep, his wet fingers wake me. If I am dressed, he undresses me. Reading, sewing, telephoning, trying to write . . . he touches the back of my neck or the inside of my upper arm and I put down the needle, the book, the telephone, my coffee cup, the thought.

"We're like this because it's all new," I say. "We're still strangers. Don't confuse our time together with real life. If we were together for a few months doing all the dumb domestic things men and women do, I'm sure we'd be different in bed, Jason. A few months." He shakes his head. "A year. Two years."

"Not me. I'll always want it. Even when I was angry with Diane I wanted to make love twice a day."

"Don't say that, Jason, please."

"What's wrong, Kate?"

"I might believe you. You're making it too hard to let you go."

He laughs.

"Where are you, sweetheart?" he asks.

I am curled at the foot of the bed where he dropped me, all nerve endings, narcissistically caught up in my own body, contracting, coming back slowly from being the exploding target in Jason's shooting gallery. First a long slow love, then a fierce manic fuck . . . seeing stars.

"Come here, baby. I'm up here."

I pull myself to the pillows. His finger touches my nipple, makes a tiny circle, scarcely touching. I can't breathe. There is a tiny wire running directly from my nipple to my pussy. I feel I'm going to come again—again after all the other comes—just from that finger on my breast. He sees what is happening, how vulnerable I am. His idle touch becomes intense, concentrated . . . power, a command, the finger circling my breast with a studied rhythm of pressure and tease. I hear the moans, shuddering, my body does it, comes.

"Oh Jason." I turn to kiss his palm, suck his fingers. He puts his other hand on the furry plane of my cunt. Down. Finds me open. Begins to rub the magic button. "Oh Jason, no more." He presses the lips of my pussy together, crushing the clitoris, sending me off into whirlpools of aching ecstasy, like a siren growing loud and louder, hotter between my legs, holding me tight because my body is arching and straining and fighting to get away, wanting him to hold on but struggling to escape his fingers, close to hysteria, coming again in a scream. Still, he does not stop. His fingers are still there, rougher now. He will not stop.

Kate is crying and kicking to get away from those hands. Knows he won't let her go.

Knows . . . nothing. The feeling is too intense. I'm being probed by hot steel. Feeling blots out everything except the sense of invasion, of being bound, helpless. "Too much, Jason. Too much." The animal voice not even recognizable. The tissues are numb. How can there be any more comes? I lie there for a moment, no longer struggling or responding. Now he has both hands between my legs, cupping me from in front and behind. Side by side, turned away from him, locked against his knees. Then the waves sweep in again. I'm giving in, giving myself in to it totally, furiously, insane and violent, beating my shoulders and his, beating my head against I don't know, something, covering my face with a pillow, screaming into the pillow fucking sucking bitching fucking oh oh oh. And another wrenching animal climax. There is a flash flicker like a train passing through a tunnel flickering awareness of my pitiful vulnerability . . . how I've exposed myself to him, my animal, my madness. That he's exposed myself to me. That I love being nothing but a cunt. Now he knows it. It needn't be his cock and hand, just a cock and a hand, could be attached to anyone. Except, of course, it *was* his.

I lie away from him, at the farthest edge of the bed, crying. I feel like I have crossed some divide. I feel like a third-degree-burn victim—flesh gone, pain blurred by drugs, lying here waiting for the skin to grow back.

Jason did that for me. I want to tell him. I want him to know nothing like that ever happened before. That he has exposed a Kate I didn't know.

"I want to say something, Jason."

"You don't have to say anything."

"I want to say . . . doesn't that frighten you, Jason? Jason, my skin is gone. You did that, Jason. You."

He is silent.

"I'm wondering what you must think of me."

Silence. And finally: "I think what a joy you are to be with."

That silence was too long. I am never going to know what he thinks. Perhaps that's a kind of protection. It's better not to know what the man you love is thinking. It's like reading his mail or going through his pockets. You always find something you didn't want to see.

Innocent Kate the simple late-blooming adventuress. I was artless, an ingenue, an amateur. With Jason I confront depths of my own sexuality I could not have imagined. I am in a state of almost perpetual heat. Penis envy. Ah, Sigmund, what a delusion. The quintessential pleasure is penetration.

"I don't want to sound like an ad for *Redbook* or Modess or . . . I did spend a lot of years wishing I were a man . . . only realizing now how glorious it is, Jason, being a woman. I wish you could feel how it feels."

"I'm happy to take your word for it."

"Jason."

"Sweetheart. I see your face."

"To be penetrated, controlled, to be possessed. And yet always to emerge, still there, still me."

"I don't think I would have guessed it about you, Kate. Your first impression is very strong, stubborn, unsubmissive. But the complexity is very appealing."

"You see, you didn't know everything, Jason. You didn't know I love *The Story of O* so much I keep it tucked between my nightgowns."

He grins. "So nothing less than an iron ring will do."

Kate shivers. "I suppose there are more contemporary versions of the ultimate submission. Iron rings being somewhat tacky these days."

"If you're talking about ass-fucking that's never been my favorite fetish."

"But anyway, Jason. Penetration isn't only passive."

I try to explain. He wants to know everything. Perhaps he is compiling an Encylopedia Sexualis of Kate. "It can be aggressive. I take you into me, I ride you, devour you . . . I'm in control."

He smiles. "The Empress Catherine. Yes, I've seen your Empress face."

Does he feel the power I have encircling his cock—the teeth little boys imagine we hide inside down there? Will I give it back? Will it be there when I let it go and he returns from his *petit mort*—as the French call orgasm, the little death?

Another step today. A dimension of womanhood I hated has become another source of pleasure. Menstruation. Jamie always assumes I do not want to make love during my period. Glass is indifferent. He can overlook it. But Jason's passion for woman is pure.

"No, I say," a demure hand over my pussy. "Not today," as his mouth moves from my toes past the knees along the inner thigh toward my pussy. "It might not taste all that terrific today," says Kate with a ridiculous little-girl circumlocution that makes even me cringe a bit. This is a writer!

"Oh," he says. "Your period. But pussy is something that always tastes good."

And he is eating me, the forbidden me. I am awed, pleased, perhaps even faintly repelled, incredibly excited. Wiggling, loving with him and against him, aching to be entered, wanting to taste his mouth.

Dozing and waking, I rouse him with my mouth on his cock, sitting on it and riding, falling backwards to the bed, letting him pull me up and wrap me in his arms, the cradled rider, feeling protected and precious, a gentle stroke getting harder, the tension mean, the angle a shade this side of unbearable, coming, feeling my muscles squeeze the last drops of his come. I lift myself away from him. Two great drops of blood fall on his stomach. Without even thinking, I lean over and lick them up.

Kate shocked. Surprised by the taste, very bland, very fresh, like licking a cut finger. Kate incredulous, delighted. Is this me?

X X

THERE IS A PHONE message from Jamie waiting at the hotel in Lyon. How did he find me? I was deliberately vague saying I might rent a car and drive from Paris to Cannes with friends game for a gastronomic detour. Jamie and I have done this trip so many times. Not that difficult then to find me.

The Cowboy is lying on the bed all the pillows propped under him reading the morning *Trib*. I am unpacking, gathering socks and underwear to wash, setting a pile of postcards on the desk. I have been carrying them with me from Paris, untouched, unwritten, along with my script, a pile of unanswered mail and two books forwarded by Holly in some perverse act of devotion.

"I guess I'll phone Jamie. It's almost eleven A.M. in New York now."

"Fine."

"I'll call collect."

"You don't need to."

The operator rings back with Jamie on the line. Jason lies there, sensitive as a cow, with an expression of disinterest on his stubbled muzzle.

"Hi sweetheart. How clever you are to find me. No, of course, I wouldn't miss dinner at Bocuse. Are you okay, darling? You sound . . . tired. I miss you too, darling. Darling, have you talked to Maggy? Are you eating your vegetables? Anything new from the zoning department on the brownstone project . . . well, of course, I remember. The hearing was scheduled this week. I miss you, Jamie. I love you, sweetheart. Yes. I'll always love you." Jason doesn't even blink. "I'm kissing you, Jamie. Good night." I hang up the phone. "Aggggh. Damn. That was awful. You didn't have to just lie there listening."

"I wasn't listening."

"Oh shit." I slam the bathroom door behind me.

In a second he is across the room, smashing it open. "Don't you do that door slamming crap to me, lady." His face is blotched with anger. He grabs my arm, hard, hurting and shaking me.

"Oh Jason." Crying, crawling into a hug. "I didn't mean to be bitchy. I have such a terrible stomachache."

He ruffles my hair. "Poor baby. Take an aspirin."

"You don't take aspirin for a stomachache, sweetheart."

"Try it. I bet it'll work." He reaches for the phone. "Give me the concierge. I want you to confirm our reservation for dinner tonight. For two at nine."

"I hope I can eat," says Kate. "If my stomachache goes away."

"Your stomachache will be gone by then, Kate. Take two aspirins."

"Jason. Please. I know all about aspirin. Aspirin is terrible for stomachs. Aspirin is for headaches, fever."

"Trust me." He hands me the bottle, takes it back, removes two aspirins and puts them in my hand.

Oh hell. I am swallowing the goddamned aspirin.

"Better," he says, prompting.

"Yes. Better." Fucking bully.

Of course, what is really extraordinary is the god-damned aspirin seems to have cured the goddamn stomach-ache.

We lie awake telling everything.

"Do you remember the first time you went down on a guy?"

"I can't. I can't. Oh, Jason, isn't that awful? Do you remember the first time you ate a pussy?"

"Oh yes. Maryanne Lakeland. A little gamey."

"How brave men are to eat pussy. How brave the first man must have been. Who was he, do you know? Is it in the Bible?"

"That's a good question. Who were the great explorers of sex? The inventors of sex acts?"

"Yes," says Kate. "Who first discovered the clitoris and figured out what to do with it?"

"His name was Arnold Clitoris. In fact, it was named after him. Before that it was known as the granted, because everyone took it for granted."

Even Jason groans.

Now I know about the pregnancies he was accused of. His first marriage to the prom queen Carole. There was a tiny red birthmark on her shoulder. She wore purple Capezios. I cannot believe I'm cluttering my brain with this trivia. I even know what perfume she wore. White Shoulders. I know about Diane and Carole and someone named Carla who fell out of bed and broke her leg in three places and one whose name thank God I've forgotten who had legendary vaginal muscles. They have all become a part of my life.

Falling in love with a man in his forties is like pledging a sorority. At twenty it's so much simpler. A man has a

mother, and a sister, a few aunts, some tame old flames, a
love letter or two. But at forty there are ex-wives, children,
mistresses, pre-marital, intra-marital, extra-marital liaisons.
My head is crammed full of all this new baggage.

He wants to know about Jamie. Why I love Jamie.
Why I sleep with other men. How can it be possible Jamie
doesn't suspect? If it were he Jason would know, absolutely, yes, he insists. He talks about Diane. I am learning
Diane in niggling detail. What she said. What she said when
he said what he said. Diane drives an orchid Camaro,
custom paint job. She has a pilot's license, and once he
caught her balling the flight instructor. Later she confessed
to one Dallas flight control engineer and a weekend with
her freefall parachute teacher. She's athletic, you see, not
like me. That's why she has her choice of tennis pros and
Kate has to make do with the United Parcel man. Diane
is a medium-size power in Dallas philanthropy. Works for
the Girl Scouts, cerebral palsy, the animal medical center,
the Symphony and hemophilia because Richard Burton
pinched her ass twice (she boasts) at a hemophilia benefit
in London. She is not a morning person. When she first
moved into his house, she made a spectacular effort to be
alive before eleven. Soon she stopped. She has the hair on
her thighs removed with wax. I have no hair on my thighs.
This never ceases to delight him. Jason indulged Diane,
waited on her . . . if she cleared her throat in the middle
of the night, he got up for a glass of water. If she shivered,
he went for a blanket. If she hated a party, they left. And
yet it is quite clear, she was his creation. Certain maso-
chistic-slave-master-Pygmalion threads seem snarled in this
relationship. She was a young small-town girl, wide-eyed,
eager and yet spoiled. He'd traveled, made money, wore
that arrogance so jauntily. She was definitely his creation.
I wonder what he intends to make of me.

* * *

Fumbling for the phone ringing in the dark. Something has happened. Someone is dying, is dead. Maggy. Jason wakes faster than me, takes the phone. "Yes. Yes." He switches on the light. "It's speaking French." Hands the phone over.

New York calling. "Oh damn, Kate, probably I woke you." My clever, world-renowned agent Harry Hinkenstadt knows damn well French time is six hours ahead of his own. "I was afraid I'd miss you in the morning. And you haven't gotten back to me or answered my letters. They're bugging me about the script. Just give me a possible date I can tell Eskins. David Brown's office called. He wants you to phone him in Cannes. Wants you to save time for dinner with him and Helen and the Zanucks, of course."

Jason turns off the light, pulls me toward him, tucking my ass into his tummy, his hand between my legs. The two of us in the dark with Harry.

"I'll set aside some writing time in Cannes, Harry. I can't remember what's in the mail. I'll try to—"

"Kate, didn't you get the stuff we sent you? Why aren't you in Cannes? Shouldn't you be in Cannes by now? Kate?"

"Hang up, Kate," Jason whispers, his hand doing some very serious erotic business now, provoking a lot of heat and a few involuntary gasps.

"Harry, I'll have to call you back. Harry. This afternoon. Good-bye, Harry."

Jason takes the phone and hangs it up, settles back on his pillow, arm locking my head to his chest. I can smell me on his hand. I kiss it. "Hey, where are you going, Jason, darling? Jason, don't go to sleep. Jason. Are you asleep?"

No answer. I touch his thigh. No response. His cock . . . shriveled little ornament, asleep. I am lying here suddenly angry. Creamy and hot. I want to make love. Shall I wake him? Am I entitled? Will he be furious? What will I say if he says no? Why do I even have to weigh all these ridiculous considerations? This man loves me. Loves sex.

Shit. "Jason." Very low into his ear, "How do you feel about sexually aggressive women?"

He stirs. "Wake me in a little while, baby, and I promise to make you happy."

Mean old bastard. Okay. So I can't fall asleep now. I will read in the bathroom. Very funny novel by a new English writer. I am even less sleepy now. And what are those little blue lines on my left thigh? They weren't there yesterday. And all those funny little freckles on my arm. They're new too. What's going on? Old age has been creeping up and taking over, all in the last forty-eight hours. When I hold my hand like this, instead of like that, the skin looks infinitely younger. My hand cream is in the other room. I should sleep wrapped in mayonnaise to keep me silky. Thank God my neck isn't decaying. Aha. There is a scraggly intruder lurking in one eyebrow. I am sitting here on the chilling tile floor leaning against the wall plucking my eyebrows at . . . God knows . . . 4 A.M.

X X I

JASON IS ANGRY with me because I didn't call ahead from Paris to reserve a room at Baumanière. The inn, it seems, was booked up, days ago. The best our Lyon concierge could do for us was a room in the hotel annex.

"I wanted everything to be perfect," Jason mutters. "You should listen to me. You don't know everything just because you've been here before." His face is grey and sulky.

My stomach shrivels and the gloom grows as he stalks through the grey stone entranceway, leaving me behind. "No room. No cancellation," he snaps, returning. Obviously he had expected the force of his presence to create a vacancy. I have lost my voice. We are to follow a porter on a motorbike. Down a muddy road to the annex—stone like the main house and grey with tall French doors, roses everywhere and a pool.

"Ici c'est beaucoup plus tranquille que la maison," the porter offers.

220

"It's much more peaceful here, he says," I translate. He glares. I feel myself turning to salt.

The room is cool and elegant with eccentric antiques, velvet, a luxurious tile bath. There is champagne in an ice bucket (ordered from Lyon when hope still flickered) and a bouquet of iris, tulips and windflowers. There are even pale blue sheets on the bed and a deep royal-blue velvet spread. I'm afraid to say anything. I am mutely hanging my clothes in the armoire—speedy and efficient because my packing and unpacking seems to exasperate him.

"I like this room," he says, coming up behind and hugging me. The tension has been terrible. I start to cry.

"Kate. What is it?"

"I don't know. I was so frightened."

He pulls me down to his lap, rocking me the way you rock a child. "I love you, Kate." I still feel strangely anxious. I would feel better if we made love. Then I'd know it was all right. He pulls up my shirt and kisses my breasts but I can feel he's just dabbling, not seriously libidinous.

"Let's go for a drive," he says.

"Do I make you feel like a sex object, Jason?"

"Sometimes."

"Oh dear."

"I don't mind."

Reluctantly he surrenders the driver's seat. I insist because I want him to see the strange black-streaked walls and peaks of sandstone blasted by the winds. They look like ancient ruins. We pass a small sign. "The Valley of Hell." Only one other car passes us on the twisting narrow road. I pull over onto a jut of shoulder to stare at the wind-etched rock. How hot and sunny it was at our room below. Here in a curve cut off from the sun it is grey and cold.

Jason is silent. I haven't learned how to cope with these moods. I start the car up and drive down to the foot of Les Baux, the tiny hillside town that leads to the ruins of what was a Medieval Court of Love. To see Les Baux now with Jason fills me with a mean edginess I must admit is guilt. Les Baux belongs to Jamie and me, discovered without warning years ago on a clear fall day when we were in love and carried rare magic with us everywhere.

Jason and I are climbing past a hideous clutter of souvenir stalls. "What is this awful garbage?" Jason is appalled. The town is even more commercial than I remembered. Ancient stone steps and cobbled courtyards, a jumble of clumsy ceramics, hideous copper ashtrays, bolts of Provençal prints, racks of postcards, nutcrackers, keyrings.

"Don't look, sweetheart. Just keep climbing." At the top there is a turnstile. For a franc, we cross over onto a grassy plain. Jason has his arm across my shoulders. He's almost smiling. His arm is heavy, protective, loving, possessive. How safe I feel. We stand at the edge of the grassy plain, the valley stretched for miles below. "Turn around, Jason. That's it. The ruins of the Court of Love. Destroyed by Richelieu. In the long winters—you know about Le Mistral, the fierce wind of Provence—troubadours wooed the ladies of the court by playing madrigals. Married ladies. Very naughty. They had no soap opera to tranquilize them in those days."

We climb along the edge of a vestigial castle walk. I tuck myself into a shallow niche. Below us some German tourists scale the walls, disdaining stairs. Jason presses against me. I am wrapped in a sudden sadness remembering Jamie leaping up these stairs, scolding me for leaving the camera behind. I smell Jason's smell and feel the rough stubble of his afternoon beard on my face, his fingers on the tiny gold locket that catches between my breasts. If I were Jeanne Moreau, I could have them both—Jamie and Jason. Like *Jules and Jim.*

Dissolve to a country road. Kate in an old-fashioned swimming costume on a bicycle. Jules and Jim pedal to-

gether behind her. I am lying in the sand under my parasol.
The two men emerge from the bathhouse in old-fashioned
swim suits. Jason and Jamie.

Our little stone annex seems to be deserted. No sign
of a chambermaid. No guests. A third of the pool is still
warmed by the sun.

"I'm going to swim naked," I announce, peeling off my
clothes. Jason looks around, shrugs, steps out of his yellow
knit bikini swim trunks.

"Where are you going?" he calls from the pool.

I return with the champagne and two glasses. He takes
a sip and sets his glass at the edge of the pool. "God damn,
this is decadence." He takes another sip. I walk down the
tile step with my glass. The sun has left the shallow end.
The air is cool. He pulls me onto his lap and paddles away
with me to the sunny end.

"Don't drop me, Jason." I hang on the edge of the
pool, sipping champagne. I always meant to become a good
swimmer. Of course, I was also going to be fluent in Italian.
I was planning to do needlepoint, modern dance, know
Africa. Now shivering slightly where my skin is exposed
to the air, riding in Jason's arms, I see myself cold. Cold,
too much a dreamer, over the halfway mark, Kate. Now
suddenly I realize I am never going to be a great swimmer.
I will not perfect my Italian. There is no time for needlepoint. I'm fooling myself about modern dance. I am always
going to be neurotic. And allergic. I'm never going to learn
to fly. A few years ago there was time for every whim.
Jason is the same age as Jamie but his skin is older. Does
he notice?

"Come inside, Kate," Jason asks. He is standing at the
doors of our room. I hear someone behind the building,
a gardener perhaps, a construction sound, a shovel or an
axe. Walking naked across the lawn in the sun makes me
feel bold, faintly wicked.

There is a fly in the room. Jason pulls the sheer white curtains across the open doors. I lie on the bed watching, waiting, knees up. Open, smoothing my thighs, caressing my breasts, half caught up in loving myself and both knowing and wondering what will happen next. Every time we fuck it is different but also the same, always the same awareness of how good it is. I lie here cool and quietly ticking like a clock attached to a bundle of dynamite. I am going to be full and burning and laughing, all senses bombed into oblivion.

In heat. Now I know exactly what that means. In heat, in a perpetual state of sexual hunger.

"You look very pleased with yourself." He smiles.

What a bizarre creature: a handsome man with a hard-on. Sticking straight out like a towel rack. Does it get in his way like the 100-millimeter cigarette? Always bumping into things. Bumping into me. "Play with me, Jason."

"What a sweet little box. It's sticky already. You're always ready, aren't you?" His teeth in my mouth are teasing. I am so high from champagne and sun. I don't want to move. I just want him to do everything. My passivity seems to excite him. Or is he angry? I don't know, only know he is fucking my mouth with his cock, making me choke on it, fucking my cunt in the way he knows really hurts, fucking me with my head hanging over the side of the bed, sliding sliding fucking me on the floor till I'm sweeping over the edge again and again and then when I feel him close, gasping, crying, coming together. All of me is pouring out—the heat, my sweat, my tears, my come.

At dinner Jason is a commanding presence. Quite a dandy in a white linen suit with the Mississippi gambler cigar. I feel invisible beside him, well certainly a mere appendage to his imperious persona. He will brook no nonsense. The fish must be fresh, the chef himself must confirm its freshness, must offer counsel. If the *spécialité* noted on Jason's personal recommended list is not being served tonight, he must know why. All this in clipped formal English. If they do not understand, send someone who does. He is making them pay for exiling us to the annex. Me he treats like a glued-together porcelain, very fragile, perhaps slightly retarded. He is loving and tolerant. A few snickers and raised eyebrows fade quickly and soon everyone is snapping to, fawning and zipping back and forth to indulge his whims.

In the car driving back to the annex, he roars, very pleased with his performance. Outside our room, he hugs me silently for a long time. The air smells of roses. Our time together is half-gone. We will be in Cannes tomorrow and I'm filled with uneasiness. Must we go to Cannes? Why can't I simply navigate us west, toward Spain, prolong our time alone. I feel uncomfortable, nervous brain dancing to the imminent collision with my real life. I won't think about that now. There is a shut-off valve. I'll reverse the reel. By sheer force of will, I can bring Kate back into the present. That face in the mirror tonight, my face, I love it. Don't know why exactly. It's the same old face, but softer and he seems so pleased with it. The blue Dior nightgown is different from anything I've worn. Rather serious, with an edge of lace barely covering the aureole of my breasts. He watches.

"Stand there." He puts down his book and his glasses. "Don't move, Kate." He comes toward me naked, his cock growing as he comes close. He's so tall. I love to kiss him standing up, feel his tummy, his cock against me, one hand on each breast. Nobody does that in movies. Nobody does that to Faye Dunaway. Not even to Dyan Cannon. He drops the straps of my gown, kisses both breasts, drops Dior's best intentions into a tangle of blue nylon on the floor.

I can taste the toothpaste and his cigar, his full soft lip in my mouth not like a lip at all but like some unknown portion of anatomy, giving against my teeth, his tongue in the corners of my mouth, behind my teeth, his hands on me —not just on the right places of a woman's body, the designated erogenous zones as specified by Dr. Reuben but on me, Kate. Won't let me go down on him. Wants to put it inside me. I'm so wet, full of him. He is slow and gentle, cradling and protective, arms around me. "I love you." I can feel the love pouring into me. "Oh Kate, I love you." Harder now and faster, eyes open watching me loving me, making me climb his cock, pushing it into me deeper. I want to keep his eyes but I'm sinking away, the intensity is pushing me backwards out of my head. I won't let me go. "I love you." Like a tattoo on my body. He is crying and coming, a fierce heaving climax, his tears wet on my shoulder.

He lies beside me, catching his breath. Then, "Why aren't you saying anything? Why do you make me say everything?"

Does my silence seem as dim-witted to him as it does to me? I want to say it. I have been biting my lips to keep from saying it. I'm already too vulnerable. If you say it, that's the beginning of his panic . . . the seed that can grow into his retreat. Men hold it against you. They always do. As soon as you admit it, they've got you . . . a treasure too wonderful and frightening to hold on to. I'm so wise. I know all that. Oh Kate, so young and so wise.

"I love you, Kate."

If I weren't so damned fucking wise, surrender would take no courage at all. Hell, let Kate be brave. Or foolish. Or both.

"I do love you, Jason."

My thigh is falling asleep, needles, under him. I will have to move. My brain is totally perverse. Why else would it make me think of Jamie, now?

* * *

Jason destroys books. He doesn't understand why that upsets me. He turns down the corners of book pages, breaks the back of the binding with a stern crack, tears off paper jackets. "They get torn and messy anyway," he explains. I was taught to treasure books. My mother used to wrap books in folded newspaper to protect the paper covers. We would never dream of underlining, touching with sticky fingers. To turn down a page was a crime. Jason does not approve of such misplaced reverence.

"Books are made to be read," he says, snapping the spine of John Le Carré's latest. "It says here, listen, Kate. There is no love possible without illusion. Do you believe that?"

I suppose I do. Illusion is like salt. It brings out the flavor. A few days later when I pick up the book, it opens at the turned-down page. "There is no love without self-delusion."

How sweet that he misread or misremembered the line. I think.

XXII

THE COWBOY HAS a detour he'd like to make to some wealthy French beef baron "just a few hundred kilometers west of here." A few hundred kilometers is nothing in Texas. "We drive that far for good barbecue." Do I mind? Monsieur Montelimon is a Western buff. Dresses like Gary Cooper, has a ranch copied from old Western movies.

Well, I say, why not? We're already a day late. It's just the Cannes Film Festival, tame, a shadow of the hysteria it used to be. Lots of the same old faces. A few new deals. I've never met a French cowboy. I imagine Alain Delon in *High Noon*.

I am to call ahead. Madame Montelimon is *"enchantée."* We must stay for dinner. Henri does chili—cheeyee, she pronounces it, *sensationel.*

The house is vaguely Spanish with enthusiastically applied Western touches, stucco main house with braided rag rugs and plaid horseblankets thrown over the back of a rocking chair. M. Henri's den is a faithful replica of a Western saloon complete with swinging door. And I wouldn't be surprised if their Spanish maid got the job because she's a dead ringer for Katy Jurado. Madame, slim, elegant, and clearly aware of the incongruity of her gingham pinafore, pours Pernod for the men and passes Fritos. "We have them sent from Fauchon in Paris," she confides.

"Owdy Owdy," M. Henri says. "Pleasetomeetcha." He speaks very little English and doesn't necessarily understand most of what he says. The men go off to look at the animals. Madame and I are momentarily stranded. Would I like to see Henri's collection of American Western art? I am delighted to note that the giant square-cut ruby on her right hand is precisely the red of her gingham. Passing through the kitchen for a whiff of Henri's chili—one wall is stone with an oven for bread and a giant barbecue—we see both men waving their arms and shouting. If they are to communicate, I must be there.

Frankly, I'm not much help. My vocabulary in cow breeding and the marketplace is limited. But no one seems too upset. There are three horses saddled outside the barn. Jason takes my arm. "You ride?" he says.

It isn't exactly a question. "Yes. Well, not really. Not recently. Not well." I haven't been on a horse since college.

"Will you be all right on a Western saddle?" M. Henri wants to know.

The horse is enormous. Jason lifts me and sort of tosses me on its back. "Monsieur Henri wants to know if I'll be okay on a Western saddle, Jason. I've never been on a Western saddle."

"It's easier," says Jason. "You've got that big hunk of leather to hold on to. Boy, those are damn silly shoes for riding."

"Jason, take me down."

"Oh sweetheart, you'll be all right. We'll just mosey on along, right, Henri? Mosey along."

"Doucement," I translate. "Slowly. *Doucement,* Monsieur Henri."

"You have not fear?" he asks. Is it possible I'm in love with the wrong man? M. Henri is more sensitive than Jason.

The Cowboy is impatient with me now. Why am I making such a crisis of this? It's not that far to fall and maybe I won't. The grass makes a cushion of sorts and the air is fresh. *"Ça va.* I'm fine." Jason squeezes my thigh proudly.

"Your horse calls himself Hi Ho Silver," says M. Henri. He leads the way. Jason gestures for me to follow. There's no point trying to post in this saddle. My shoes are no help at all. I seem to remember the feet go at an angle. Hi Ho snorts. Or could be he's laughing. M. Henri's horse moves into a bumpy trot and then a run as the wood ends on a grassy meadow. Hi Ho knows he's got a coward in the saddle. My heart is pounding and I'm hanging on, just hanging on barely, as the horse leaps a tiny stream. We slow and the two men, oblivious of my hysteria, are talking about cows. Jason looks to me for a translation. I am so angry I cannot speak.

"Kate, darling, explain to Monsieur Henri about the housewives' beef boycott."

I cannot quite catch my breath but I am explaining, sweating, still gripping the pommel, my hands cramped and white. The Cowboy must know damned well I'm terrified. He smiles. "I love you with your hair flying," he says. "Your face is shiny."

My knees are trembling. I wonder how much longer I'm sentenced to sit on this stupid animal. Why am I doing this? The horses skitter sideways. M. Henri leads off across the field, he and Jason side by side. Hi Ho follows all on his own, splashing through a shallow stream, splattering my pants with mud. My throat aches with rage. Perhaps it is only minutes, maybe half an hour. The stableman holds my horse and raises a hand to help me down. I can't move.

Jason lifts me off the horse. My legs are still trembling. He supports me.

"If something is wrong, Kate, you discuss it with me later. I know you're bored but I don't want to spoil their dinner."

Bored. I could punch him. I am certainly not bored. Madame Montelimon shows us to a room in the guest house, a riot of sateen Victoriana. "Cute, eh," says Jason. "It's a cathouse. An old-time brothel."

"*Charmant,*" says Kate. The minute she leaves us for a siesta before dinner, my smile unfolds from its freeze. I can feel the tightness in my face as if I'd made some deep new permanent wrinkles. There is an old-fashioned claw-foot tub in the bathroom, an electric towel warmer and a bidet draped in fringed velvet. Jason takes my hand. I pull it away. He catches it again and holds it tight.

"You are wonderful with people," he says. "So relaxed. It's so easy for you. Well, of course, you meet people all the time. But still you have a special quality. You're real. So many celebrities are on all the time. Condescending and phony."

I am laughing in spite of myself. "I'm not exactly a celebrity. I'm not a star and I don't play the star. Besides those people never even heard of Kate Alexander."

"Well, even more impressive then. You could have spent the afternoon telling them how important you are. I thought you'd enjoy being anonymous for a change. Escape having to tell all those Hollywood stories, all that crap. Even now, they have no idea you're anyone special." He pats my hand. "To them you're . . . Monsieur O'Neill's woman. The Texan's woman. How do you like that, Kate? How does that feel?"

"Curious."

At dinner M. Henri is clowning. "You are lucky," he

says. "I like you too much to cook you my special Texas chicken fried steak." I translate.

Jason makes a face. "Chicken fried steak. You love it or hate it. No one is ever indifferent. You make a white gravy with the leftover grease."

"And we have a wine you don't find every day in the drugstore in Houston," M. Henri adds, pouring a silken sweet Yquem for us to drink with the delicate pink foie gras Madame Montelimon serves on thick toasted croutons, an incongruous elegance leading up to Henri's peppery rich chili. Madame eats only a small bowl of bean sprouts.

"I am always dieting," she explains. She asks about the Women's Liberation Movement in America. For the average Frenchwoman, the law is unjust, she explains. "But for me, there is a certain equality. Everything is written into our marriage contract. The cows are Henri's but this is my land. If we divorce, his cows will go—out, out, gone."

"Yes, it is written into the marriage contract," M. Henri agrees. "She has an apartment in Paris. I own an apartment in Paris, too. I have my family house in the Loire Valley. The condominium in Marbella is in my name. But I would never divorce you, my love. A Frenchman is too practical."

"Henri has his cows."

"And Marie has her lovers."

"Oh Henri." To me she says: "Henri has such an imagination."

"It's nothing to destroy a marriage for," says M. Henri.

"The cows?" says Marie.

"The lovers."

XXIII

CRAWLING ALONG THE CROISETTE in the stop-and-go traffic of Cannes fills me with unhappy forebodings. Jason is irritable in traffic anyway and he has yet to smile this morning.

"Wouldn't we be happier in a little country inn?" he says, again.

"Oh, we would be, darling, infinitely happier. But that inn on your list is so popular. They'll never have a vacancy at last-minute notice, not during the Festival. Besides, it's far from Cannes. We'd be trapped in traffic like this hours every day."

There are clusters of familiar faces in the lobby of The Majestic, self-conscious bronze-gelled suntans in safari jackets eyes darting clicking off the scene. Someone waves to me across the room. I hear my name whispered. Kate Alexander. Jason grins and puts a proprietary arm across my shoulder. Edie Feiler, the syndicated gossip columnist, dashes up to kiss me on both cheeks. Actually our lips never touch skin. We're kissing air. "Aren't we French," she says.

"Aren't we." Kate the hypocrite squeezes Edie's hands affectionately. She has a dingle and dangle of gold on every finger, delicate "brass" knuckles in 18-carat gold. Her hands are like wrinkled paper towels. She is older. How does she stand it? Edie is hanging on like a leech and I'm going to have to introduce Jason. He is smiling that sweet lazy smile that masks exasperation, intolerance, his whole range of antisocial potential. Then the man at the desk, Claude, recognizes me. A perfect diversion.

"Oh, dear Madame Alexander." He bubbles a polite welcoming blah blah in French. "Just sign this card. We'll take care of the rest."

Jason takes the pen. "I'll sign."

Claude looks to me questioningly. If I nod even a tiny assent I will betray the Cowboy. He does not want my permission. Or is it my imagination that he's so sensitive here about who's with whom? He signs and drops our passports on the desk.

"Oh, but the passports are not necessary," Claude protests in French. Jason ignores him, leaving the passports behind. Across the sea of safari jackets is the bar. I can see Eleanor Perry all in black with a circle of admirers, disciples and Festival effluvia. Jason has my arm in a commanding grip. Well, Cannes at Festival time is something of a grotesquerie. Here we all are, the lions, the Christians, the snakecharmers, Queens for a Day, last year's overnight comets burning out. Jamie never got used to it. I'm not sure I am myself. Why did I bring him here? I hope I wasn't just trying to show him who I am in case he's forgotten. That would be disgusting. But it's Cannes that makes this adventure tax-deductible for me . . . my supposed purpose for being here. If only he'd go off to sell cows for a few days. The thought that he could leave gives me a chill. My stomach cramps. I lean my head on his shoulder in the lift going up. His arm, so possessive across my shoulders, moves to my waist.

We have a suite. I paid my own way here this year but Jamie insisted I take a suite. "When you're being lionized in Cannes it doesn't matter if you don't have a suite. But when you're just along for the adventure without official status, it pays to look rich," he reasons. "Stay at Cap Ferrat if you like, Rabbit. It's only money." There is a pile of messages in the box hanging on the door, two letters and a cable from Harry, hello from Vincent Canby, please call Roger Ebert, a note from Liz Smith, a letter from Maggy, two phone messages from Jamie.

Jason is running water into the tub. "Want a bath?" he asks.

"I'll make some calls first." Oh the past does keep creeping in. What am I going to say to Jamie?

"Take a bath first. Let me be your slave," says Jason. "Soap you all over. Massage under water. What's wrong, Kate?"

"Jamie called twice."

"Come into the tub with me."

"I'm not in the mood, darling . . . you know."

"That wasn't a dirty invitation. That was a clean thought. Champagne? Come into the tub with me, sweetheart."

"What am I going to say to Jamie?"

"What do you want to say to Jamie?"

"I'm afraid. I don't know. I was always such a good liar. I never had much actually to lie about. I never went with anyone who mattered. I love Jamie. I never stopped loving him. The playing around . . . it was just good times, adventures, feeling great."

"A flying fuck here. A flying fuck there."

"You make it sound nasty. What I did felt wholesome. Nothing to threaten Jamie and me. I deliberately avoided anything complicated. There is my work too, you know. I don't have time to fall in love."

"It's cruel to let Jamie just drift on—"

"And it's cruel to be honest when you and I both know I'll go home. You'll go back to Texas. I won't see you for a while. Diane will come back. Everything will eventually fall into place. I'll get over you."

"Oh, that's your plan. You'll just go home and take a good hot bath and pick up where you left off, lying like a bitch, fucking some stud whenever you get horny."

"Shut up, you prick. Shut up." I'm punching his arm. "Shut up. I'm not going home. I'm staying with you. Shut up."

"Okay." He holds me in his arms as if I'm a fragile package, a clever child who has finally given the right answer to a tricky question. I wish I could disappear into this man. I could just let him take care of everything. I could be nobody. I could be myself, a woman, his woman. It would be so easy, could peel away all the superficial garbage of my life. Of course, I mustn't forget it's Kate Alexander screenwriter sometime poet minor novelist he's fallen for. Don't know how much all those titles mean. Nobody has ever loved me for what I am. Only for what I do. Even Daddy, so proud of his brilliant Kate. Only God will love you for yourself alone and not your yellow hair.

He is shaving.

I am not saying much of anything to Jamie. Just the usual. I love you. I miss you. Are you getting enough sleep? That's Jamie to me. Are you eating your vegetables? That's me to Jamie. He drove up to see Maggy. The house is full of ladybugs. There is a new baby, not hers, thank God. The house voted to call him Dylan but the mother insists on naming him Hans Christian Andersen because she loves Danny Kaye. "Miss you, Jamie. Please miss me."

Jason may not be as brilliant as Claude Rains in *Deception* but I bet my skill as an adulteress would give Bette Davis an anxious chill.

He paces. He broods. He whistles. Jason pretends to read but he is listening. Listening, hell, he is monitoring, editing my telephone conversations. This suite is not big enough for the two of us when I'm trying to work. We need a château with a soundproof tower.

"I'm sorry, Jason darling. I'm sorry. Just a few more calls. I'm sorry, love." I do believe I've said I'm sorry three hundred times this morning and it isn't even lunchtime yet. If I suggest he go down to the pool or find someone for tennis, it sounds as if I'm dismissing him. If I hint, I'm patronizing. When he is good he is very very good but when he's annoyed, what a complex man. "Where are you going, Jason?"

"Nowhere." Slam door.

Blank sheet. Somerset Maugham said write anything. Even if it's just your name. It feels as if a century has passed since my meeting with E. Jay Eskins. I haven't even thought about the script for days. My mousy little scientist with her manufactured pheromones. Harry said Carol Burnett is begging to see the script. Carol is a genius but she's too funny to be my myopic little Bunsen burner, Dr. Doris Rinehart. Slapstick could kill it. Thank God the world's fifth greatest director agrees. E. Jay is high on Ann-Margret. I struggle to envision Ann-Margret as a mousy little anything. Barbra Streisand's name's been mentioned. Isn't it always? And why not, since we're all in this for money. Sheet still blank.

How can I concentrate when I'm choking in a kind of murky anxiety. I'm not happy with Jason sunning alone at the pool. Not that I don't trust him. Not that I trust him either. The bodies here are spectacular. The bare-breasted hopefuls with their golden cocoa-buttered skin and straight hay-colored hair walk by his chaise twitching tight little asses as if they were auditioning for Vadim. I watch him watching. What does he think? If I ditch the old bag I can wallow in all that young flesh. Let the wizened old crone sit chained to her typewriter. I can sneak away. Sure some of these nymphets hope to be discovered but others are bored or hungry and want to be serviced. One enterprising twenty-year-old sent him a photo of herself nude. It was in our mailbox yesterday afternoon when we came up from lunch. He opens it in the elevator and flashes a glance to me.

"Not bad, eh."

Twenty-inch waist. Legs that go on forever. Foxy face and a mop of carrot curls. And oh yes, the tits. Enormous. High. Pointing straight out, the most remarkable defiance of gravity since Jane Russell in *The Outlaw*. Maybe someone snapped the photo as she was standing on her head.

"I saw her on the beach coming on to you this morning," says Kate, subdued.

"She's a real redhead."

In the room he tosses the photo in the wastebasket. Doesn't rip it up, I notice. Phone number on the back.

"Jamie's girl, the one I told you . . . the time he left me. She was twenty-three."

He is silent, peeling off his clothes. "I really think there's a limited aesthetic in young bodies. It's like preferring a cartoon to a painting."

"Oh Jason. You're remarkable."

Sheet still blank. It feels as if I've been staring at this same blank sheet of paper in my typewriter for days. Actually an hour. A nap might help. Half an hour. And perhaps it will help me sleep if I play with myself. Just a little. Kate has her hands, both hands between her legs, the sheet bunched into a hard knot, rubbing it against herself. Working up a splendid fantasy. Honey and harem pants and tiny tattoo of a strawberry just inside a creamy white thigh. When suddenly. Just a feeling. No sound. Just a sense. The Cowboy is standing there.

"Is that how you do it?" he asks. "Why do you use the sheet?"

"I don't really know. Maybe somebody told me you mustn't touch yourself down there, little girl, so I started using the sheet."

"Always a sheet."

"Well, a towel is nice, kind of rough. Or my pajama bottoms."

"You wear pajama bottoms."

"I wore pajama bottoms till I was twelve."

"You've been playing with yourself since you were twelve?"

"Jason, do you really want to talk about this?"

"Do you really *not* want to?"

"Seven. I think I started at seven."

"Why are you playing with yourself? You can't possibly be sexually frustrated. Or is that an arrogant assumption coming from me?"

"Oh Jason, darling. I've never had so much unbelievable sex in my life. This . . . this kind of helps me nap when I'm nervous." I reach for his hand and pull him down beside me. He sits on the edge of the bed, cold and curious and not intimate at all.

"Do you come?"

"Jason darling . . . do we have to talk about it?"

"Hey, I'm not the one abusing the sheets."

"You walked in without knocking."

"This *is* my room." Icy.

"Sometimes I come. Sometimes I just make myself tired and I nap. It doesn't feel like anything you do when you touch me. It's different. A pale substitute."

"If you must play with yourself let me show you how to do it right."

"Oh Jason, how lovely." Kate is giggly and goose-bumpy and instantly interested. "Teach me. Be my instructor. I'm just an innocent little girl and a virgin and I need to be taught all about my body."

No answer. He puts his hands between my legs, finds my clitoris and does all the things he always does that drive me wild.

"Aren't you going to undress, Jason?"

"I'm not your lover. I'm your instructor. I don't undress and get into bed with my students. It's not professional."

Kate doesn't give a damn. She is so caught up in what's happening between her legs. "Oh professor. That's so good. Good. Good." Teeth clenched.

"That's an excellent response, my dear. Now you do it yourself."

"Don't you think I've had enough, professor?"

"You need practice, young lady. Proceed."

"Is this right?"

He slaps my hand, a sharp slap. "Don't be coy. Do as I taught you. Or you'll be punished."

"Jason, aren't you getting your fantasies mixed up?"

"Don't call me Jason."

"All right, all right, Herr Professor. It just doesn't feel as good when I do it." Whiny small voice.

He slaps my arm.

"Jason." Shocked. "We're not playing reform school."

He slaps my ass.

"Jason. It's a game. Stop that."

"Stop whining. Rub harder. Put your fingers inside."

"I never put my fingers inside."

"Put your fingers inside. Put this candle in. Here."

"Darling, Jason, that hurts."

"Stop whining, young lady. Or I'll give you something bigger and harder."

"Oh Herr Professor, wonderful. Please give me something bigger and harder."

He laughs. Thank God. He drops his pants and puts

himself inside me. Fucks me wild and fast. I'm snuggled into him, meek and small. "You were so mean, sweetheart. You really scared me. It's so hard to tell where you start and the game ends."

"I'm beginning to be rather confused myself."

XXIV

THE PHONE RINGS waking us both. Jason picks up the receiver, listens, then holds it to my ear. Dawn light filters into the room.

"Kate, it's me." Jamie. "Goddamn it, Kate: You cunt. You whore. Kate, goddamn it." He is shouting and crying and banging I don't know his fist, foot, a hammer, something.

"Jamie, talk to me, sweetheart. Talk to me please, Jamie."

"Cunt. Slut. Cheap ugly slut. Kate. Kate, how could you fool me?" He is crying.

Holly comes on the phone. She is crying too. "Oh, Kate, he's terrible. The room's a mess. He's ripped up your clothes, oh dear, I shouldn't tell you. He's smashed the little monkey on your desk. Papers thrown all over."

"What does he know? How did he find out?"

"The Cannes Film Festival . . . Kate, you must be

crazy. I can't believe you two just walked into Cannes, open, together. I denied everything. He called and made me come here. He's in a rage. I think he wanted me here to keep him from total mayhem. Chick Williams called. Your terrific friend, your champion, your adoring Chick Williams. Trading gossip with Ginger. Ginger . . . we all know she's not to be trusted. That's why Chick called her. And Ginger called Jamie. Oh Kate, I'm so sorry."

"Can you do something for him, Holly?"

"Do something? Tea. I made tea. He won't take Valium. He won't take a drink. He let me stop him from smashing stuff in the living room. We were just sitting here. I was holding his hand. He was telling me how wonderful you are. How vulnerable. How loving. How brilliant. You know. Then he made me get you on the phone."

"Will he talk to me?"

There is a long silence at the other end.

"Not now, Kate."

"Take care of him, Holly. Tell him I do love him."

Jason takes the receiver out of my hand. What is he saying? Murmuring things. Comforting me. I'm so numb, feeling hollow. We didn't have to come to Cannes. We didn't have to be so obvious. I wanted to tell Jamie myself whatever there is to tell, I'm not sure. I can't imagine me in a life without Jamie. I suppose I am going home with Jason but somehow I didn't see that meant giving up Jamie forever. Maybe I could have told him in a way he would have accepted . . . he would have waited. Was I going to keep on lying forever?

"I should go home and talk to Jamie. Fix things up."

Jason has me wrapped up his arms, my face pressed against his shoulder. Holding me like a child. "You're not going home. He needs time to cool down. If you like, on the way back to Houston, you'll stop in New York for a day or two to get your things. You'll talk then."

"I didn't realize we'd actually decided."

"I've decided."

I can't quite believe it. Kate Alexander of Central Park West on a ranch somewhere outside of Houston. How do people find the bare minimal comforts of life west of the Hudson? What do they do for Scotch salmon and Moishe's black pumpernickel without Zabar's? I can see Kate as Joan Crawford playing Vienna in *Johnny Guitar*. Stalking about in black Levi's with a gun on my hip. Bet that's not the Kate Jason sees.

With me Jason is so loving, playful, funny and open. But with my friends he closes up. I should have realized dinner with Bud Hildreth was a mistake. I love Bud. He is the one director I've worked with where there was a true sense of collaboration. The two of us, me at the typewriter, Bud on the floor—his bad back. Testing ideas and twists of plot, back and forth. Bud insisted I come on location to watch how it worked, make changes as shooting dictated. So I sat there eating dust in a dry little Arizona town watching the star, Lena George, seducing dear Bud and distorting the script. The last third was so bad, the studio said, a new director came in to reshoot it. The critics didn't know what to make of our film, *Cabbage Patch*. I never saw it. I couldn't bear to see it. Well, that's a lie actually. I did see it. I'd like to forget I saw it. I sat there sweating and wanting to disappear hearing that obnoxious dialogue knowing everyone thinks I wrote it. I didn't feel like talking to Bud for a long time. Then when he had a few bad movies in a row and couldn't get a job, I wrote him a note and introduced him to some money men and now we're friends again. Bud wants us to collaborate. He has an idea and a wildly successful agent who wants to become a producer. The conversation is highly technical, narcissistic, boring. Bud's endless puns are exhausting. Our time together is so precious. I should be shot for spoiling it with this.

But the Cowboy could be less impatient. His silence is

oppressive. Poor Bud is stammering. And I am talking too much to fill in the silences? "Why don't they take away these dirty plates?" Jason is itchy. "I can do without dessert," he announces.

"No dessert for me either," says Bud, obviously intimidated.

"If nobody minds, I'll have, hmmmmm . . ." Across the way an elegant Frenchwoman is eating something creamy in a cage of spun sugar with a red sauce, probably raspberry. She is thin, so thin, tan and smooth (not that awful leathery brown the Palm Beach ladies get) with a long thin unlined neck, almost breastless, very bare in overlapping triangles of sheer peach silk with a perfect profile, bridgeless straight nose, pale blond hair in a soft neat knot. If you are what you eat, I should eat what she eats. "I'll have whatever that is."

Jason makes a face. Bud orders coffee. Jason sighs. "Cigars," he says. A busboy arrives with a pyramid of cigar boxes. Jason is impatient with so large a choice. "Upmann," he says. "Upmann. Upmann." But the English pronunciation sounds quite different from the French. The boy is rattled, drops the box. It spills. The captain rushes over. Now they are warming a long fat cigar on a candle, wonderfully preposterous ceremony, but Jason will not give them the pleasure of watching. He stares straight ahead. He tastes my dessert, dismisses it, pops two chocolate truffles into his mouth, one after the other.

"As long as we're still here, I'll have a brandy." He orders a rare Armagnac, unwittingly, I bet. "Why are you eating that?" he asks. "It's too goddamned sweet."

"I love the sauce."

"Let's get out of here, Kate."

Bud stares at the tablecloth, embarrassed for me.

"If you're restless, sweetheart, why don't you let us wait for the check. You take the car. Bud and I will sit awhile and call a taxi."

The Cowboy looks at me, shocked. Lurches out of his chair and out of the room.

"How about a cognac, Bud, or an *eau de vie?*"

"Go after him, Kate," he says.

"I'm going to have a stinger myself."

"Jesus, Kate. A stinger after that beautiful food. You don't drink."

"All right. I'll just sniff some *poire.* I love the way it smells but it's too strong to drink. Tell me your idea, Bud," says Kate. "And who is this agent? Is he serious? How much money does he have to gamble?"

I am inhaling my pear brandy like a cocaine-addict because if I stop I have a very grim feeling I'm going to be sick.

"Sweetheart. Jason." No one. He's not here. The chambermaid has straightened the room, turned down the bed but Jason isn't here. *"Quelle heure est-il?* . . . what time is it?" I ask the operator. Quarter after one. His clothes aren't even . . . I throw open the closet door. Still there, his clothes are still there, his shoes, a pile of worn underwear. I'm dizzy, a little bit drunk, crying, disgusting, mascara running down my cheeks. A big greasy spot on the front of my seagreen silk tunic. What a slob. Doesn't deserve $350 silk anything. I could have seen Bud in New York. I should have gone after Jason, spoiled bastard. Bully. Poor guy. Cannes at Festival time would make anyone feel crowded. We were so good together in the isolation of our truffle and foie gras freefall. I could have skipped the Festival. So what if I miss a little exposure, don't come up with a bon mot for Rex to quote.

I am sitting here in the tall tapestry armchair with a cloth folded over my nasty puffed-up eyes, waiting. I will give him Bette Davis in *Now, Voyager,* send him away: "Don't ask for the moon. We have the stars." Bette knew what to do about puffy eyes and wrinkling epidermis. She smashed the mirrors, let them carry Errol Flynn off to the tower. "He never wanted me. He wanted my kingdom."

Jason, my power-hungry consort. "Is it true you wanted my throne?" Some throne, Kate, a free pass to the Walter Reade theaters and a friend at Zabar's who lets me cut ahead of the line at the delicatessen counter.

I wake. The time is six and a quarter hours, the operator says. He is not here. I take off the spotted green silk, throw it into a crumpled ball for the cleaners, cream away the blue and black streaks of makeup. Too tired to wait for the tub to fill, I bathe with the sting of an especially assertive Danish shower. There is a big hooded terrycloth robe on a hook. Still wet, wrapped in the robe, I sit in the soft dawn light filtering through the curtains till I fall asleep.

He is here. My mouth is dry. I try to swallow, choke. His face is vacant. He drops into the chair opposite mine. At least he is looking at me, silent but looking at me. I exist. I can see him leaving me. If Bogart could leave Bergman . . . this beautiful blue-eyed peacock can certainly leave me. Garbo and I need very little, Jason. All we ask is eternal love.

"Kate."

"I'm sorry, Jason."

"I was a shit, Kate. Totally unreasonable."

"No, darling. You are infinitely reasonable." Oh God what a lie. If the Hays Office were still around, I'd be struck dead on the spot. "You are the soul of patience. You're so good, Jason. Movie people . . . what a tight little world to just be suddenly thrust into."

"I know this world very well, Kate. Don't forget."

"We'll go. Get out of Cannes."

"No. We'll stay. It's only a few days. You want to see the new Altman movie. You need to be here. We'll stay."

"Please sweetheart, I want to go. Let's go to one of

the fabulous inns in your notebook. We'll just disappear. No one has to know where we are. We'll swim and sun and talk. I'll write and you'll read and whenever the typewriter keys stop, we'll make love."

"All right."

He holds my face, pulling the skin taut, looking at me sternly. I can smell brandy and perfume on him. Shit, I even recognize that perfume, Jolie Madame. Now where the hell has he been? The goddamn bastard. I can smell it faintly on his fingers. Pussy. I push him away.

"What is it, Kate?"

Yes I'm furious but my rage is exhilarating. I can't believe where it's taking me. Ripping off his shirt, tearing open the zipper of his pants. His cock, that smell of pussy and come. "What are you, Jason, some kind of fucking satyr?" The two-faced bastard. I run my teeth up and down his silly soft cock. Hand pressing hard into his balls.

"You don't know the first thing about fucking around, you bastard. Infidelity . . . you're pathetic. You're an amateur. You could at least have taken a shower, you bastard. Get out of that lousy chair, you fucking amateur. Get out of those clothes. You stink. Jolie Madame. I want to see if what you've got there is good enough for me."

He smiles his lazy smile of drunken amusement. Stumbles. Stands. Steps out of his pants, tugs at his dark blue abbreviated French shorts, drops to his knees, pulls me to his mouth. I can feel the scratchy stubble of his beard as his tongue and teeth begin a Jason courtship. The rhythm of my breathing changes. Bone-melting heat, a rush of blood.

"You're doing well enough for a fool and a charlatan," Kate cries. "You're good, you know. Did she tell you how good you are? Don't stop. Now that's a bit boring. You better try something el—agh." He really bit me. "You animal." Pushing him off, pushing him back to the floor. "You can just lie there. I'll put it in. Don't move. I'll do it. I said,

I'll do it." I am sitting on it, thighs locked against him, watching his face, his eyes closed. He's smiling. Lifting myself, riding it, rubbing myself against him, making myself come.

Suddenly he grabs me. Holds me still. Thrusts against me, deep and hard, making me gasp. We're really fighting now.

"I'm the one, Jason. *I'm* fucking you."

But he's stronger. I can only keep control if I make him give in to what I make him feel. Now I'm squatting on him, my knees pressed together hiding his face, one hand behind me holding his balls in a neat little package, lifting slow, falling hard, turning the tension tighter, so close to coming, so close and then, damn mean bastard, he pulls me off him, throws me onto the floor.

"You can't do that," I'm crying. "Stop, Jason. I'm the one." He twists me over onto my face, both hands grabbing my ass, pulling it toward him, shoving into my pussy from behind, deep and deliberate, hard, battering into me so hard. I lose my breath with every bang.

Even this time, I can't win. He won't let me fuck him. Won't let me make myself come. He has to do it. Oh, don't I love that. "I love it, Jason," says Kate, laughing. Just then he shoves against me, knocking me flat on the floor. "No. Jason. Not there. Not in my ass." With my hand, trying to put his cock back where it belongs. He twists my hand. He has me pinned. "No. Jason." Oh God what a scream. "Wait. Wait." Ripping into me. Pain. Tearing impossible pain. Tearing into me just as I tensed. "Stop. Stop."

"Stop screaming."

"Take it out."

"I want it. Stop crying, Kate. I want it."

I let myself go limp. Feel him come deep inside me.

"Stop crying Kate."

"Don't move, you fucking sadist."

"I'll be gentle."

"It's too late."

"You loved it."

Silence.

"You loved it."

"You're crazy."

In a fury at this dumb bullshit. I'm crying. He starts to get up. "Jason." I reach for him. "I. Don't. Love. It." He holds me. "You will."

I wake late, embarrassed and uneasy. Jason is smiling and scratching and stretching, affectionate . . . as if nothing has happened. He's asked the concierge to suggest a real estate man to find us a villa. "But won't that be extravagant? A villa for just these last few days."

"Let's see," he says, off to look at some sprawling villa in the hills above Cannes "down the road from Picasso's place," he marvels.

And I am trying to reach Jamie. Twice earlier I tried the apartment. Sandy, the cheerful unknown voice of the answering service, is embarrassed. She says Mr. Alexander has left instructions not to give me his number. His secretary is embarrassed too. "He's out of town," she tells the long-distance operator, from the tone of her voice, clearly a lie.

"He's living with her," says Holly. Back to Audrey so fast. Was she waiting all that time? Or did she never go away? Maggy promises to speak to him. Maggy persuades him to talk to me.

"It shouldn't have happened to us, Kate," Jamie says.

"I know."

"We're really good together. Nobody I know, none of our friends have anything like what we have."

"Jamie, I don't know how to explain it. Maybe it's just something I have to go through. Maybe I'll come out at the other end looking for you."

"Oh Rabbit. There's no one like you. No one will

ever know me the way you do. No one knows how wonderful you are. They think you're brilliant and funny and successful but they have no idea how good you are."

"I know I'll be back, Jamie, if you'll take me back."

"It won't be the same, Kate."

"No. You're right. It won't be the same. But it could be better. I love you, Jamie."

"You know, Kate, you're a fucking cunt."

Jason finds me huddled under the covers, miserable, eyes swollen, hair damp and tangled. "Of course, you're upset," he says. "You don't just cut off a love of all those years without pain. It's that vulnerability I love." He cuddles me with a look that makes me wonder if he isn't seeing Carroll Baker curled up in a baby crib. The three faces of Kate. Cunt, Baby Snooks and pussypie. Somewhere in there must be me.

Next time I'm alone I have to write Jamie. Somehow, explain. I keep seeing him standing at the door of my office looking for something to throw, something precious but not too precious. Or has he lost that strange and wonderful capacity for measured violence? How dare he smash my toy monkey. He gave it to me inside a lapis box for Christmas, the monkey nestled in peanuts. That was the Christmas he came home from Audrey to me. And we were so fragile and careful and awed to be together, healing.

I keep seeing Jamie in shock and anger because I remember the pain of Kate in that first terrible week that *he* walked out. Sitting on the floor next to the bed by the phone, hysteria poised, waiting for him to call and say he'd changed his mind, bad joke, Audrey, big mistake. Like a script girl on the set, I have all the details of the scene recorded in the pain notebook of my head. Legs stretched out like a giant doll, woman in shock, barefoot, staring at a fuzz of dust under the bed, shivering in Jamie's old torn paint-stained sweatshirt, his smell, his faint almost imperceptible smell on the shirt, rain, even rain, like a Hemingway novel, unable to move, as if I'd been hit by a truck. Eyes fat nearly closed shut from crying, terrible heaving wrenching sobs that suddenly stop because there is no one to hear. There is a razor next to the phone. Oh yes, reduced to cliché. Nothing too serious contemplated, just a gentle nick or two timed to greet Minnie the cleaning lady who can call the police who can call Jamie who will come and then won't he be sorry. Forget the razor. Can't have the police. Can't have the *Daily News.* Can't face the headline: Central Park West Adventuress Can't Take Tat for Tit. Right there beside the razor, a macabre gastronomic touch, Jamie's prized Rudolph Stanish omelet pan. I hid it when he packed. I won't let him make perfect omelets for some twenty-three-old morally superior home-destroyer who wouldn't know a perfect omelet anyway.

Maggy shutting the window, mopping up the rain. Holly walking in and out. The patient semicomatose. The phone. Sympathetic friends.

"Kate, you have to pull yourself together."

"No, I don't."

"She isn't even that pretty."

Don't tell me. When did you see her? You call yourself a friend. Fuck off. Go away. "What do you mean? Jamie says she's beautiful."

"She's young. That always helps. But actually rather plain, small, thin. Big mouth."

Jamie loves big mouths.

Then Jamie finally calling, crying too. "It's a mistake, Kate. As soon as I walked out the door I knew it was a mistake, impossible to leave you."

"Then why did you keep going?"

"I had to. Have to see . . ."

"What do you have to see? You know already. Even if you come back it isn't going to be the same."

"Well, yes, Kate. But maybe it can be better."

And then my mother. "I know I never seemed to understand you, Kate, and you don't want to talk to me but I can't bear to see you sitting there like a highway accident victim. At least comb your hair."

I look at her. So thin and lined, meticulously groomed, stylish in her fuzzy mohair knit with the high cowl framing her heart-shaped chin. Even she can see I've been hit by a truck. I've made my point, I guess. "I'll get into bed for a while."

Everyone talking over me, the victim. Kindly old Dr. Kildare is taking my pulse.

"It's a strange anaphylactic reaction," Kildare says. "She is allergic to reality."

I recovered. I managed one whole telephone conversation without tears, and four strips of bacon for breakfast, and the typewriter. Let M. Marc do something drastic with my hair, hated it. Bruised purple days. Good friends meaning well, asking me along. The third, the fifth, the extra woman at dinner. Blind dates: the lame, the sick, the doddering old. For two weeks I was manic, went everywhere, tried everything, never said no. Then battered and disenchanted I came home and worked. And I did everything I could to make Jamie come back. Did really outrageous Bette Davis in *Jezebel* tricks. Like calling Jamie at her apartment sometime after two in the morning. Hearing her choked waked-up voice.

"I can't bear it, Jamie," I say. Crying. "You don't know how it is."

"I know."

"You don't know. You're with her. Why are you doing

this to us?" Tears into a kind of hysteria not faked, no, not for a minute faked, all painfully real but . . . self-conscious, all the time knowing damn well, I'm getting to him. Imagining her lying there beside him—young body, pale but firm, oh my yes, firm and smooth, big mouth, dark hair on the pillow, suffering as she hears Jamie's voice breaking, listening to him loving and sad on the phone, knowing that it's me.

"Don't make me cry," he says. "Please, don't make me cry."

Now I'm in bed with them the rest of the night. Okay, so it's sick. I may not be Scarlett O'Hara, but I bet I'd look right fetchin' in a gown thrown together from our blue velvet curtains.

And Jamie came home. Now it's me gone away. His broken heart seems very efficiently patched. Who says estrogen is everything? Morally superior brunettes with firm young bodies are apparently very big medicine.

X X V

NEVER MIND the villa. The inn he wanted stubbornly all along has an unexpected vacancy.

I have to laugh. Jason's inn is the same handsome old farmhouse where I spent two stolen sex-crazed days last year with a certain rogue director I'm not going to name because he does love his wife. I'm fond of her too. It was just an adventure.

As soon as I've said—"Oh, I love this place. I've been here," Jason's face clouds. I could cut out my tongue.

"With Jamie?" he wants to know.

"No."

That damn lower lip comes out and he ignores me as the proprietress leads us along the garden walk to a small cottage with a tiny walled garden beyond a grapefruit tree. There are two ducks and a guinea hen strutting across the lawn. She is proud of the room, all blue flowered print.

"The hyacinth suite," she says. There are books, fruit in a bowl, two fruit knifes and a graceful basket of flowers. I smile but Jason is sulking.

"Darling, you're not going to be angry. It was nothing. A tiny adventure. Nothing like us."

"I can't show you anything. You've been everywhere."

"Jason, you've shown me . . . how can I tell you? Myself. Feeling I didn't know I could have. A depth of sexuality I never knew before. You make me feel . . . reborn. Brand-new."

"That sounds like sex, don't you think?"

I look at him. Sulky, hurt. I suppose he's right. That's just how it sounds. The peacock is insecure. "Oh Jason. The sex is unbelievable. But sex is just one element. It's everything, all the things we are. Your head, your wit, the way you look, the way you look at me . . ."

"The way I sing off key."

"Your sensitivity. Your intelligence."

"My neatness. My aptness of thought." He smiles. "There's another song, you know," says Jason. "It goes, 'You only love me because I'm good in bed.' "

"Jason. I'm warning you . . . I haven't heard that song. And I didn't write it."

Tonight is the first time we've gone to sleep in a bed we've not made love in. I'm trying not to read messages of cosmic significance into this unhappy development. My militant feminist friends might say, if you want him, why don't you reach over and take his cock in your mouth? What is this obsolete sexist passivity? The dilemma is I want sex all the time. I never want to get out of bed. He teases me for my voracity. His word: voracity. What does that mean? The dialogue in the room yesterday. I didn't force him to be so good in bed. Do I make him feel like one wonderful cock in a never-ending parade? I bet my parade is no match for his parade. One afternoon without fucking, one evening, one tender good-night kiss, let's not make a federal case out of it.

I wake. He is holding me. "You were crying in your sleep," he says. "What were you dreaming?"

"Was I? I can't remember."

"Try. Maybe it'll help."

"Jason, please. I'm half asleep. I don't want to try." I open my eyes. "You were making love to me in the dream, Jason. And there was a line of men beside the bed waiting their turn. With their flies unzipped. And their cocks out. And I . . . I said . . . 'Next.' Oh Jesus. Is that what I said? I don't want all those men."

"But you *must* want them, Kate. Who put them in your dream?"

"Maybe that's the way it was before, Jason. Not the way I want it to be. And it was never just fucking. I was just being free, Jason, tasting everything. Voracious is not a word I'd use. I was practically decorous . . . a lesson in passionate moderation." That's Kate. A little exaggeration never hurts.

"How many men do you consider moderate?"

"What do you mean?"

"I mean how many men have you been to bed with?"

"Oh Jason, I have no idea. I don't count."

"Is it that many then, so many you can't begin to count? Try, sweetheart. Never mind before you married, just count how many since . . . since you started, ah, playing around."

I've told him too much. The endless sex stories, our erotic foreplay. "Jason, you're not serious."

"I'm not sure how I got into this but yes, I think I'm serious."

"I'm counting. Give me a minute."

He snaps on the light, fumbles for stationery, hands

me his pen. "You're good on paper, Kate. Make a list." The man is a nut. I start to laugh but his expression forbids it. Is this for real or is it another erotic game? Fear cuts through me, a perverse nerve-tingling fear, an aphrodisiac. "Four, five and ummm is six, seven, twelve."

"What was that, five in one night? An orgy?" He takes the paper from me. "I don't want scratches. This isn't a gin rummy scorecard or a fucking laundry list. Who was the man who brought you here? And write down the women too."

"There aren't any women, Jason." I haven't told him everything. I don't have to tell him everything, the bully.

"But you'd like to go to bed with a woman, wouldn't you?"

"I don't know, well, yes, probably I'd find that exciting. I want to try everything that feels good. Yes. But not just any woman."

"What would she look like?"

"Jason, please." He has my hand in his, the soft pad of his thumb making circles on my wrist. "Must I?" He squeezes my wrist. "She would be thin, little round breasts, perhaps slightly boyish, with pink nipples, you know those kind of raised aureoles, with a firm neat little nipple."

"My, you know a lot about nipples." He pulls down the covers and begins to make love to my left foot. It tickles.

"I see them in the gym, Jason. And in *Playboy*. And in dirty movies."

He looks up. "Oh, you didn't tell me you were a porno fan."

"Not quite a fan, Jason. Just curious. Shall I tell you my porno movie fantasy? Jason, I can't talk when you're doing that." He stops. "I am wearing a skirt that buttons up the side, nothing underneath, no panties . . . and you play with me and make me come right there in the movie theater."

"We'll make those poor creeps in their raincoats jump out of their seats," says Jason. "Kate Alexander, the Porno Queen." He takes my hand. "The man you came to this inn with. Did he do this to you?" He licks between my fingers. "Did he do this?" He licks my eyes, my ears, bites my mouth. "Answer me when I ask a question."

His jealousy is wonderful. "Yes, he did all those things."

"Did he do this?" He rolls me over and puts his tongue in my ass, sucking, biting.

"Yes. Yes." He puts his head under me so I'm sitting on his mouth. "Yes that too, Jason. Oh Jason, you make me so hot."

"The lady is hot. Did you hear that, friend? Guess who just walked in the door, Kate. You remember Kate, don't you, friend? You two were here last year, I believe. Stretch out on the bed, Kate, spread your legs as far as you can. Very good. Lovely, isn't she, friend?" Jason leans over, takes both my breasts in his hands. "Great boobs, eh, friend. She loves it when you do this. And this."

"Jason, you're hurting me."

"Don't pay any attention, friend. She loves it when you hurt her. A little. Try it, be my guest." He rubs and bites. His hand on my mouth muffling the scream. "Remember how much she loves to have you rub her clit? Oh please, do, go ahead. I'll just watch. In fact, if you like I'll just raise her ass a little . . . isn't that ass something? Don't you love the line here, the way the hips flare . . . those two sweet dimples. If you promise not to be too rough, I'll let you fuck her."

"Thank you," he responds in a perfect imitation of Cary Grant's voice. "You honor me with your hospitality."

I can't help giggling.

"Don't laugh," he commands.

I am fighting Jason's stranger. I know we can drive

down any road and there will be a Gothic castle with grey stone chambers and chains and strange men even animals to whom he will make me submit. It's a game and it's real. The stranger is biting my neck, shaking me, entering me with nasty fingers, a rough dream demon, pulling my hair, shoving his cock into my mouth, holding my wrists to the bed, making me a prisoner. Fucking me into the headboard, over the edge of the bed. I'm grabbing at the wall to keep from falling. He grabs my ass again, licking it.

"No, no. Jason. I know you think I'm just playing the game." Struggling to get free. "Not in my ass. I mean it, Jason," No, no, no, too frightened to make it not hurt that much. One hand muffles my screams.

I feel him watching me sobbing, trembling, trying to contain my rage. He takes me in his arms.

"You like it now, don't you?"

He can kill me if he likes. I'm not going to answer.

Late, much later, I wake. He is lying there, watching me sleep. It must be almost morning. I can see his eyes. He looks as if he's been crying.

"Are you having trouble trying to sleep, Jason?"

"Kate. I don't like what's happening to me."

Waking, sitting up. "Jason. What is it?"

"I'm not like this. I don't fuck like this. I don't need submission. Pain doesn't turn me on. You're bringing out something in me that must be there but I don't like it."

"Jason, you do like to be in charge."

"I don't have to fuck someone I love in the ass to get my way, Kate. If it sometimes seems I like to be in charge it's perhaps because I'm the take-charge type. Don't confuse masterfulness with brutality."

"Jason, I love how you take charge."

"You can't love a sadistic ass-fucker."

Silence.

"I think you do in some part of your head, Kate. And that worries me. You're provoking me over the edge, Kate."

That worries me too.

"We won't play that game anymore, Jason. I'm looking at a self I don't like to see, too. Come, love me sweet. I'll just hold you, Jason."

XXVI

WE ARE LYING side by side in the sun on canvas chaises, always touching. If the full moon brings out his Mr. Hyde, sunlight seems to tenderize Jason around the edges. Today he is a creature halfway between Winnie the Pooh and Dietrich's eager Professor in *Blue Angel*. Running around in circles to please me. Arranging pillows and angles of chaises in relation to position of sun. Fetching fresh-squeezed grapefruit juice. Making up preposterous news items and pretending to read them from the morning paper.

"Do you have a plot for your novel?" he asks.

He has decided I should write a novel. Immediately it exists for him. My novel. Of course I have wanted to write another novel for a long time and a retreat to far Texas would be the ideal time. "Perhaps I should write about sex. Sexual fantasy or a sexual obsession," I say. "I have some characters in my mind but I don't know what I'll do with them. A successful woman about to turn forty and her idyllic life, or so it seems."

"I have a plot for you," he says. "She is married to a man who constantly sabotages her work because he feels overshadowed by her success. She meets a man whose wife has left him to find herself, the classic Women's Lib cliché . . . the wife thinks she can never grow or become her own person unless she leaves this guy. But your heroine is attracted to him because he is strong and can handle her strength and her success."

"I love the irony, Jason."

"Use it," he says with an exaggerated sweeping gesture as if it were a family heirloom. I'm not saying that's a plot and I'm not writing it off as hopeless but I love his literary counsel and I'm awed by his illusions.

"Can you be interrupted?" Jason has been at the pool most of the afternoon. He is pink on brown and lightly peeling. "If it's not a good time, don't stop. I'll wait."

"I can stop." I always stop. He can never wait. I have never written a script with a tinier percentage of my concentration but E. Jay is in London and I've promised the final revisions on *Queen Bee* by courier from Nice on Friday. I have two days and a morning till flight time.

I follow Jason down stone steps. Each crack is filled with tiny pink flowers. The gardener is cutting the lawn. The air is heady with an intense smell of green.

"I've hidden something. A beautiful present for you," says Jason. "If you can find it."

"Oh Jason." I hug him. And run to the pool shed. Not there. To the tile terrace and the barbecue with its eighteenth-century shaft that works on weights and the mystery of physics. Not there. "Is it in plain view? Is it outdoors, Jason?" Across the pool three plump old men and a freakishly tall teenage boy are taking tea.

"It's outdoors. When you come near, you'll see the blue tissue paper. If you don't find it, you can't have it."

"Jason, that's cruel." I sit at the foot of the steps for

a moment studying the full sweep of garden. Where would he hide it? The spot must be obvious. That's what Jason would do.

"You'll never find it just sitting there, Kate. I think I'll give you a time limit."

"I can't work with a time limit, Jason."

"You have three minutes."

"Jason, don't be a shit."

He seizes my arm, pulling me to my feet. "I'm not a shit, lady. I'm a nice man who loves you and has bought you a beautiful present."

When he's like this, I'm frightened. Hiding my face in his cheek—the fat men are staring, I whisper: "Jason, you're taking a wonderful time and making it into a punishment." He looks at me, hurt. He takes my hand and leads me.

I can see a spot of blue in the grapefruit tree. The limb of the tree is exactly the height of my nose. He hands me the package. "Jason, darling, I'm sorry."

"Open it," he says, dropping to the ground in a hidden spot behind a hedge, pulling me down beside him.

"Oh Jason, it is . . . absolutely beautiful." A dress, sheer and fragile, tucked with a narrow edging of handmade lace. "Is it old?"

"Empire, the woman said."

"Oh dear, Empire ladies were tiny."

"Not this one. Try it on."

Incredibly, it fits, well, just barely. I hope there is a seam I can have released where it pulls across the bosom. "It's not like anything I've ever owned, darling." God, that's an understatement, nothing could be less me. "I shall have to buy myself a reticule, wear little white gloves."

"You do like it, don't you?"

"I love it, sweetheart."

"I love you in it."

"Is it part of some fantasy you have?"

"Oh no. I just love that delicate ladylike you."

"Unbutton me."

"You don't like it."

"Darling, I love it. I love it. I just want to go for a swim."

XXVII

___

HARRY INSISTS I talk to Hilary Lakein. I've told Harry I'm taking a sabbatical but he hasn't quite come to believe it. It seems NBC Television has given Hilary a big chunk of money to do something dramatic of quality on daytime television—to stagger afternoon minds numbed by game shows and soap opera. She's asked to discuss it with me. And since she agreed to drive up here from Cannes, I surrender. Can't hurt to have a drink and listen.

Jason is playing golf with some cattle chum from Texas. He comes looking for me, finds us on the terrace sipping iced tea, is barely civil . . . stalks away.

"It's just talk," I try to explain back in the hyacinth room after Hilary flees. "I gave her a few ideas. She wants me to do a script. I don't have to commit myself to anything definite now."

"Damn it, Kate. Tell your agent to lay off. Stop playing with yourself. You're stale, Kate. This time away from movies will revitalize your mind. How long has it been since you took off a real stretch of time? Haven't you always dreamed of being lazy . . . reading as much as you please."

"I swear to you Jason, Hilary's project is more than four months away."

"Four months. Kate, you said you were taking six months. You said nothing would take you away from the ranch for at least six months. What the fuck are you talking about?"

"Jason, I don't remember ever saying six months. I said I'd think about it."

"Think about it. What the hell does that mean?" He shoves me onto the bed.

"Jason, stop pushing me around."

"Are you coming home with me or not?"

"Jason, I'm scared. In six months I'll be nobody. Everyone will have forgotten I exist."

"You'll be halfway through your novel. You'll be writing something no one can delete or pervert or fuck up." He shakes me. "Kate, damn it. You are coming home with me."

I love his rage. "Jason. Hold me tight." You got me, Mr. Christian. I'm signing on.

"You'll learn to ride well," he's saying. "I'll let you have breakfast in bed, well anyway, coffee, every morning and fresh fruit. We have it flown in from California. We'll fish together and camp out if you like. I have some camping equipment so luxurious I'm embarrassed to be caught in it, and a tiny cabin on a lake."

Yes. And I'll weave and slop the hogs and make friends with the natives and chew your blubber and braid mesquite, whatever that is.

"Jason, you're not ready." We are to drop the manuscript of *Queen Bee* off at the Nice airport for the courier, then celebrate with a very special lunch at The Moulin de Mougins. He's ordered lobster fricassee in advance. "Jason, we can't possibly do everything if we don't leave . . ." I look at his watch. "Fifteen minutes ago. Jason, please." He is the world's promptest man. It just isn't possible he's doing this now deliberately.

"No need to get hysterical," he says, plugging in his electric razor with a languor two beats this side of slow motion. Why do I keep feeling I've seen this before? Is he trying to *Gaslight* me? Do I see the lights flicker? "Have the concierge call the courier service and arrange for them to pick up your envelope at The Moulin."

"Jason. Now. At the last minute. Are you mad? You expect a courier to find The Moulin and then make it back to Nice?"

"Give me two minutes. We'll get it to the airport." The roads are curved and crowded. This is the Riviera in Festival . . . a Sunday. Everyone from St.-Jean-de-Luz to Monte Carlo is clogging up this fucking highway today. He is swearing, switching lanes, furious.

"Jason, we'll never make it."

"Get out the map and see if there's any other way we can go. Kate, I'm really sorry."

"Jason. The map isn't here. Jason, the map's always here. Where is it?"

"Didn't you take it into the room to look up . . . something."

I remember. That shuts me up. The flight is gone when we arrive. Jason takes my envelope and with his usual efficient, commanding snap-to, arranges for it to make the next plane to London. The pilot will deliver it himself. He is pleased with his invention and enterprise. I don't trust myself to say anything. I can't think of anything I want to do less than . . . lunch. I don't trust myself to say that either.

The lobster fricassee looks beautiful. I manage to look interested in the string bean salad. Truffles do seem to calm the outraged stomach. But I can't handle the country cheese with herbs in its mantle of crème fraîche. So rich. So voluptuous.

Jason has discovered the Belgian businessman at the next table has a cousin in Irving, Texas. He is trading a pouf of our chocolate soufflé for a wedge of something frosted in chocolate and praline.

"I'm going to be sick, Jason," I say into his ear. "Let me get a taxi. You stay . . ."

"You won't be sick," he says. "Have some coffee."

"I want a taxi, Jason."

"Don't move from that chair, Kate."

I am not moving. I can't move anyway. It's too late. I'd never make it across the floor and up the two stone steps to the desk. My teeth are clenched and every shred of will is concentrated on not throwing up at this table. I am thinking. Blue skies, sunny days, coffee beans, good thought, coffee beans.

I'm not sick at all. Just deathly silent all the way home, pretending to doze. Thinking.

In the room, Jason peels off his clothes. "Tell me now, Kate."

"I'm not sure if I know what I'm feeling. It's a feeling of . . . dread, I think, Jason. Like I'm disappearing. Everything you say makes sense. When you're talking, I agree . . . accept everything you say. What you're doing. What we're doing. It's all for me. For my work. And I know it isn't deliberate but it's almost as if you won't let me work. How could you let me miss that courier? Why do all my friends sound like idiots suddenly? Have they always been idiots? Am I really going to give up films, calmly drop everything—I haven't told you but Bergman has asked me to come to Sweden to work with him on a project we discussed months ago—*Bergman,* Jason, I can't really believe it. You want me to do whatever I want to do . . . as long as I stay close to wherever you are. Am I crazy? Am I crazy wanting to go to Bergman? Am I crazy wanting to go with you? Oh shit. The fucks that pass in the night were so simple."

"What about your novel, Kate?"

"I haven't got a novel, damn it. That's your idea." I start to walk away.

"Listen to me, lady." He grabs me.

"Want to fight, Jason? Want to punch me? Want to slap me around a little? Show me who's stronger. Hit me, and I'll hit you back. You'll win but at least I'll fight back."

"Kate, I've never hit anyone. In bed, playing out your fantasies, yes. But never for real. I feel like you're asking for it. Provoking me to be something I'm not. I've always loved strong women. I want a woman to be my equal. But I sense your need to feel strength, to be taken care of and I find it provoking a streak of bullishness . . . call it domination, whatever it is. I don't like that part of me at all. I know I'm hurting you in bed sometimes. I hate it and I see that you love it. You scream and weep and pretend you want to get away but you love it. Submission, that's what you're asking for. That's the fantasy in your head when you lie there holding your wrists together as if they were shackled . . . letting me do everything to you."

"But what happens in bed is for bed, not for life."

"I know that quite well. I want you to feel totally free to be anything in bed with me. But somehow it seems to creep into what we do outside of bed."

"You're right, Jason. I do love it. I was seduced. I let go. It was so wonderful to just let you take care of everything, like crawling into a cocoon. Your strength was terribly appealing . . ."

"Stop saying was."

"The way you order people around, get things done, make people jump. I love it. Your time schedules, your organization, your sweetness—the massages, the gifts, running for sun lotion, finding raspberries at three in the morning, reading aloud to me. There's some dumb core in me that finds it tempting—to be a Stepford Wife. But unless you were planning to do a prefrontal lobotomy, I'd always be running off needing to be Kate Alexander."

He is holding me, crooning to me. "We'll make it work, Kate. You'll have running-off room. I'll do everything for you. I don't know any other way to be."

"I need to sleep, Jason."

He starts to undress me.

"Jason."

"Just to sleep," he says. He lies down beside me. I fall asleep in his arms. Not very comfortable, actually. But he won't let me go. We are really good. All that love. All that fierce wonderful fucking. The games, the teasing, tenderness, even the power struggle. I can't bear to give it up.

I wake. The clock says after six. Jason is gone. I feel weak, empty, euphoric . . . like a patient recovered from a terrible fever. We are going home. Jason refuses to believe we can't make it work. I know he's right. I must talk to Jamie.

More than forty minutes to put the call through. I doze. The ring wakes me. I tell him that I need to see him. Jamie is very quiet. "Jamie darling. I love you. That's the one constant in all this. I never stop loving you. Please talk to me."

"All right, Kate. Come home. But I won't come to the airport. I'm not tough enough for a scene in an airport. Let me wait for you at home."

Jason is in the garden. I hear him banging about.

"Jason."

His hair is wild. The movie star teeth. When he comes into the room I feel the same shock I felt at the Plaza-Athenée. Blue eyes, blue skies, blue denim workshirt. I'd forgotten how beautiful he is.

"Jason." He stands at the side of the bed. I put out my arms. How tender, how subtle . . . how exquisitely delicate he is tonight.

Much later halfway into sleep, I am thinking I hear him say: "Maybe Bergman can wait a while."

I'm too far away to answer. I'm sure we can work that out.

Next morning I wake when he docs. "Sleep some more," he says. "I'll go into the main house and confirm our flight." He comes quietly into the room near noon, rattling tissue paper, waking me again.

"I was getting worried," he says. "Nobody can sleep that long." He looks so fresh and healthy. "These irises will have to do for your funeral or your survival, whichever you choose." He hands me a small box. Inside, exquisite Victorian earrings, gold set with seed pearls.

"Oh Jason. Now I'll have to survive."

"I'm not going to kiss you if you're still weak."

I pull him toward me. "I'm practically cured."

"Hmmm. Yes. That sure feels good to me." Running his hand under my nightgown. "You've been a good patient, my dear. But there is a lingering fever that the good doctor must cure. Have you noticed any symptoms?"

"Fits of drowsiness."

"How about a fierce burning between your legs? You feel that? A classic symptom. Be brave, now. I shall apply a cooling hand."

"Oh doctor, it feels better already."

"That's a sign of a good prognosis."

"Oh doctor, what is that terrible-looking instrument?"

"Don't be frightened, my dear. This is my fever reducer. Open wid. "

Modern medicine is full of miracles. Here I am loving Jason. Loving Jamie. Loving Jason's cock. I love and fear the Kate he's shown me.

X X V I I I

JASON IS A DEMON in airports. Air France's service manager at Kennedy recognizes him at once. Like magic, we are waved through customs without opening a single bag. My taxi drops him at a Braniff departure gate. He kisses me, that same voluptuous mouth I imagine I'll feel like a tattoo on my mouth forever. "Soon. Come quick."

The elevator man has a nervous smile. I have a feeling he is registering his disapproval. Does everyone know everything? He lingers at our floor, lining up the suitcases, waiting to see the big reunion scene. The door opens. Jamie is standing behind it. He grabs my bag, the canvas tote, the attaché case, the typewriter. Hugging me. Both of us crying. Oh, we're so wonderfully incurably corny.

Oh, Jamie. Here we are hugging and sobbing and touching, the kind of leaky fumblings grown people do in real life. It would all be too slow, too boring for the screen.

That's why we have the fades and dissolves and Godard leaps. To spare you. Let's get to the dialogue. He loves me. He'll never love anyone the way he loves me. No one will ever love him the way I love him. What we had was so special. There must be a way to save it. This is not crisp snappy dialogue. But it's us. I believe him.

He doesn't talk about Audrey.

I'm not saying anything about Jason.

"Come in the cave, Rabbit," he says. And here we are lying under the table locked together, trying to make it feel like it used to feel. I'm remembering all the times in the cave holding each other, endless comfortings, the pregnancy that wasn't, the shock of Maggy's arrival, the desecration of *Cabbage Patch,* the waterfront city that was never built because of snowballing payoffs and fraud finally exposed . . . too late to save Jamie's dream. The survival of Audrey. All those welcoming homes for the wayward Kate, giggling and abloom from the mischief he never suspected. We just fit. It feels safe. I cannot possibly leave this man.

"Can we try again, Jamie?"

He studies me, very solemn and slow. "We can try."

"Should I try to explain?"

"Not now. I think it's probably safer if we don't talk about it for a while."

Jamie brings me a glass of champagne in the tub. I am floating in bubbly foam. He looks at me curiously, or so I imagine. Is he looking for some damage, some evidence of enemy occupation? He is naked. I find myself not quite able to look. His body is so different from Jason's. I'd forgotten how smooth Jamie is. He kisses me and then I hear him in the bedroom, a strained breathing . . . doing situps. Something new. Dedicated no doubt to keeping the forty-two-year-old man in shape for the twenty-three-year-old girl. The tiny potbelly was always good enough for me. I love his belly. And me, with my seventy-five-dollar Dior nightgown, and that little girl giggle I seem to have perfected for Jason. Shall I dig the blue nightie out of my suitcase? Jamie paid for it. Give him his due. What a shitty idea. How can I do this? Come to Jamie so fresh from Jason. Perhaps Kate is some kind of emotional monster. No real feelings. I know damn well I've not given up Jason. I just have to concentrate on one step at a time. Till I know . . .

"Kate."

I feel so shy. Coming home. I walk the three thousand steps (make that twenty) to bed naked, still wet, wrapping the towel around me, hair piled on top of my head, smelling of bubblebath, a little, and Cabochard, a lot—the perfume Jamie chose himself after sniffing six scents "definitely not you." I lie there pressed against him, his hair in my mouth. I feel I belong but he's still a stranger.

"We're not saying anything," Kate complains.

"I had so much I was going to tell you."

"Well, you can talk, Jamie. I'm feeling numb from no sleep but I can listen."

"What makes me so angry is not that you did it. Your fucking around doesn't upset me half as much as the deception. I can somehow accept another man's cock inside you but I find myself enraged that you fooled me." He is silent. He turns out the light. That means he is ready to sleep. There will be no making love. I am disappointed but quite frankly, relieved. I burrow into the pillows. "Stay next to me," says Jamie. "Spoon me." He tucks his ass against my tummy. Cotton candy stuff, I know. But that's the way we are. Even when nightmare-dream, cramped spine or sliding blanket move us apart in the night there is always a patch of my skin touching a patch of his skin in a message that is sweet but probably neurotic so I'm not going to examine it.

Drifting between awake (overtired . . . wishing I'd made a list of all the things I must do tomorrow) and dream (me having it out with Audrey in a scene from *The Women*), Jamie moves his hand between my legs. I press my hand against his cock, cup all of it with my hand, circle its softness, startled to wake with a cock not Jason's in my hand. A sudden memory of how the fatness of Jason's cock would fill my pussy. Oh damn, I wish I could turn off the power in my head, shut off subversive teasing memory. Make myself see black.

Jamie is eating me. I concentrate on the blackness behind my closed eyes. Everything just slightly off, too soon, not enough, too gentle, too aimless. And yet I feel all that love. Jamie's mouth sucking and biting. All thought obliterated by loving Jamie loving me.

I reach for him. His cock is still soft. Going down on Jamie, smelling his elusive sweet smell. Nothing happens. He pulls me away, pulls my face to his face. "I really want to, Kate." He puts his face in the pillow. "I don't know what's wrong. Maybe I'm angry. Or too hurt. Maybe I'm punishing you."

Hugging him. "Oh Jamie, it will get better fast. You've forgotten how wonderful we are. How good we can be. I'll be sweeter and thinner and neater. I'll smile in the morning and clean out the closet that attacks you whenever you open the door. Maybe I'll learn to swim. Oh Jamie, and tennis."

He groans. "Easy, Rabbit. If it's the secret sloth in you I can't live without, so much virtue could destroy us."

"I'll start with a modicum."

"Better."

He sleeps. Now I am wide-awake, lying here trying not to remember anything that might disturb that home-again feeling, planning breakfast, a diet, making guest lists, planning parties, friends too long neglected, thinking it's almost July and maybe we'll take a whole month in Bridgehampton. And if I really want to start pure I might even be brave enough to swear off the Jerry Glass habit. What

sweet vengeance. To top all Glass's insults and neglect
with a cool "farewell forever." Screaming comes in a doggy
bed are not exactly essential to happily ever after. But
Jason is essential. And Jason will never put up with being
my "Back Street" man. Oh damn. Could I ever be monogamous again? Too cosmic a question to face just now. I'll
think about that tomorrow. Now I'll just think about loving
Jamie loving me. I think there should be a comma there.
Loving Jamie, Jamie loving me.

Quiet morning. A long time ago Jamie came to understand my morning slowness, the armor of silence. But this
morning he is especially quiet, disappearing into the kitchen
to brew deep dark espresso. The perfume of fresh ground
coffee beans filters into my consciousness. "Sleep another
half hour," he whispers kissing my ear, disappearing into
shower-shaving sounds.

It's afternoon in Paris. How can I still be sleeping?
Awake, on my feet at least, peeing, watching him shave
still angry after all these years at the irritation of razor
against stubble, hugging him from behind, coming truly
awake in the shower, knowing I must call Jason, hugging
Jamie again in my towel, halving oranges for juice. A long
strangely sad embrace at the door. And he is gone to work.

Left to dreary confusion. What will I do about Jason?
Suitcases, carpet bag, laundry piling up on the floor, clippings and papers everywhere. The proposal from Bergman.
An Everest of mail to go through, *Women's Wear,* mag-
azines, department store catalogues, books with letters
asking for comments, galleys—everything screened and
marked by Holly "must" "debatable" "forget it." Lists of
phone calls intercepted by the answering service, calls
catalogued by Holly, notes from my housekeeper Minnie.

Telephone rings. It's Jason.

"Are you all right, Kate? You sound funny."

"Jason, it's so hard. I didn't think it would be . . . so painful."

"I shouldn't have left you. I should have come with you."

"You offered, Jason. We agreed that it would be too terrible for Jamie. Jason . . ." I don't know what to say. The sound of his voice reminds me of . . . crazy. *Let's Pretend*. Saturday radio. "Cream of Wheat is so good to eat, so we have it every day. It makes us strong . . ." I'm giggling.

"I missed you last night," he says.

"Nobody making voracious demands?"

"I put my pillow between my legs so I would feel warm and loved. You see I have my insecurities too." He laughs. "When the toothfairy comes, she goes right for my pillow and guess what she finds. How long is it going to take, Kate? Do you want me to come for you? I can get away for a day or two this weekend." Silence. "Kate, you're not saying anything."

"Jason. I have to sort everything out. I just got up. I haven't spoken to Jamie or Harry or thought enough about how to respond to the Bergman thing."

"Bergman is a real breakthrough for you, I know."

"Sweden could be a great new market for you, Jason."

"I don't think I'd make a good tag-along man, Kate."

"Let me call you tonight, Jason."

"Kate, tell me what you're thinking. I must know."

"I'll call tonight, darling."

"I love you, Kate."

"I love you, Jason."

Telephone rings. Can't take another one like that before coffee. I have to sit down. "Bumble mumble (didn't quite catch the name) from *Time* magazine. Your agent told me you'd be back today. We're putting together what might be a cover story on where the Women's Movement is going. It's summer and news is slow, of course the Middle East could explode or something political, but for now, it's scheduled as a cover, timed for the release of your movie, *Wonder Woman*. It was screened night before last in Pasadena, you know, and audiences apparently went wild."

"Oh no. I didn't know. I was on the plane. I'm just back. Well, could it be tomorrow then? Give me time to comb my hair, unsnarl my thoughts."

Adrenalin pumping tidal waves. "My God, Harry. *Time* magazine. Tell me about the sneaks. What happened? She said they loved it. *Newsweek* too? No, they haven't reached me yet. Maybe there's a message here somewhere. I can't believe it, Harry." Calling Jamie. *"Time* magazine. Maybe the cover. She didn't say what on the cover, could be me, could be Wonder Woman. And *Newsweek* too, Jamie. I could be the Bruce Springsteen of the month. Oh Jamie. Jamie, is something wrong?"

"Kate, don't go out. I want to see you."

"Jamie, are you all right? What is it?"

"I'll be home in an hour."

All the alarm bells are ringing. Mustn't panic. Sweeping the mess under the beds, Jamie hates mess, throwing everything into closets and drawers. Me. Doing me. His favorite faded pink oxford shirt from the old Brooks Brothers button-down days. Hair combed full and free the way he loves it. No makeup, well, a look of no makeup, a puff of blush, a dull matte glow. Telephone ringing. Won't answer it. Minnie is vacuuming the library. I have to send her out on some errand. Have to stop eating these damned smoked almonds, they're stale anyway. If I could sort out the cleaning and laundry, I could send Minnie with that. And the drugstore. And the florist. "I want dozens of daisies, Minnie. White. Second choice yellow. At least six dozen daisies. And stop somewhere for lunch,

Minnie. My treat. Jamie's coming by from the office and we need a few minutes alone."

Only eleven o'clock. Too early for a drink. But it's practically the cocktail hour in Paris. My drink is mostly orange juice, a big healthy squirt of lemon and just a dash of rum, hmm . . . another dash of rum. Practically sheer unadulterated Linus Pauling. Lots of ice. Music. No music. I need some kind of music. Jamie loves Billie Holiday. Why doesn't somebody alphabetize these fucking records? Must be 500 albums . . . here is Billie. Keys in the door, Jamie. Jamie isn't looking at me. Can't look into my eyes. He's hugging me, looking into the crook of my neck so he doesn't have to look into my eyes.

"It isn't going to work, Kate."

The sun is pouring into the living room. What a fine sunny room this is . . . too sunny. Soon I'll be reupholstering the sofa because the sun is fading the blue. Already the blue is faded to a funny shade of teal.

"I love you, Jamie. I'm so happy to be home."

"I thought it would work, Kate. But it isn't going to. I love you. I'll never love anyone the way I love you."

"Why do you keep saying that?"

"Good morning heartache," Billie sings. "Might as well get used to your hanging around. Good morning, heartache. Sit down . . ."

I'm staring at Jamie, listening to Billie. Can't stand that Billie. "Turn off that damned music, Jamie."

"Maybe the wound is still too fresh," Jamie is saying. "I feel like I can't really trust you, Kate. You have too much power to hurt me. I don't want a woman who's never here. You go away so much. People are always trying to sell you or woo you, sign you up. I stand there like an obsolete vestigial appendage—"

"Oh Jamie, you know that's not—"

"I love you too much. You'll go away again. I don't ever want to feel that pain again. I can't stand that pain. Oh Kate, it's impossible. No one will ever love you the way I love you, Kate. This shouldn't have happened."

"Jamie, stop saying that. If you love me, love me. Don't leave. That's crazy. How can you go?"

"Audrey is nothing like you. Next to you . . . she's nothing next to you. Not even formed yet. Maybe I find that appealing. For her I'm something very special. I know everything. I bring everything to her. Maybe I like that, that Pygmalion thing. Anyway, she isn't so complicated, Kate. She's simple, what you see is what's there. She has no ambition at all. She's quite dependent on me. There's no—"

"But *I* need you, Jamie. Who could be more dependent than me? Bring new things to me, Jamie. I'd love that. Take me places we've never been. Teach me things. I'd love it. Jamie, you make me sound jaded and a thousand years old. I'm not complicated. I'm so simple. You know everything about me. You love me the way I am, all the bad things, all the good things, all the ways I really am that nobody else understands. Jamie, that's why I'm here. All these last days, everything that happened, I never stopped loving you."

"It should have worked. We were so good."

"Jamie, you can't leave. You always said you couldn't live without me."

"Maybe I can't. But I don't have the strength to take so much pain."

"Jamie." Getting a little crazy now. "Jamie, you can't live without me. I promise you. You can't. You can't go. All right, go. Get out. I can't stand you like this." Laughing. "You bastard. I can't even cry today because I need to save my eyes for *Time*."

"I know I'm selfish to tell you now." Jamie is crying.

"Don't cry, Rabbit. You'll mess up your eyes. I'll be so proud of you in *Time* magazine. I love you, Kate. I'll always love you."

He's in the bathroom gathering up his shaving things. "Don't take that toothbrush, damn it." He drops his toothbrush back into its hole. "You better leave that toothbrush here. You'll be back."

"Kate, don't get hysterical."

"Stop telling me what to get, Jamie. You aren't taking care of me anymore. I am hysterical. I will be hysterical." He stands at the closet, staring at the rows of suits, jackets, shoes. The suitcases. His fishing gear. "I wouldn't take any winter things, Jamie. You'll be coming back."

"I won't take anything now." He slides the door closed, staring at me with that mournful face. As if I'm not me. As if I'm already dead. I feel myself turning into something I'm not, a pitiful creature, a woman abandoned by her man. I do not want Jamie's sympathy. I'm hopelessly miscast. This just isn't going to happen. I can see myself in the mirror behind him. I look better now than I have in years. I'm wearing the shirt he loves to see me in. He's holding me and crying.

"Stay, Jamie. We can make it work." What a line. Who writes this dame's dialogue? Certainly not me.

"Rabbit, I have to go," says Jamie. "Will you be all right? Is Holly coming? I have to go."

"I won't be all right, damn it. Eventually I could even commit suicide . . . if this were final . . . which I cannot believe. What the hell are you smiling about?"

"I was just thinking you'd never write a line like that." He laughs. "You do need me, Kate. I know that. You need someone. But you're a survivor. You're really angry now because you don't like surprises. I know that. I didn't do it this way deliberately. When you called from France, I came running. I was so relieved. I thought all I wanted

was to have you back. I was wrong. But you'll survive. I'm
not worried about that, Rabbit. Be strong, Kate. Be fine."
Be strong, shit. Be fine. What does he mean giving
me that Hemingway garbage? Be strong. Be fine. He's
gone. And I'm not crying. Isn't that remarkable? Incredible
what vanity can do, and knowing that Jason is waiting. It's
too much to think about now.

Minnie comes in through the kitchen a few minutes
after Jamie goes, bustling and making more noise than a
horned rhinoceros in heat. Very tactful. I'll cry tomorrow.
Agreed, Kate. Then Jamie and I will sit down and have a
cool rational talk. I know I can get Jamie back. I did it
once. Too bad Bergman has already made *Scenes from a
Marriage.*

What does the victim do when she's wounded? What
does she do in her last five minutes on earth, the blood
trickling from her cracked heart, staining her faded pink
oxford shirt? She arranges daisies, six dozen white daisies.
Mustn't let go now. Mustn't fall apart till I've charmed
and disarmed the lady from *Time.* The *woman* from
Time. A sister, let us hope. A sister will be predisposed
to treat me kindly. I ought to be grateful that old-fashioned
female competitiveness is considered counterrevolutionary.
Ironic, when I've been so competitive all my life. I would
feel much more comfortable if they were sending a man.
Even a team would be good, Jimmy Stewart with notebook,
Myrna Loy with camera. Kate, very crisp, skinny, wonderfully aristocratic, terribly Mainline and all aglow like Hepburn in *Philadelphia Story,* but not spoiled or arrogant at
all. Like me.

Holly is leaping all over the house, delirious about
Time. "Monsieur Marc can send Richard tomorrow morning at nine or he will do you himself at the shop if you

can get there by eight forty-five. I think you should get Scavullo. Look what he did for Martha Mitchell."

"If I only could, Holly. Do I dare insist?" She relays my request for Richard.

"Kate, can't you tell me what's happening? Are you back? Are you leaving?"

"Oh Holly, I don't know. I can't even think about it now. Do you think the shoemaker can do anything with these shoes. You could start the mail. I wrote answers longhand on the bottom of the 'must' letters. What do you think I should wear for the interview?"

I suppose this is how I will function if they ever announce the world is about to end. A quick trip to M. Marc for a comb-out. A few minutes of indecision at the closet. Shall I be tailored and elegant or soft, monochromatic or subtly sexy, irrepressibly earthy? How will we meet Armageddon, barefoot with toes painted Teddy Bear rose or in our Chelsea Cobbler boots, kicking to the end?

Holly is clipping and filing. "Do you realize Brigitte Bardot is over forty?"

"Holly, I can think of more cheerful topics of conversation."

"But it is good news," she says. "Brigitte says life goes on." She looks at me. "I'm just chattering. How about a cup of papaya leaf tea, Kate?"

"Papaya leaf tea sounds awful. That's just what I need. I'm not sure I've sorted out what happened. Maybe it's all still happening. In a way, it was quite self-revealing, Holly. I kept meeting people who never heard of Kate Alexander. At first I enjoyed that. Then finally, I became uncomfortable. He's so bright. So strong. Oh Holly, he was so fucking good in bed."

Holly blinks. The tea burns my tongue. "Wait," she says. "Let it cool."

"But what matters, Holly . . ." Oh fuck . . . here

comes the mist, mustn't cry. "Jamie is going, says he is going, says he is not coming home." Holly looks crushed, her eyes fill. "Don't you cry, Holly. Jesus Christ, what is this? A goddamn fucking soap opera? I've just got to get through today and tomorrow. Jamie loves me. He'll come back. He came back that other time. Holly, be cool and cheerful. Be Anne Baxter in *All About Eve,* if you like. Just help me get through today."

"What about Jason?" Holly asks.

Oh, yes. Say the magic word—Jason, Jason. I'm working on that, Holly. Subliminally. Tomorrow. Tomorrow.

Holly is returning phone calls, putting off invitations and requests, postponing all decisions. And I have crawled into my bed-nest with a notebook to make a list of deeply perceptive, humble, witty, irreverent things I want to say to *Time.*

Maggy calls. "I love you, Kate. You'll always be my mom."

"Maggy, don't sound so full of doom. Of course I'm your mom. He'll be back. I promise. He just needs time to sort things out. How is the family? The baby? Your film? I'll call next week."

Mustn't be alone tonight. I could stay home and do my nails and eyebrows and deep sleep beauty facial. The thought depresses me. I don't want Noni. Can't face questions now. Definitely not Glass. Though a good fuck always agrees with me. Great fucking is a better beauty pickup than silicone or estrogen or sleep. Too bad Estée Lauder can't put it in a bottle.

Mother calls. "I just hung up from talking to somebody at *Time* magazine," she says. "They want baby pictures and high school graduation, your college yearbook."

Oh damn, they're really doing a job. "For God's sake, Mother, don't give them anything with a date. I was born in 1938, Mother."

"Yes, I was there, dear."

"I'm thirty-eight, try to remember."

"You can't fool *Time* magazine, darling."

"I can't but you can, Mother. You've got three generations of Puritan heritage in that face."

Vincent Canby calls. Oh Vincent. They're calling you too.

Holly hands me a note. It's from Michael. "I'll be at The Algonquin. Call." Michael, my dirty Jack Armstrong with his ice-blue eyes and his silver studs and the zippers. What do you think, Kate? Fate is providing amusing alternatives.

Holly tiptoes into my room pinning the organdy curtains back to let in the sun. "Wake up, Miz Kate. Mistah Rhett is back."

"Jamie. I knew you'd come."

I am standing here in the burned-out hulk of Tara with all my faithful darkies gathered about me. Minnie, Malcolm X, Martin Luther King, and Sidney Poitier. Sidney is slicing a watermelon. Everyone hums a mournful hymn. Holly is trying to lace me into my girdle.

"You gwine have to lay off them chocolate mousses, Miz Scarlett."

"I'm leaving, Scarlett," says Jamie.

"No. Oh my darling, if you go, what shall I do?"

"My dear, I don't give a damn."

Holly jerks the strings tight.

"I'll go crazy if I think about losing him now," says Kate. "I can't let him go. There must be some way. I won't think of it now. I'll think of it all tomorrow at Tara. Tomorrow, I'll think of some way to get him back. After all, tomorrow is another day."

I have to call Jason. I'm not sure what I want to say.

If I'm ready to say it. Nobody said I was sentenced forever to sit at the typewriter. I never signed it in blood. I never planned to write screenplays. I was going to be a novelist. The movies just happened. With Jason I could just be. Stop running. Be me.

If I want to get Jamie back I can. Jamie loves me. He couldn't stop loving me. Jamie knows me, trusts me . . . trusted me. I can get Jamie back. But that can't just be an exercise in power, Kate. You have to mean it. Well, I mean it. I realize I can't just let go of Jamie. Jamie would never keep me from doing the Bergman script. Shit. Either way it could be everything I want or a mistake.

You could give them both up, Kate, and just get back to work. Sure I could. But that wouldn't be me.

Enough of this tap dance, Kate. Make up your mind.

You must be kidding, friend. Don't you see Kate never makes up her mind. She drifts. Lets fate decide. Reacts, responds . . . some Amazon. What a fake.

I *will* decide. Tomorrow.

Thank you, Miz Scarlett.

Just one more chorus, friends. Ladies and Gentlemen of the Press, introducing Kate Alexander, screenwriter of the week. Coming attraction. Now playing. Wonder Woman of Central Park West. Smile. Beautiful smile. What did she say?

Cheese.

Oh yes. Cheese. Lovely smile.

The telephone. Oops. Which one is it?

"Hey, woman, why aren't you here?"

Don't recognize the voice. "Well, I was just . . . where are you?"

"The Algonquin, where else? Steal an hour for me."

"Michael. It's so late. So many things are happening."

"Just an hour, baby."

Good God, Kate, you wouldn't.

Wouldn't I?
You couldn't.
Just once . . . for my complexion.
Kate, you're impossible.
That morning-after glow. You feel so . . . powerful.
Oh Kate.